6840401416 1 767

TRUTH WILL OUT

Recent Titles by Pamela Oldfield from Severn House

The Heron Saga
BETROTHED
THE GILDED LAND
LOWERING SKIES
THE BRIGHT DAWNING

ALL OUR TOMORROWS
EARLY ONE MORNING
RIDING THE STORM

CHANGING FORTUNES
NEW BEGINNINGS
MATTERS OF TRUST

DANGEROUS SECRETS
INTRICATE LIAISONS
TURNING LEAVES

HENRY'S WOMEN
SUMMER LIGHTNING
JACK'S SHADOW
FULL CIRCLE
LOVING AND LOSING
FATEFUL VOYAGE
THE LONGEST ROAD
THE FAIRFAX LEGACY
TRUTH WILL OUT

TRUTH WILL OUT

Pamela Oldfield

British Library Cataloguing in Publication Data

Oldfield, Pamela.
Truth Will Out.
1. Missing persons–England–Hastings–Fiction.
2. Ransom–Fiction. 3. Detective and mystery stories.
I. Title
823.9'14-dc22

ISBN-13: 978-0-7278-6785-8 (cased)
ISBN-13: 978-1-84751-150-8 (trade paper)

All Severn House titles are printed on acid-free paper.

Typeset by Palimpsest Book Production Ltd.,
Grangemouth, Stirlingshire, Scotland.
Printed and bound in Great Britain by
MPG Books Ltd., Bodmin, Cornwall.

PROLOGUE

Friday, April 8th, 1921

Maude stared at the letter in her hand. Did she recognize the handwriting? She didn't think so. The envelope looked cheap.

Her Aunt Biddy glanced across at her from the far side of the kitchen table. 'What's wrong, Maudie love?'

'Nothing, probably, but . . .' As her voice trailed off she held up the letter for her aunt's inspection, took up a knife and slit the envelope. Withdrawing the single sheet she unfolded it and began to read aloud.

'*Dear Mrs Brent, I shall be attending promptly at four thirty, Friday, for the interview* . . . That's today!' She glanced nervously at the clock on the dresser. Ten past two. Plenty of time.

'What's today? What's happening?'

'That's just it – I don't know.' She read on. '. . . *and look forward to meeting you. Your husband assures me that I will suit and, if that proves to be the case, I look forward to a satisfying relationship. Yours faithfully, Alice Crewe*.'

Biddy Cope, a comfortably round figure in a voluminous apron, was as baffled as her niece. 'Alice Crewe?' she repeated. She stopped rolling pastry and looked thoughtful. 'Do we know an Alice Crewe?'

'I certainly don't but Lionel obviously does. "*I will suit*." Suit what exactly?' She frowned. 'What on earth does it mean?'

'I once knew an Alan Crewe but that was years ago. Or was it Arnold? Could be a relation of this Alice . . . Or maybe it was Adrian Crewe. Oh dear! My wretched memory. No! *Adrian Trew*. That was it.' She smiled. 'He worked in Grandfather's emporium. Nice curly hair . . . He could sell anything, that man. Father used to say he'd sell ice to the Eskimos!'

'It could be an April Fool's trick from Lionel – you know what he's like! But if so it's a week late.'

'Last week he sent you that so-called declaration of love – "eyes so green" . . . "your hair's dark sheen" . . . Some such nonsense.' She laughed at the memory. 'He'd disguised his handwriting but you still guessed it was him. But your face when you first read it!'

'Lionel's such an innocent.' Maude rolled her eyes in mock despair. 'I wonder if he'll ever grow up!' She read the letter aloud again, frowning.

Her aunt's initial fear had faded. 'Whatever it is, if she's expecting to be interviewed, it must be possible for you to turn her down. You don't think he's hiring staff, do you, because I can manage perfectly on my own.' Alarm flickered in her eyes. 'I don't want any flibbertigibbet girl in my kitchen, getting under my feet and muddling me all up!'

Maude nodded and smiled reassuringly but her aunt's words had dismayed her. Biddy, a spinster, had lived with her family for as long as she could remember and had acted as an unpaid housekeeper – not because the family had demanded her services but because she loved to be busy and to feel useful. Latterly, however, she had started to become a little vague and Lionel had commented on this once or twice.

'I don't think he would hire anyone without consulting me first,' said Maude.

'But that's just what he is doing, by the sound of things.' Her aunt sat down on a nearby stool and regarded Maude with wide eyes, suddenly fearful. 'It's because I burned the rock cakes yesterday.'

'Of course it isn't!' Maude tutted impatiently. 'Rock cakes are supposed to be a bit on the rocky side – yours were a bit too crunchy, that's all. We scraped off the burned bits and they were fine. Anyway, how could he have organized this Alice person so quickly? She'd hardly have had time to write the letter, let alone post it!'

Biddy was still worried. 'But if it is about me . . . it might be a maid or a cook.'

'Then I'll send her away. It will be that simple, I promise you. But Lionel will be home before she arrives and all will be revealed.' She glanced round before leaving to take one of her frequent walks to Folkestone beach to feed scraps to the gulls that congregated there when there were no fishing boats to offer richer pickings. The bolder birds could be rather alarming but Maude was used to them and enjoyed their noisy clatter. 'What are you making?' she asked her aunt.

Biddy brightened. 'I thought I'd do a Bakewell tart,' she said eagerly. 'I came across some ground almonds I'd forgotten about so I thought I'd use them up. It's Lionel's favourite, Bakewell tart.'

It wasn't, but Maude had been brought up not to contradict her elders and she didn't want to argue with her aunt.

She said, 'I'll take Primmy with me and hope we don't meet any large black dogs. Primmy hates them! I'm always having to apologize to the dogs' owners for the way she behaves.'

Ten minutes later Maude set off for her walk, warmly wrapped in a tweed skirt and jacket and matching beret, and carrying some scraps of bread for the seagulls. It was already early spring and today the weather was fine but Lionel insisted that she took no chances. He lived in fear of her catching a chill and she understood his anxiety and tried not to fret at his well-meant restrictions. She had caught a cold when she was fifteen, which had developed into a severe bout of pneumonia and congestion of the lungs. In fact for several days she had been seriously ill and had hovered between life and death but had mercifully survived.

As soon as Lionel heard the account from her aunt he had become over-anxious about a possible recurrence and Maude was 'confined to bed' for the mornings until eleven o'clock when she rose, washed and dressed in time to go downstairs for lunch. It was irksome being treated like a semi-invalid but Maude had become used to it during her year-long marriage, and her aunt played her part by bringing breakfast on a tray and doing most of the cooking.

The house was built on rising ground overlooking Folkestone harbour and the walk to the beach took around fifteen minutes. Maude paused for a few moments to watch the queue of eager passengers waiting to board the boat that would take them across to Boulogne. She and Lionel had made the trip once, on their honeymoon, but Maude had been queasy in the slight swell and had not enjoyed the sensation of being away from firm ground. Although the return journey was smoother, she had been extremely pleased to see Folkestone reappearing through the mist when they returned.

Today she stood on the beach feeding the raucous gulls while Primmy raced up and down across the shingle in search of something to carry home as a prize. Last time it had been a dead seagull, which the dog refused to surrender. Slowly Maude made her way down to the water's edge and watched the small boats bobbing at anchor on the incoming tide – a sight she usually found very relaxing. Now, however, Maude's thoughts were anxious and centred on the mysterious Miss Crewe.

Moving further along the beach she met and spoke to Tom Wheeler, the deckchair attendant, about the programme of Sunday morning music promised for the bandstand.

When she finally turned to retrace her steps she spotted Lionel hurrying towards her across the shingle, waving to catch her attention. Instinctively, at the sight of him, a smile lit up her face.

Lionel was a slim, handsome man, with fair hair and a moustache – he was as fair as she was dark. His eyes were hazel while hers were blue-green. His hair was fine and fair and well-behaved and he wore it fashionably parted in the middle. Hers was dark chestnut, curly and often unruly. As soon as he reached her, Lionel gave her a fierce hug.

'Mrs Brent, I believe!' he said with a grin – his usual greeting.

'Mr Brent. Fancy meeting you!'

'It's a small world.' He kissed her, and slipped an arm through hers as they began the walk back. 'Have you forgiven me – for the surprise?'

'The letter, you mean? No I haven't. You've given us cause for concern. What on earth are you up to?'

'I knew if I suggested it you'd say no so I thought I'd surprise you, but I think you'll like each other and I do want you to give her a chance.'

'If she's to help Aunt Biddy the answer will be a definite no, I'm afraid. She'd hate—'

'It's not exactly for her benefit, dearest, it's for you. You need care and your aunt is getting older and rather frail. She's doing much too much and Alice will ease her burden by looking after you.'

'But I don't need looking after, Lionel,' she protested. 'You make too much fuss of me. I'm perfectly healthy. Ask the doctor if you don't believe me. The pneumonia was years ago! If I can survive that, I can survive anything!' She glanced down at the dog and groaned. 'Oh no, Primmy! What have you found?'

Ignoring her comment, Primmy trotted proudly beside Lionel carrying part of a dead crab.

Lionel looked annoyed at the interruption. 'I disagree, Maude. You're very brave and you make light of your frailty but I'm your husband and I intend to protect you from yourself, whether you like it or not.' He smiled suddenly. 'Where would I be without you?'

His smile disarmed her as it always did. Maude knew she was loved and Lionel was the centre of her world. If anything happened to him, she would be devastated. If anything happened to her she knew it would break his heart.

He went on eagerly. 'If the two of you like each other, and I know you will, she will live in and be a companion for you. And before you say you don't need one, I must remind you that for most of the week while I'm at work, you have no-one to talk to except an elderly lady who is becoming distinctly doddery and likes to spend all her time cooking! I love your aunt dearly – you know I do – but look at the quality of your conversations, Maude.'

'My conversations? What d'you mean?'

'How often do you discuss art or books or the state of

the theatre? When do you discuss the state of Europe . . . or the winner of the Nobel prize?'

'How often do *you* discuss them?' Her tone was indignant.

'Frequently at my club. I'm not criticizing you, Maude. I'm simply afraid that your world is much narrower than it should be. You're a very intelligent woman.'

In spite of herself, Maude still felt slighted by his comments. 'So is this Alice person constantly watching the operas at Covent Garden . . . or reading *The Lancet* for the latest medical discoveries?' Maude glanced up at his face and recognized the determined set of his jaw. Her husband could be hard to move when he had set his heart on something and now it seemed it was Alice Crewe. She changed her line of attack. 'Isn't a companion rather old-fashioned, Lionel? I mean, aren't they intended for elderly widows or spinsters? I'm young and I'm hale and hearty and—'

'You are nothing of the kind, Maude. But you're right in one respect. Miss Crewe was exactly that – a companion to an elderly widow who has just died. The poor young woman was at her wits' end with nowhere to go and Barlowe at the gallery was asking if anyone needed a governess or a companion. I thought of you.' He held up a hand to forestall her objections. 'The fact is I think we could take the pressure off Biddy. Miss Crewe could run up and down for you more easily than your aunt and you would have someone more your own age to talk to.'

They left the beach and started back along the road while Maude tried to think of further reasons why Alice Crewe should go elsewhere. The fact was she was becoming intrigued in spite of her initial objections.

Lionel said, 'The old lady travelled widely and she must have talked to Miss Crewe about her earlier life. I'm sure you'll find her interesting to talk to.' He took a quick glance at her face and added, 'There's something else. She doesn't cook!'

They both laughed and Maude relaxed and punched his arm playfully. 'That's not nice!' She decided not to mention the Bakewell tart. Lionel was always complaining that the lighter puddings he preferred – stewed fruit, jelly or ice cream – rarely appeared on the table. Instead pies, steamed puddings and hearty fruit crumbles were carried in relentlessly by a beaming Aunt Biddy, who made certain that none of it was ever left.

As they came in sight of *Fairways*, their house, Maude sighed. She could see that her kind-hearted husband was hoping to offer the unfortunate Miss Crewe a new home and a job. He had convinced himself that he would be helping his delicate wife. They had four bedrooms so they could easily accommodate her. Maude could not object on that score but, still wary of the project, she felt there must be a way out of the dilemma, if only she could find it. She said no more on the subject but before they reached home Maude had made a decision. Bringing a stranger into their small household was a risk she was not prepared to take. Reluctantly she was going to disappoint her husband. Alice Crewe would not be joining them.

In fact, Alice Crewe was not at all what Maude had expected and as they sat down together in the elegantly furnished sitting room, she was forced to make an immediate reassessment. Several inches shorter than Maude, Miss Crewe was a friendly, bubbly person with surprising warmth. She reminded Maude of a cheerful gypsy in her dark-red skirt and white jacket. Her neat straw hat was decorated with dark-red ribbon. Only her sensible shoes suggested that she might previously have been someone's paid companion.

'Of course I miss the poor Mrs Patterson, the funny old dear,' Miss Crewe confessed with disarming honesty, referring to the death of her former employer. 'But four years is a long time and pushing a Bath chair to and fro along The Leas twice a day was hard work. And not very exciting, to be frank. I read to her from the Bible first thing in the morning and last thing at night.' She leaned forward confidingly. 'She was dear soul but, considering her wandering past, strangely terrified to step outside the routine she had devised for herself. It probably made her feel secure. Probably felt more vulnerable as she grew older.'

'Were you the only other person in her life?' Maude asked curiously.

'No. There was a Mrs Hacket who came in each day and prepared meals for us. Not breakfast but a simple cooked lunch, mostly steamed fish and mashed potatoes, and the inevitable sandwiches for tea.' Her rueful smile faded abruptly. 'Am I talking too much?'

Maude smiled. 'Not at all. I'm interested. So you haven't travelled yourself?'

'Oh no. We did go to Italy once for a holiday but she was very nervous and rather critical of the hotel and its staff. I got the impression she had once been used to better things. She did most of her travelling before she needed me. "Globetrotting" she called it. She was troubled by arthritis in her hips towards the end and was forced to give up her wanderings.'

'May I ask how old you are, Miss Crewe?'

'Twenty-three last time I counted!' She looked round the room. 'I thought there was a dog. I'm not allergic to dogs or anything.'

'Primmy is almost certainly sulking in the kitchen with Aunt Biddy because we've thrown away a dead crab she found on the beach. She's a rather wild cross terrier "of dubious extraction" – my husband's description – but she knows that all tasty titbits come from my aunt. She spends too much time in the kitchen, I fear.'

'I understand you're a semi-invalid.'

'Oh no! Certainly not!' Maud rolled her eyes. 'I assure you I'm not!'

'Mr Brent used the word "delicate". He says you have to stay in bed until eleven each morning. I thought . . .'

'That's my husband's idea but I don't always obey the rule!' She rolled her eyes humorously. 'He thinks I do and that's what matters. I was once very ill and was near to death but I'm perfectly fit now. Mr Brent, however, worries about my health and insists that I take life slowly and carefully . . .' She tailed off and shrugged.

'I suppose he means well. I mean, he obviously has your best interests at heart.'

'I'm sure he does. He's a wonderful husband. I'm very fortunate.' Suddenly Maude felt that Miss Crewe, being single, might think she was gloating so she searched for a new topic. 'What is your health record, Miss Crewe?'

Miss Crewe grinned and her round face crinkled and her dark button-black eyes shone with mischief. 'I'm as tough as old boots – or so Mrs Patterson claimed. I told her, "I have to be tough to push that Bath chair of yours!"'

Maude was trying hard to be rational about the woman. Alice Crewe seemed very open, had a sense of humour and in many ways seemed very suitable for the job Lionel wanted Maude to offer her. True, she was the sort of woman Maude would like as a friend – but did she want her as a companion? A friend would come and go. A companion would be permanent. Did she want a stranger hovering around her all the time?

'What are your interests?' she asked. 'There would be plenty of time when I would want to be alone. What would you find to do here? It's a far cry from London with all the theatres and art galleries. Apart from the sea and the ferries coming and going to France—'

'I've never been to a theatre but Folkestone has a few, doesn't it, and I read a lot of books. I'm also very keen on learning chess. The dear old soul taught me the basic moves. Do you play?'

'Not really. I have a chess set that belonged to my father. He intended to teach me but then he was killed – and my mother died of a broken heart. That's what the doctor said.'

'When was that?'

'About eighteen months ago. My father was a well-known artist – you may have heard of him. Arnold Cope. As their only child I inherited this house and I still have many of his paintings stored in the cellar where it's cool and a few more in the attic or tucked away under the stairs.'

'I'd love to see some of them,' Miss Crewe said eagerly. 'I don't know much about art but I might learn something.'

Surprised, Maude frowned. 'Actually, my husband thought you were quite well informed about art and music.'

'Oh! Did he?' She looked startled. 'I–I suppose I may

have exaggerated a bit,' she confessed. 'I was so keen to be considered for the job.'

Maude laughed. She found the young woman's candour refreshing. 'It doesn't matter, Miss Crewe. As for the paintings – I sell them quite regularly, mostly through the Barlowe Gallery in London in which, since my father's death, I now have a fifty per cent financial interest. Since our marriage my husband spends a great deal of his time promoting the gallery in different ways.'

'It sounds interesting work.'

'It is but it's not work as such. He isn't employed but does it for the pleasure of it – and to help me, of course. He genuinely enjoys it. He says it has opened up a new world for him. He helps Mr Barlowe mount the exhibitions, which we do regularly, and also travels widely to seek out new artists who we might ask to exhibit. He's away from home quite a lot, actually.'

'So you don't only sell your father's paintings.'

'No, we don't, but my father was very well respected and his work is still very much in demand, thank goodness.' She decided to match Miss Crewe's honesty and added, 'They provide a useful income.'

'Your husband told me a little about your parents. It must have been terrible to be left alone like that.'

Maude shook her head at the memories. 'But shortly after they died I met Lionel and we were married. It was what is called a whirlwind courtship but I've had no regrets. We're very happy.'

'It all sounds very romantic. So where did you actually meet?'

'Through the Barlowe Gallery! Lionel bought one of my father's paintings and was so impressed he asked if he could come down here to Folkestone to see more of his work.' She smiled at the memory.

They were silent for a few seconds and then Maude heard herself asking about Alice's former pay and conditions – how many hours she worked a week, what accommodation she expected and what time had been allowed by her previous employer for a holiday.

'I shall discuss these terms with my husband and my aunt,' Maude told Alice. 'But you must understand that nothing is actually settled. Mr Brent has surprised me with this idea and I need time to think it over. We'll write and let you know our decision.'

Later, when she talked to Lionel, he continued to encourage her acceptance of the plan. 'You don't have to employ her, dearest,' he told her, 'but I confess I will be seriously disappointed if you don't. I shall feel so much happier if you have someone like Alice to keep you company. I have given this a great deal of thought and to me she seems to be ideal and would fit in well here. '

Maude smiled. 'If it were up to Aunt Biddy she'd get the job. Before Miss Crewe left, the three of us sat a while over a cup of tea and she told us that she has a weakness for food of all kinds but especially cakes and pastries! My aunt now thinks of her as a very discerning young woman.'

'So she did impress you, Maude? I thought she would.'

'Except that she had rather deceived you, Lionel, about her familiarity with the arts. Or did you deceive me?' She laughed. 'She's never been to the opera in her life and knows nothing about art or music!'

He held up his hands by way of a defence. 'Oh! Poor Miss Crewe. I dare say most people lie at interviews . . . and maybe it was me that exaggerated. I thought she'd make a lively, cheerful friend for you, Maude. Please don't upset me by saying I was wrong.'

Looking thoughtful, Maude still weighed the arguments in her mind.

Lionel went on, 'I would want her to have her own rooms. That is, a room as well as the bedroom. It would have to be the box room next to her bedroom but we could make it cosy. A shelf for her books, maybe, a small table and a comfortable chair. That way she needn't share our space all the time.'

'I should hope not, Lionel,' Maude said quickly. 'She isn't going to be one of the family. I mean, we're not *adopting* her. She will want to be on her own some of the time but . . . but available at others. At least, I imagine that's how it works.'

'Whatever you say, Maude. She can certainly have the box room.'

Maude nodded. 'Primmy liked her, too.'

He rolled his eyes in mock exasperation. 'Oh well, if the dog approves . . .!'

'Stop it, Lionel! You know what I mean. Maybe we should offer her a probationary period. Say two months to see how everything works out. Then if I don't enjoy her being here or . . . or she doesn't fit in . . .' She shrugged. 'She goes.' Suddenly her eyes widened. 'Oh dear! I forgot to ask for a reference!'

'She sent one. It was very complimentary. I'm sorry, dearest, I forgot to show it to you.' He glanced round the room, patting his pockets as he did so. 'Now where did I put it?'

When asked, Biddy hadn't seen it and Lionel failed to discover it. 'I'll give it to you when it turns up,' he told Maude. 'But I do recall it was quite flattering but written in a shaky hand about a year after Mrs Patterson became ill.' He got up from the chair, stretching his arms. 'I feel stiff. I think I'll take a stroll around the garden. D'you feel like joining me?'

Maude hesitated then shook her head. 'I think I'll write to Miss Crewe before I change my mind, and offer her the two months' probation to see how things go. I hope I don't regret it.'

He gave her a kiss as he passed. 'I'm sure you won't,' he assured her. 'And your Aunt Biddy will be in seventh heaven!'

ONE

Friday June 2nd, 1922

It was five to eight in the morning and Maude lay in bed waiting to hear the front door close. As soon as it did she smiled to herself as Alice's footsteps sounded on the stairs. The door opened and Alice's head appeared.

'All clear! He's gone.'

Maude threw back the bedclothes and slid her feet on to the rug. Life had changed since Alice Crewe moved in. She had rapidly become one of the family and everyone enjoyed her presence in the house. With unerring judgement she had found her place somewhere between a paid companion and a close family friend. She was the sister Maude had never had and also proved herself a willing student of cookery, learning fast from Biddy and fully appreciative of her talents.

Maude secretly admitted that she enjoyed Alice's young company but she was careful not to exclude her aunt from their gossipy chats, which wasn't difficult because these mostly took place during long walks on the beach when the weather permitted.

Lionel had no idea that his wife no longer had breakfast in bed except on Sundays, when Lionel was not travelling to London to the gallery or further afield. Each morning, after his departure, Maude washed and dressed and hurried downstairs to join Biddy and Alice in the kitchen, where the latter was transferring the untouched contents of Maude's breakfast tray to the table. When Alice had first suggested the deceit, she had used the oft-quoted excuse: 'What the eye can't see, the heart can't grieve over!' No-one had argued with her.

Now the three women settled comfortably round the kitchen table and began to eat porridge with honey followed by Biddy's cinnamon bread, generously buttered.

Maude waited for the right moment and then said, 'Lionel is planning a holiday for me. He's booked a week's stay at a private guest house in Hastings. The Romilees Hotel.'

Biddy frowned. 'Romilees? That's new to me. Where exactly is it situated?'

'Somewhere on the hill opposite the pier.'

'You mean behind where the new White Rock Pavilion will be? Does it have a view?'

'I suppose so. Our stay there starts at the end of next week, on Saturday. I feel rather mean, leaving you both behind, but my dear husband thinks we need a little time to ourselves.' She shrugged.

Biddy said, 'No offence, dear, but I'd rather stay here, to tell you the truth. I never have been one for holidays. I went to Exeter once with your mother, to a so-called boarding house. All that way to stay with some friends of hers who owned it. It was after she recovered from the pleurisy, before you were born. It was nice enough but I didn't think much of the food. Not enough of it and nothing I could call substantial.'

Alice grinned. 'You mean no big nourishing puddings!'

'Exactly.' Biddy folded her arms. 'Flimsy food. That's what I called it. An hour after a meal you needed a biscuit.'

Maude said, 'I didn't know Mother had ever had pleurisy.'

'Didn't you?' For a moment she struggled with her memory. 'Well, maybe it was something else. I forget. It was something that began with "p" . . . Or was it? It might have been after the jaundice. Your mother was never well for long, poor soul.'

Primmy woke, stretched and wandered to the back door. Alice got up from the table and let her out into the garden.

Maude poured herself a second cup of tea and handed the teapot to Alice, who refilled her own cup.

Biddy looked at her niece. 'I think Lionel's right. You should have some time together. We're quite a houseful and you've only been married for a year or so.'

'Like a second honeymoon,' Alice agreed. 'He's being very thoughtful as usual.'

'Of course he is, Maude. Don't worry about us. Alice

and I will have a grand old time here, won't we, Alice? We can get up to all sorts of mischief. When the cat's away, the mice will play!'

'A grand old time? What are you implying?' Maude challenged, laughing.

Alice said, 'We could give a wild party and invite all sorts of undesirables!'

'You don't know any undesirables!' Maude stirred sugar into her tea. 'Or maybe you do!'

'Precisely. I might be friends with an axe murderer, for all you know! Or my favourite uncle might have been a forger. Bank notes and such like.'

Not to be outdone, Biddy said, 'We could run off with the family silver while you're both away.'

Maude ignored the suggestion. 'Anyway, the plan is we're going to take gentle strolls along the cliff tops at Fairlight, and maybe picnic on the beach. Fresh sea air!'

'You can do all that here in Folkestone,' Biddy pointed out. 'What's so special about Hastings? It's rather gone down in the world, hasn't it?'

'Don't say that!' Maude said indignantly. 'Lionel thinks—'

'It used to be popular with invalids with lung troubles who needed fresh air,' her aunt continued unabashed. 'And the sun and sea bathing was highly recommended, but that's mostly gone now. Hastings isn't what it was although it's trying to recover.' She cut another slice of bread. 'Your grandmother lived there all her life and she used to go on about all the wealthy people who came down from London in the summer, but now it's only day trippers and the like. Noisy, no money, here one day and gone the next! At least Folkestone has avoided that particular problem.'

Maude shrugged off the criticism. 'Well anyway, Lionel thinks the change will do us good. He may need to spend the odd day in London at the gallery but there's a train service, although it's very slow and not especially punctual.'

'So he'll be leaving you on your own some days.' Alice got up to let Primmy in again and gave her some scrapings from the porridge saucepan. 'You'll find that a bit odd, won't you? You might be lonely without your devoted aunt and your faithful companion.'

'I shan't be alone exactly,' said Maude. She knew Alice was teasing her but insisted on taking the comment seriously. The same thought had occurred to her but she wasn't about to admit it. 'There'll be other people staying in the hotel, presumably, and the staff will be on hand. I might even take some charcoal and a sketchbook and do some sketching in the gardens. Apparently they have a very attractive garden. A small lily pool . . . and a small aviary.'

'Forget the birds,' Biddy suggested. 'They'll be difficult to sketch with all that fluttering. Unless they are parrots. They do at least sit still on their perches most of the time. I'd go for the lilies if I were you.'

'You ought to be able to sketch, Maude,' said Alice, 'and paint, with such a famous artist for a father.'

'You'd think so but I'm not much good at it. Still, it would pass the time.'

Biddy suddenly lost interest in the conversation. The idea of herself and Alice being left to their own devices depressed her. There would only be Alice to enjoy her cooking. Poor Lionel would miss her puddings. She stood up abruptly and smoothed her apron. 'I think I'll make a bacon roly-poly for supper,' she said. 'All those in favour?'

Two hands rose obediently.

Biddy's smile returned.

The following days seemed to rush past while Maude spent a great deal of time trying to decide which clothes to take with her. She knew they would be expected to dress for dinner so she spent a cheerful afternoon with Alice, shopping for a suitable outfit to augment the dress she already had. They finally agreed on a lavender skirt and a lightweight jacket in the same colour but with white trim at the cuffs and collar. Maude began to look forward to the trip. The fact that they wouldn't be too far from home allayed her fears about her aunt and Alice being left to fend for themselves and Lionel gave strict instructions that if anything went wrong in his absence they were to be telephoned at the hotel immediately.

'Not that I expect anything to go wrong,' Maude told Lionel earnestly, as they undressed for bed. 'But if it does . . . Aunt Biddy is becoming rather vague and—'

'You don't have to tell me that, Maude. I can see it for myself.' He reached for her hand and gave it a reassuring squeeze. 'So stop worrying, my love. If anything does happen we'll summon a taxi and be home in no time.'

The following afternoon, Thursday, Maude was relaxing on one of the garden seats with Primmy beside her when the dog sprang to her feet, stared down the garden and started barking furiously.

'Primmy! You made me jump!' Maude scolded and turned to see what had excited the dog. To her surprise she saw a figure half hidden in the bushes and she watched in some trepidation as the dog raced forward.

'Who's there?' she cried, jumping to her feet. 'I can see you!' Glancing back at the house she hoped someone would notice what was happening and come to investigate.

Primmy had found her quarry and was yelping with excitement as she pranced round whoever it was. Eventually a male voice cried, 'Call him off!'

'Not until you come out of those bushes!'

The voice grew shriller. 'Get down, damn you!'

It occurred to Maude that the dog might be in danger from the stranger. It was unlikely to be the other way round because Primmy was noisy but not aggressive. Maude took a few steps forward and then called, 'Primmy! Come here. Good girl!'

'Get *away* from me, you stupid animal!'

The intruder had not hurt the dog so far and Maude felt a little braver. She also assumed that the intruder hadn't been bitten by the dog. When the dog returned she caught hold of her collar and called out, 'Come out at once or I shall call the police.'

Almost at once a wiry figure appeared from the bushes and stepped gingerly into full view, and Maude saw with relief that he was no more than a very young man who was obviously more frightened than she was.

'I'm not a burglar,' he cried. 'Don't call the police. I've brought a package for a Mr Lionel Brent, that's all. I've done nothing wrong.' He edged a little closer. He was thin with unkempt hair and what Maude thought of as a foxy face. The sleeves of his jacket were too short for his arms and one of his bootlaces was undone. Maude could see no sign of a weapon and no hint of hostility in his face. So who on earth was he and why was he bringing her husband a package?

At that moment Alice appeared and called Primmy to her. 'What is it, Maude? Can I help? Shall I fetch Mr Brent?'

Maud realized at once that this was a clever bluff on Alice's part because they all knew that there was no man in the house. Lionel was miles away in London. Maude was full of admiration for her friend's quick thinking. She replied, 'It's all right, Alice. The young man has brought something for Lionel.'

The young man held out a bulky envelope. 'I was told to deliver this – for a shilling – but I was only to give it to Mr Brent.' His voice quivered and Maude began to feel sorry for him. She guessed him to be about eighteen and obviously he had been tempted by the promise of a shilling.

She held out her hand. 'I'll give it to Mr Brent later on. He's my husband.' From the corner of her eye she saw that her aunt was now also watching from the front steps.

The young man shook his head. 'I have to give it to him and only him. He was very determined about that.'

'Who was very determined? You're speaking in riddles.'

'I can't say. More'n my life's worth.' His voice had grown sullen. You tell him I'm here. Say Jem's here. He'll know.'

Maude realized suddenly that he was no longer frightened. It was unfortunate that Lionel was absent but she must follow Alice's lead. She said, 'He's ill in bed. My husband. A slight fever. He's sleeping.'

He considered this, his head on one side. 'I won't get a penny if I don't give it to him.'

'To Mr Brent. I know. Well, he can't come down so there's an end to it.' Maude gave him what she hoped was a stern look and hardened her voice. She didn't want him to think she was at all wary of him.

'So you say!'

She ignored the remark and said sharply, 'You won't get your money so get along!'

'But I have to deliver it, see, otherwise . . .' His eyes had narrowed suddenly as if he suspected her of lying.

'But he's not available and I'm not having you littering up the garden while you wait for him to retur—' She left the word unfinished and said instead 'to recover'. Even to her own ears it sounded rather unconvincing but Maude, sensing that he posed no threat, pressed home the point she was making. 'So please leave and be quite sure that if you set foot on our property again I shall call in the police and have you arrested for trespass.'

For a moment he considered his options then shrugged. He turned away, stuffing the bulky envelope back into his pocket, and Maude, Biddy and Alice watched him in silence as he stumbled back through the bushes and presumably climbed back over the fence.

'All very strange,' Maude muttered as she made her way back to the front steps to join the others. They released Primmy and she raced off in his direction but, finding him gone, returned looking crestfallen and threw Maude a reproachful glance.

Maude explained the whole encounter to Biddy and Alice and they agreed to watch at intervals from one of the bedroom windows, just in case he came back, but there was no further sighting and even the dog lost interest in the stranger and retired to her basket.

When Lionel came home Maude held his briefcase while he took off his raincoat, and she told him about the intruder.

'Didn't need it,' he grumbled. 'Not a sight of rain all day.'

'You're not listening, Lionel. I'm telling you that this weird young man was lurking—'

'I saw him,' Lionel told her. 'A bit of a scared rabbit, wasn't he! He was waiting for me on the station platform. He must be a bit dense.' He tapped his head.

'But he had a package for you. An envelope.'

He nodded impatiently. 'It was a package of information from the guest house, which I'd requested but they sent the wrong stuff. I wanted to know what was happening in the town in the way of entertainment during our stay.'

'So where is it now?'

'I tossed it in the station rubbish bin. The leaflets were for August not June.'

Maude stared at him. 'But why send someone like him? All that cloak-and-dagger stuff and . . . and a shilling . . . and refusing to give it to me! Why not put it in the post? Don't you think that's very odd?'

Lionel shrugged. 'No good asking me why they sent him. Maybe he lives in Folkestone. I don't know. It seems an odd thing to do but there's no harm done.'

'But I nearly called the police. He frightened me, Lionel. I keep thinking that if we had already been on our holiday in Hastings, Alice and Aunt Biddy might have been in some kind of danger. Even if he was harmless it would be unsettling.'

'But they weren't here alone, Maude, and nothing bad happened so do stop worrying.'

Lionel's attitude was reassuring and Maude began to feel that perhaps, after all, she had made too much of it. 'Primmy was marvellous. She rushed straight at him, barking like a lunatic. The young man was almost as scared as I was and—'

'My poor love!' He hugged her briefly. 'Just forget about it.' His expression changed. His eyes shone. 'Now I'll tell you about *my* day. We sold the last of your father's paintings to a French chap. For a good sum!' He whispered the amount in her ear and her eyebrows shot up.

'Goodness! Father would be astonished.'

'Monsieur Laconte was just browsing but it took his eye right away. He knew the name Cope and also recognized the landscape. He was determined to have it.'

'That's wonderful news! Well done, Lionel!' The encounter in the garden was already fading from her mind. 'So when does the gallery want the next batch of pictures?'

'In a few weeks' time. I don't want them to be too readily

available. Let the clients wait for them! Maybe next month.' He loosened his tie and unfastened his collar as he headed for the stairs. He would change from what he called his 'business clothes' into something more casual and was looking forward to his evening meal.

In the kitchen Biddy was stirring the leek and tomato soup, which would precede a chicken and bacon pie. Her mind, however, was busy replaying the incident of the intruder. Something about it jarred but she couldn't put a finger on it. The whole story seemed odd. Why should anyone send a dim lad like Jem to deliver a few brochures or leaflets or whatever they were? All the way from Hastings to Folkestone? And why had he come creeping in over the fence instead of coming straight to the front door? Perhaps he was fantasizing, making out that he was spy on a secret mission. Boys liked to do things like that, she imagined, and although he looked older he might have been a bit backward. A bit childish, even . . . She tested the soup, pushed the saucepan to the back of the stove and replaced the lid. As she did so the nagging worry became clearer. How had the young man known that if the women folk were lying about Lionel being in bed with a fever, there was a chance he was in London and would return by train? In other words, why had he waited for him at the station to hand over his package?

Biddy wiped down the table, trying to remember what she had planned for the evening meal, to follow the soup. Stepping into the larder she surveyed the shelves in the hope that something would jog her memory. She believed that so far nobody had noticed that she was becoming very forgetful and had decided to keep a little notebook somewhere so that she could make notes and refer to it, but so far she had forgotten to buy the notebook.

Seeing some cold chicken she smiled. Chicken and bacon pie! Of course. As she carried it from the larder and set it on the table, Alice came into the kitchen in search of her gardening gloves.

Biddy pounced. 'You're always losing them, Alice. You

should return them to the potting shed after you use them.' It made her feel better to know that someone else, someone *younger*, also had a faulty memory. Before Alice could reply she went on, 'Funny "how d'you do" this morning, wasn't it? I can't rest easy in my mind. That strange young man and—'

'It was odd, true, but Mr Brent seemed to understand it all. You should forget about it. We all should. I'm not letting it bother me.' She opened the dresser drawer and found the gloves. 'I thought I'd give Maude a hand. She's trying to tidy up the roses, which have gone a bit straggly.'

'But how did he know he should wait at the station? We didn't mention it.'

'Whoever sent him must have known he works in London some days. He was set on earning that shilling and can't have been as daft as we thought.'

'But we said Lionel was ill in bed.'

Alice grinned. 'We're obviously terribly bad liars! Quite a compliment in a way. Anyway, who cares? I'm quite looking forward to a week here alone. I mean, just the two of us. We can get up later than usual and—'

'I expect we'll find plenty to do,' Biddy told her firmly. 'We could sort out the linen – maybe even turn some of the worn sheets sides to middle. The days will drag if we do nothing.'

'I hate sewing! I'm paid to be a companion.'

'You can't be a companion to someone who's not here and they're hardly going to pay you for a week for sitting around!'

'I didn't ask them to go away. I'd go with them if they wanted me to go on earning my money.'

Confused by the logic, Biddy ignored this line of reasoning.

Alice investigated the contents of the saucepan and, brightening, reverted to her vision of their week alone. 'We could get out that old croquet set,' she suggested, 'and have a game on the lawn!' She noticed the cold chicken. 'Let me guess – chicken pie!'

'Chicken and bacon pie. There's not quite enough chicken.'

'Mmm! Lovely.'

Biddy smiled at her warmly. Going in search of the butter, lard and flour distracted her, and she pushed her doubts aside and concentrated on the job in hand. She cut the butter and lard into the flour then broke it up into smaller pieces with her fingers. She lined a pie dish with the pastry, reserving enough to cover it, then broke up the chicken and a lump of cold ham and added them to the dish along with a small chopped onion and two diced carrots.

She said, 'We'll have to be careful when they're away, always to keep the outside doors closed – and locked – in case the mystery man comes back.' She glanced surreptitiously at Alice to see if she would also consider the idea sensible.

'He won't,' she said confidently. 'Why should he come back?'

'I don't know. He might know we're on our own.'

'But if Mr Brent is at Hastings in the hotel, why would they send someone here?'

'Ah!' Flummoxed by this obvious question, Biddy felt horribly foolish and was again reminded uncomfortably of how woolly her mind had become. 'You're right,' she mumbled, embarrassed. 'I wasn't thinking straight.'

To her relief Alice didn't laugh at her mistake. Instead she said, 'So we'll have nothing to worry about.'

She whisked out of the kitchen into the garden to help Maude and left Biddy to complete the pie and turn on the oven. As she placed a gauze cover over the pie while the oven heated up, she visualized the complete meal set out on the dining table, and the usual sense of security returned. With a smile on her face, she began to hum a favourite hymn.

The Barlowe Gallery was situated in Wentnock Street in London and at quarter to nine the following Saturday it was still closed. Opening times on Saturday were from ten thirty a.m. until seven p.m. but Lionel was already there. His secretary, Jane Dyer, would be in some time around half past nine. She had replaced Mrs Breck, who had retired eighteen months ago after twenty-one years of loyal service. Miss Dyer claimed to have studied art history and was reasonably knowledgeable but, due to her shy manner, lacked her predecessor's easy way with the clients. Lionel, although secretly disappointed, did appreciate her office skills. She managed all the paperwork with clinical attention to detail and nothing was ever mislaid or unaccounted for. She could be trusted to fetch things from the safe when necessary and, although her tea making could never match that of Mrs Breck, she was willing to run the occasional errand, which Mrs Breck had considered beneath her dignity. Jane Dyer also performed well on the telephone and several buyers had commented on her efficiency and pleasant manner.

His hope had been that she would blossom as the years went on but at twenty-one she still lacked confidence. She lived at home with her widowed mother – a strict churchgoer who had brought up her daughter with Victorian values that many young women were beginning to abandon. She dressed primly and wore no make-up but she was slim, pretty and eager to please and he felt she gave the gallery a certain elegance. In fact, on the few occasions when she was absent, it felt rather dull without her. Glancing at the clock, he saw that he had twenty minutes before she was due to arrive, and set about attending to various matters that he felt needed last-minute attention before setting off for their holiday in Hastings. He telephoned Barlowe and then rang an artist who lived in St Leonards, and arranged to meet him during their holiday – meeting for lunch in the Romilees Hotel on the third day, to be confirmed. His wife had understood that he couldn't resist the chance to kill two birds with one stone. Time was money.

He then unwrapped a painting that had been delivered the previous day just as they were closing. The artist was new to them but he was hopeful. Lionel set the painting up on a spare easel and stood back to study it. It was a watercolour of boats at anchor in Folkestone harbour and he knew from experience that it would find a buyer within a week or so. There was something about the sea that touched people. In this particular painting the sea was calm and the boats seemed to rock gently. It was a tranquil scene and would appeal, he imagined, to people with fraught lives. Normally, once a picture had sold from a new artist the gallery would commission further pictures . . .

He heard a key in the street door and glanced up, pleasantly surprised. Miss Dyer was five minutes early. Smiling broadly, he crossed the room to let her in.

Startled, she cried, 'Mr Brent! I thought you were going on holiday today. I didn't expect to see you here – not that I'm objecting.' She blushed faintly.

'We are off to Hastings, Miss Dyer, but it will probably be later in the afternoon before we arrive there. I wanted to check up on a few things here before I go. A couple of phone calls . . . Would you be a dear and make me a cup of tea?'

'Of course, Mr Brent, and would you like a butterfly cake with it? My mother made them and I brought two in but you can have Mr Barlowe's and he needn't know.'

He thanked her with a conspiratorial wink and she hurried away to the kitchen, beaming broadly.

TWO

The Romilees Hotel was situated on high ground opposite the pier from where some of the rooms enjoyed a sea view. It boasted ten bedrooms, three of which were single and one of which was a family room with three beds. The rooms were named after flowers and the one that had been booked in the name of Brent was the Rose Room, which meant that the eiderdown was of pink silk, the wallpaper design was pink and silver stripes and the matching lampshades were edged with pink fringing. It was one of the rooms with a sea view.

Penny and Meg worked together in the room, stripping the bed and remaking it for the couple who were due to arrive in the afternoon.

'Mr and Mrs Brent,' Meg informed her colleague. 'He's something in London, I think. Arty. A bit posh so might get a decent tip out of them. They're coming about four.'

'How "arty" exactly?' Penny pushed a stray lock of frizzy ginger hair back under her white linen cap. 'You mean he paints pictures?'

'I s'pose so.'

They smoothed the pillow slips and hauled the eiderdown from the chair over which it had been draped.

Meg glanced up at the wall above the bed. 'I wonder what he'll think of that?' The picture showed a bowl of blowsy roses from which a few petals had fallen on to a highly polished table. The colours were brighter than might be expected and the picture frame was of intricately carved wood.

'What's wrong with it? I like it. It's lovely.'

Meg shrugged. 'It's a bit like the lid of a box of chocolates.'

They arranged the eiderdown and stood back to approve their work and give the room a final inspection before the beady-eyed owner made her rounds.

Meg gathered up dusters and polish and put them in the bucket. 'We went to see the show on the pier last night. Didn't see you there.'

'We didn't go after all. Tom felt a bit upset because he had another run in with the chap next door to him – the funny one who hardly ever went to school.'

'Jem, you mean. When he did go he was in my class.'

'Not often, then. Anyway he disappeared for two days last week and his mother worried herself to death about him.' Penny ran a critical finger along the window sill, frowned at the dust she had accumulated and wiped it on her apron. 'When he came back again my Tom saw him out the front. Stupid like, he started teasing him and called him "Runaway" to his face and then had to run away himself because Jem went after him and grabbed him round the throat!'

Meg stared at her. 'He never did!'

'I tell you, he did! He threatened to strangle Tom with his bare hands! His mother was screaming at him to let go. Jem's mother, not Tom's. Rider, that's their name. Funny crowd.' She regarded herself in the mirror, adjusted her cap and smiled at Meg. 'Good, was it? The show?'

'Not bad. It was just sketches and suchlike. A comedian – Alfie Parks – and some dancers . . . and a magician. Wahoo the Wonderful Wizard. That's what he called himself.'

'And was he?'

'What? Was he wonderful?' Meg considered the question. 'I s'pose so. He pulled a rabbit out of his hat and things like that. We were near the back so we couldn't see all that well but he did tricks. Mind you, my Alan knew how it was done. Some of it. You draw attention to something with one hand while you do something else with the other. I forget what it's called.'

Penny checked that the wardrobe was empty and knelt down to look under the bed. The chamber pot had not been used, thank goodness, and no-one had left a sock or a stocking. She had once found an earring, which she had handed in, and a ten-shilling note, which she had quickly tucked into her apron pocket. No such luck this time. She said, 'I bet the magician had dark hair. They always do. It's to make them look sort of mysterious and dangerous.' She clambered to her feet. 'You think about it.'

'He *was* dark, actually.' Meg frowned. 'But my Alan's dark-haired and he's not mysterious and dangerous.'

'I mean magicians, silly, not ordinary people! It goes with the black top hat and the black cloak. It looks sinister.'

'And the black wand! He had this magic wand . . .'

They headed towards the door, taking the brooms and other cleaning equipment with them.

On the way Penny gathered up the discarded sheets and pillowslips. She said, 'Mind you, my dad's got dark hair and he can be dangerous. Ask my brother. Dad clips him round the ear every time he says "bugger".' She mouthed the last word.

'Lots of men say that.'

'Not a boy of ten! My mum says he learned it at school . . . But s'pose a magician hasn't got dark hair? Then what?'

'Probably wears a wig.' She sighed. 'Right. What's next?' She pulled out a list and glanced at it. 'The Daffodil Room.'

They went out, closing the door behind them.

Much later the same day, Biddy settled Primmy in her basket with a biscuit, turned off the lights in the kitchen and checked for the second time that the doors and downstairs windows were locked. Alice waited halfway up the stairs.

She said, 'It's funny without them. Sort of creepy.'

'Oh, don't talk so daft, Alice!' Biddy began to haul herself up the stairs, relying heavily on the banisters. 'How can it be creepy with two people in it if it's not creepy with four people?'

'I don't know but it is.' As Biddy came up, Alice moved up to make room for her and reached the landing first. 'That top stair always creaks,' she said accusingly.

'Don't look at me.' Biddy puffed as she hauled herself up, hand over hand. 'They're not my stairs.'

'You ought to live in a bungalow, then you wouldn't have to drag yourself up and down.'

'I don't drag myself down, do I? It's only up. Up is the problem.' With a last gasp Biddy reached the top and stopped to rest. For a moment they both were aware of the gathering silence.

Alice said, 'So what time shall we get up tomorrow?'

She had asked this question several times already and Biddy still wasn't sure what to say. Coming to an abrupt decision she said, 'Half an hour later than usual.'

'Half an hour? Is that all?'

'We'll see how it goes. I might make it longer if we get the jobs done.'

'She shouldn't be giving us jobs to do. We're not servants. You're her aunt and I'm a companion.'

'Oh, don't start that again, Alice. She hasn't given us jobs. I have. I like to help around the place; it's my home, my family and I can't sit about doing nothing . . . Anyway, sleep well. See you in the morning.'

She set off in the direction of her bedroom. Putting on her light, she made straight for the chair in the corner and, sitting on the side of the bed, began to undress, folding each garment carefully and piling them on the nearby chair. Once she had removed her corset she let out a sigh of relief and reached for her nightdress. She cleaned her teeth, climbed into bed and reached beneath the pillow for her diary.

She wrote: '*Sat 10th June. They've gone and it's very quiet without them. Alice finds it creepy, silly girl. Nothing much to wash up after dinner and don't know what I shall cook tomorrow for just two. Can't think why they had to go off for a holiday. The week will go so slowly. I don't think Maude was so keen on the idea but Lionel was determined so she didn't want to disappoint him. Hope we don't see that weird chap again in the garden but it's unlikely as he won't know that we're just the two of us unless he is a burglar but he can't be because Lionel seemed to know about him but . . .*'

She paused. Surely if anyone tried to break in Primmy would bark like mad and the intruder would be scared off. Maybe they should bring Primmy and her basket up on to the landing . . . But then she wouldn't hear the intruder until it was too late. In her diary she crossed out the word '*but*' and started a new sentence.

'*Anyway I hope Maude enjoys herself even if he's going to pop up to the gallery once or twice. She'll be quite safe at the hotel and might meet some nice people to talk to while he's away. It certainly is strange here without them. I shan't sleep a wink.*'

Next day, breakfast in the dining room of the Romilees promised to be a relaxed affair and some of Maude's nervousness faded. The room was sunny and the various conversations politely muted. There were mixed garden flowers in a large bowl on the sideboard and seagulls swooped to and fro outside the window. It was strange to be away from home and she missed Alice and Aunt Biddy, although she would not admit it to Lionel. She was grateful for his concern and felt it would be unkind even to hint that the holiday might prove less than perfect. Breakfast was at nine and Maude and Lionel found themselves seated at a small table in the large bay window with an elderly couple on one side and a young couple with a son on the other.

They said their 'good mornings' and then Lionel handed Maude the breakfast menu and she chose scrambled egg on toast. When the waitress arrived Maude added a pot of tea for two.

Lionel glanced up at the waitress. 'I'll have the kippers,' he told her.

'They're very good,' she assured him.

'And some toast and marmalade.' His charming smile made her beam as she wrote down the order and scurried away in the direction of the kitchen.

Maude smiled at him. 'And what is the plan for today, Lionel?'

His handsome face lit up at the question. 'I thought we'd walk along to the other end of the town and take a look at the East Cliff Railway. It's quite an attraction, apparently. We'll be back in time for lunch.'

The elderly man leaned across to them. 'And a very good lunch it is, too, sir.' He smiled at Maude. 'My wife and I have always said that Romilees do a quite splendid Sunday lunch here. No expense spared. Fresh vegetables, first-class meat and all cooked to perfection. It wouldn't do to be a vegetarian in this hotel!'

His wife nodded enthusiastically. 'And it's all served with a smile. Nothing too much trouble.'

'Your first time here, is it?' He smiled at Maude.

'Yes it is.'

'You'll be back, my dear lady. Mark my words, you'll be back. Bracing sea air, entertainment on the pier . . . You can even swim in the sea if you care for that sort of thing. Not that we do – never fancied immersing ourselves in cold salt water – but there are plenty who do. Our amusement comes from watching their antics!'

He was distracted at this point by the arrival of egg and bacon for himself and his wife, and Maude and Lionel were once again free to discuss their day.

'After lunch you must have a rest, Maude. A sleep on the bed for an hour or so to let the meal go down.' He held up a hand as she started to protest. 'I know you slept well but you must allow me, darling, to know what's best for you.' He took hold of her hand and gave it a gentle squeeze. 'Don't I always, Maude?'

She nodded. Outside the sun shone and everyone was predicting that the fine weather would continue. Maude decided not to criticize the holiday in any way at all. Lionel had planned everything so carefully with her happiness in mind. She must appreciate his efforts. She counted her blessings. She had a wonderful husband, a comfortable home, good health, no money worries – a life many people would envy. It was up to her to enjoy every moment of their holiday together. She would forget about Alice and Aunt Biddy, who would no doubt be enjoying themselves in their own way. Primmy would be well looked after and in a week's time they would all be reunited again. Thus reassured, she glanced round the room.

At the next table the young boy was refusing to eat the

cornflakes that had been brought to him, insisting that they didn't taste right. Discreetly watching him, Maude wondered, not for the first time, when their own first child would announce his or her existence. Lionel wanted a child as much as she did but so far there had been no sign that she might be expecting a baby. Neither she nor Lionel had referred to this fact but she was sure he was as anxious as she was to start their family.

When they did have children, she wondered how she would cope. The woman next to her was being very patient but the father looked increasingly embarrassed and suddenly took away the offending cornflakes and asked the waitress to remove it.

'There now, Billy!' his mother said, disconcerted. 'See what you've done! You've made Daddy cross.'

'I want porridge, Mummy.'

'You chose cornflakes, Billy.'

'I meant to say porridge.'

The father said, 'You turned down egg and bacon and you turned down porridge.'

His mother caught Maude's eye and shrugged helplessly. Maude smiled in sympathy, wishing she could say something helpful but unable to think of anything.

To distract from his son's behaviour, the father turned towards Lionel and Maude. In a falsely cheerful voice he said, 'I'm William Hurst and this is my wife, Susan. I hope you enjoy your stay at Romilees. We come every year for a week and always feel better for the break.'

Lionel introduced himself and Maude, and they talked about Hastings and were told what it had to offer while Billy began to sniffle and then to kick the table leg. He cast sullen looks at his father and fiddled with the cruet and dropped his serviette on to the floor and tried to kick it under the table. These small rebellions were pointedly ignored but the waitress returned with a full breakfast each for Billy's parents.

Then the waitress said, 'Compliments of the cook and she has made Billy some porridge – if that's all right with you.'

Mrs Hurst clutched her beaded necklace, Billy sat up straighter in his chair and Maude held her breath, wondering what would happen next.

After a tense silence Mr Hurst gave a slight nod. 'Just this once, then. Say "thank you", Billy.'

'Thank you.'

The waitress placed the dish in front of the boy, smiled and walked away. His parents exchanged enigmatic glances and, abandoning their conversation with Maude and Lionel, concentrated on their food without speaking.

It was a small, insignificant episode, Maude told herself, when they finally left the dining room, but it had marred her first breakfast at Romilees and left her feeling vaguely disappointed. She hoped it wasn't an omen.

After lunch she took the obligatory nap and woke up at five to four. She remembered where she was and that Lionel must be somewhere in the hotel waiting for her. Sitting up she took a deep breath and tried to clear her head. The walk to the end of the town had been longer than she expected and had tired her. Too much fresh air, she thought ruefully, for there had been a stiff breeze blowing and she had been grateful that Lionel had kept an arm round her waist.

It had left her with an appetite and she had eaten too well at lunchtime, hence the heavy sleep into which she had fallen as soon as her head hit the pillow.

Levering herself into a sitting position, she slid from the bed, straightened the eiderdown and crossed to the window. No chance of seeing Lionel, she realized. Their window looked out towards the sea, and the gardens were to the side and rear of the house. He would no doubt be in the lounge or the garden, reading one of the many newspapers and magazines supplied for the guests.

With a last glance in the mirror Maude went downstairs and looked into the lounge. He wasn't there so she tried the gardens. The elderly man from breakfast was leaning back in a deckchair with a newspaper over his face because the sun was warm for June and the gusty breeze had dropped away. Returning to the house she discovered a games room where Billy and his mother were playing table-tennis, and two women whom she didn't recognize sat at a small table playing a card game that was unknown to her.

Mrs Hurst looked up, smiling. 'Did you have a good nap? Your husband said you walked too far. He felt rather guilty.'

'I slept rather too long,' she confessed. 'Now I can't find him. He's probably tired of waiting for me to wake and has gone down to the beach for a stroll.'

Billy knocked the ball across the table and his mother missed it. Maude retrieved it from the corner of the room.

'Mummy! You're not watching. You're not playing the game.'

'Hush dear. I'm talking to Mrs Brent. Be patient.'

At that moment the owner of the hotel appeared in the doorway with an apologetic look on her face. Her name was Alison Cobb and she ran the Romilees with the help of her younger brother, Derek Jayson. Maude guessed the woman to be in her early fifties but the man was considerably younger.

'I'm sorry, Mrs Hurst,' she said, 'but we do ask people not to stay on the table-tennis for more than an hour to give others a chance to play. Miss Stevens and her sister are hoping to be next.'

Mrs Hurst looked flustered. 'Oh dear, have we been here that long? Then we must make way for the sisters.'

Billy's face crumpled. 'Oh that's not fair! Mummy kept talking and talking and now—'

'Hush, Billy. We'll have another game tomorrow.'

'But I was winning!'

Impulsively Maude said, 'We could go for a walk to the ice-cream shop. It's only five minutes away. Would you like that?' She looked at Mrs Hurst for permission. 'Perhaps you would like to come with us.'

'Oh, that would be lovely. How very kind.'

Billy dropped his bat on the table and moved impatiently towards the door.

As they went out they passed the Stevens sisters coming in.

Mrs Hurst sent Billy upstairs to fetch her sun hat and then they made their way to the ice-cream shop where Billy spent ages choosing a strawberry cornet. On the way back he said, 'He's gone to buy a surprise for you.'

Both women stared at him.

His mother said, 'Who, dear? What are you talking about?'

'Mr Brent.' He looked up at Maude between licks of his ice cream. 'He was going out. He winked and said it would be a surprise.'

'Really?' Maude made a few mental checks to see if she had missed a birthday or an anniversary of some kind.

Mrs Hurst beamed. 'A surprise? Well, that's lovely, isn't it? What a thoughtful man, your husband.'

She sounded wistful, thought Maude. 'I'm very lucky, Mrs Hurst.'

Back at the Romilees she returned to her room to wait but after half an hour went back downstairs, sat in the lounge and ordered tea and biscuits. Time passed and at last she realized that she was becoming anxious. What on earth could Lionel be buying for her that would need such a long search? And what were they supposed to be celebrating?

Finding her still alone twenty minutes later, Mrs Cobb sat down in the next chair and rolled her eyes. 'This heat doesn't suit me,' she confided. 'Especially when I'm run off my feet. One of our waitresses is off sick and we have non-residents in for dinner tonight. That's an extra four. I'm rushed off my feet. My brother said, "For goodness' sake, Alison, sit down for ten minutes!" He'll hold the fort. It's the telephone business. I handle all the bookings and I don't let him interfere with that side of things in case we get in a muddle. A double booking could do a lot of damage to our reputation.'

She stopped for breath and then continued. 'You can invite someone to join you for dinner, you know, if you have friends in Hastings. Most of our guests forget that although it's in the brochure.' She fanned herself with her hand. 'Are you enjoying yourself? Did you find the bed comfortable? All our beds are feather mattresses but occasionally we have people who require a firm mattress – usually because of back trouble or suchlike.'

'Very comfortable, thank you.' Maude glanced at the grandfather clock. Where on earth was Lionel? Soon she would start to worry in earnest.

Mrs Cobb pulled out a handkerchief and dabbed her forehead and then noticed that one of the teacups on Maude's tray had not been used. 'Mr Brent not joining you?' she asked.

'He hasn't come back yet. I'm rather surprised but I'm told he went out to buy something for me – a surprise of some kind – but I am getting rather concerned.'

'Concerned? Why, how long has he been gone?'

'That's it. I don't know because he wanted me to take a nap after lunch and I did . . . So sometime while I was asleep he . . .'

'Probably met an old friend. Men do like a gossip, just as much as we do.'

'I don't think he knows anyone who lives around here. He would have mentioned it.'

'Well, try not to worry. I'm sure he'll come back soon. By the way, I hope you'll both join us in the lounge tonight at eight thirty. We always have a little *soirée* to round off the week. I know it's a bit old-fashioned but the guests seem to enjoy it and some are very talented. Do you sing or play?'

'Er . . . not really.' Maude was finding it hard to concentrate. She wondered just how long Lionel had been gone from the hotel. Could he, perhaps, have had an accident of some kind? Maybe been knocked over by a motor car . . . or been mown down by a runaway horse. *Oh! Stop this, Maude!* she told herself. *You are being ridiculous* . . . But he must realize by now that she would be worried.

'You could read a passage from a book if you wished. Most people can do something.'

Maude detected a note of reproach.

'It passes the time after supper, Mrs Brent. Have a little think.'

Without warning Maude felt a frisson of fear. It was quarter to six. She saw Mrs Cobb's mouth moving but heard nothing but a faint roaring in her ears. Her main emotion passed from anxiety to an intuitively deep awareness that something was wrong. It obviously showed in her expression because Mrs Cobb looked at her in alarm. 'Are you all right, Mrs Brent? You seem very pale.'

Maude pressed her two hands against her chest and whispered, 'Something has happened to him!'

'Of course it hasn't. What on earth could happen to a grown man in Hastings? This is a very safe town, Mrs Brent. You really mustn't let your imagination run away with you. Your husband hasn't been away that long and he won't want to come back to a panicky wife, now will he? Do try to stay calm, Mrs Brent. There really is nothing to worry about.'

THREE

Half an hour later, Alison Cobb stood in their small private sitting room and regarded her brother irritably. 'What on earth are we to do?' she demanded. Even though there was no way they could be overheard, she spoke in a whisper. 'That wretched man! Where can he be? What is he up to, messing us about like this? And his silly wife, working herself into such a state over nothing! What are we supposed to do about it? The police weren't really interested and why should they be? He hasn't been gone that long. I just don't know what to do about our little *soirée*!'

Derek was staring out of the window. His hands were thrust into his pockets defensively. 'Don't ask me! How should I know?' He was very like her but in his late thirties. There was strong family resemblance but he had so far kept his youthful charm. He was never short of female admirers but had never felt inclined to marry.

She tugged at his arm. 'At least talk about it, Derek. We have to deal with the situation. Mrs Brent is in her room, no doubt crying her eyes out by now. The police aren't taking it very seriously. Doing next to nothing.'

He turned. 'You can't say that. Constable Wickens is asking lots of questions and he says the Folkestone police are going to send a man to Brent's home to see if he's gone back there. If he's got amnesia that's quite possible.'

'Amnesia? But he was perfectly well this morning.'

'A blow on the head might cause it. If he has been knocked down . . .'

'Knocked down? Oh, what nonsense. He's probably having a drink or two somewhere and lost track of time. I just don't want this bit of bother to get out, Derek.'

'But how could it hurt us? It's not our fault he's late back. Might even give us some *good* publicity. I mean, we called in the police when Mrs Brent deemed it necessary. We're playing our part.' He was brightening. 'Might even do us some good in the long run.'

Alison closed her eyes. 'That's so like you! Always thinking about yourself. Lord help your wife if you ever find one!' Words failed her while she admitted grudgingly that her brother did have a point. If they remained calm and acted sensibly they might well come out of the situation smelling of roses.

Opening her eyes with a snap, she said, 'Right! Then we're going on with the *soirée*. That's settled. We can't let the other guests down. Can't ruin their holidays. Mrs Brent will stay in her room and—'

'She might not. She may not want to be alone. We should have called a doctor to give her a sleeping draught. I suggested it but she wouldn't agree.'

Alison sighed. 'She says she wants to stay awake to see him the moment he comes back.'

'*If* he comes back.'

Her confidence faltered suddenly. 'If? What on earth do you mean? Of course he's coming back!'

They stared at each other.

Suddenly, in her mind's eye, Alison saw the headline in the paper:

ROMILEES GUEST MISSING

Shocked, she sat down heavily in the nearest armchair. 'This is ridiculous! He'll probably walk through the door at any moment.'

Derek poured himself a stiff whisky and before she could complain he said, 'Let me get you a sherry, Ali.'

She shook her head. 'And don't call me Ali. You know I hate it.' As she looked at him she saw fleetingly the young boy he had once been. Such a disappointment. She had grown up longing for a sister. Occasionally she wondered why she had persuaded him to invest in the hotel after her husband died. It had seemed a good idea at the time but today she wondered if it had been a mistake. He didn't really enjoy it the way she did and she sometimes felt a little guilty.

He finished his drink but before he could decide to pour another she returned the bottle to the sideboard. 'We must think positively,' she told him briskly. 'The police think the press might get hold of the story, if there is a story, and if so you'll have to deal with them, Derek. I shall try to carry on as usual and . . .' She recalled her earlier decision. 'As soon as the police have finished their questioning, I shall announce the *soirée* and pin up the programme. We'll give everyone a free glass of that cheap champagne we can't sell – what a mistake that was! – by way of compensation for the disruption.' Derek started to interrupt her but she ignored him. 'Yes. That's what we'll do. You deal with the police and the press while I hold the fort. We must try to protect the guests from any more disappointments.'

'Protect them? What d'you mean? Disappointments? They're secretly loving it.' He grinned. 'Something interesting at last to write on the back of their saucy postcards.'

'Really, Derek!' Recovering from her fright, Alison threw a glance skyward as she hurried towards the door but stopped halfway to take the list of 'entertainers' from her pocket and read it aloud. 'Mr Hurst, an amusing anecdote from his childhood . . . The Stevens sisters, a duet. You'll have to play for them, Derek. They've brought the music . . . Young Miss Elroyd will recite a narrative poem, and her mother is going to play something from Gilbert and Sullivan . . . It's quite a mixed bag. Should be long enough but if not—'

'I know.' He rolled his eyes humorously. 'I'll play and we'll have a sing-song!'

She laughed. 'Don't pretend you don't revel in your moment of glory. You've always loved showing off at the piano. Mother was always praising you. She never praised me.'

'I practised, that's why. You never did.'

'I hated piano lessons . . . Oh Lord! There's the phone. Answer it, Derek, please and if it's that chap Hemmings from the *Gazette*, be nice to him! Get him on our side whatever you do. Offer him a free night's bed, breakfast and evening meal for two as long as he's fair to us in his article – and as long as it's not July or August.'

An hour or so later, Alice and Biddy were standing on the *Fairways* lawn, trying to decide how croquet was meant to be played. They had carried out a box containing four long-handled mallets, four large balls – red, green, yellow and blue – some cast-iron hoops and what Alice referred to as a coloured stake. They had spread these out and were awaiting inspiration. Primmy had examined these items with interest but, finding them lifeless, had withdrawn to the shade of a tree and now watched the proceedings closely in the hope that some excitement would follow at some point.

'It's simple,' said Alice. 'You have to hit the ball through all the hoops and whoever does it first wins.'

Biddy was leaning over the box in search of instructions. 'It can't be that easy,' she argued. 'There are rules and things but I've forgotten them . . . and how do we know where to put the hoops? I've seen it played but I was a child and it's all a bit hazy now. I do know it's not just a straight line of hoops and it's not random, either.' She pursed her lips. 'I think there may be some things missing . . . And two players may not be enough. It might need people to play in pairs.'

She straightened up from the box, one hand to her back. 'There are no instructions. I suppose over the years they've got lost. I can't recall when they were last used.'

Alice laughed. 'If that's so then we can't even start! Unless we make up our own rules. Croquet for two players.'

Biddy began to protest but changed her mind. 'I suppose we could,' she conceded. 'Since we've dragged it all out here. I know it should be played on a special court – a large grassy area marked out in some way.'

After a short discussion they agreed to set the hoops out randomly, a few yards apart.

Alice said, 'We'll take it in turns to have one go at each ball and score a point if the ball goes through the hoop. We'll have to ignore the stake thing because we don't know what it's for.'

Before Biddy could reply Primmy leapt to her feet and raced off round the house in the direction of the front steps.

Biddy said, 'You go and see, Alice. Your legs are younger than mine. I'll catch you up.'

Primmy was yelping with excitement and Biddy soon saw why. Alice was standing on the front steps holding on to the dog's collar while trying to speak to a policeman who was eyeing Primmy nervously. Biddy hurried up to them. The policeman was a heavy-looking man with a greying moustache and Biddy guessed him to be around forty years old. He introduced himself as Sergeant Taylor.

'I'm Biddy Cope, the only family member here today. I hope there's nothing wrong, Sergeant.'

'Nothing to worry you about, ma'am,' he assured her. 'Just an enquiry from the Hastings force about a Mr Lionel Brent. Seems he's wandered off somewhere and they're looking for him. They think he might have come home.'

'Wandered off?' Biddy stared at him in shock. '*Wandered off?* Lionel? There must be some mistake.'

'That's what I said.' Alice turned to him, releasing Primmy who rushed round and round the policeman legs, longing to be noticed.

Biddy said, 'Mr Brent wouldn't wander off. Why should he? He's at the Romilees Hotel in Hastings with his wife until—'

'Except that he isn't,' the sergeant insisted. 'My information is that he went out after lunch and hasn't been seen since. No explanation about where he was headed. Wife's very anxious and—'

'Oh! Poor Maude!'

'She thinks he's been in an accident but nothing's been reported, according to the hospitals.' He fumbled in his pocket and found a page of scanty notes. 'Wife, Maude Brent, has spoken to the Hastings lot as we speak and has suggested that he might have developed amnesia and be trying to reach his home. The Hastings lot are checking with us, you see, asking for us to help them out.' He glanced up enquiringly. 'I take it you haven't seen him.'

Alice shook her head. 'It doesn't make sense,' she muttered.

Biddy said, 'He wouldn't just get amnesia. I might, but not Lionel.'

He shrugged. 'Might happen if he got a bang on the head. Concussion. That sort of thing. Could have fallen and banged his head. Could have been attacked.'

Alice looked at Biddy. 'I suppose it's possible,' she said slowly.

The sergeant looked from one to the other, pencil poised. 'Nothing to add, then? No insights into what may have happened? Anyone in Hastings he might know? Anyone he might be visiting?'

They regarded him blankly. Primmy, desperate for attention, jumped up at him.

'Get down!' he roared and, although he hadn't touched her, Primmy gave a little yelp of terror and fled up the front steps to relative safety.

'You've frightened her!' Alice told the sergeant indignantly. 'She wasn't going to bite you. I told you she was friendly.'

He brushed bits of grass from his uniform. 'I don't like noisy dogs,' he replied. 'She ever bite the postman? The butcher's boy? I bet she has.'

'Well, you're wrong because she hasn't! She doesn't bite. She's just young and excitable.'

Biddy intervened quickly. 'So what's the next step, Sergeant? If Lionel is officially missing, what do you have to do now?'

'Nothing.' He shook his head. 'Refer it back to Hastings. It's their problem. They're Sussex. We're Kent. We're just helping them out.'

'But who can we ask for further news?'

He shrugged. 'Best bet is probably the hotel where the wife's staying. So, before I go, have either of you got any ideas what may have happened or where he might go?'

Alice shook her head but Biddy said, 'There was an odd chap round here the other day. Said he'd brought something and had to hand it over personally to Mr Brent.'

At that moment Primmy made another attempt to ingratiate herself with the stranger. She trotted cautiously forward, stopped about three yards from Sergeant Taylor, wagged her tail and then gave three short barks and moved forward again. The constable eyed her with obvious irritation until she barked again and then he lunged suddenly forward. 'Hop it! I've told you once.' He grinned as Primmy turned tail and fled.

Alice said angrily, 'You've got a cheek! I told you, she's not much more than a puppy.'

'And I told you I don't like noisy dogs.' He rolled his eyes. 'This odd chap?' He looked at Biddy.

She hesitated, not wanting to accuse him of anything serious. 'He was . . . unsavoury, if you know what I mean. A bit odd. He made us nervous.'

'I'd forgotten about him!' cried Alice. 'Biddy's right. He was really scruffy and sort of belligerent, wasn't he?' She turned to Biddy. 'Did he say what his name was?'

'Belligerent? But he didn't actually threaten us, Alice. He was odd, that's all, and he seemed to know Lionel, but Lord knows how.' Biddy shook her head. 'Gone missing! It's incredible. It was supposed to be a holiday.'

The sergeant asked a few more questions, made occasional scribbled notes but he seemed fairly disinterested, Biddy thought. Not on his patch so why should he care?

The policeman finally nodded. 'Well, I'll be on my way.'

Alice said, 'You haven't written much down yet.'

'I'm not investigating the case, Miss. Just been asked to see if he's here.'

He gave them a mock salute and they watched him in silence as he collected his bicycle.

When he'd gone Biddy said, 'I can hardly believe this is happening!'

Alice slipped an arm through hers. 'It'll be all right,' she told her, without much conviction. 'Don't upset yourself, Biddy. I promise you it will be all right.'

Maude sat on the edge of the bed and tried to breathe slowly, in and out, in and out . . . She had talked to a Constable Wickens until her head was spinning but had refused the idea of a sleeping pill because she was terrified by what she might be told when she woke up. She needed to be alert. If Lionel were to be found injured or had finally made his way to a hospital, she wanted to be able to go there at once. If, as she still hoped, Lionel was going to return to the hotel in one piece, she wanted to be awake, to throw her arms around him and hold him close. She clung to the idea of amnesia as the least worrying explanation. She yearned to be back at home with Aunt Biddy and Alice but it made more sense to wait here. The Hastings police seemed to know what they were doing – at least she hoped they did.

There was a knock on the door and she felt a cold rush of fear. 'Not bad news,' she whispered. 'Please God, not bad news.'

It was Mrs Cobb. 'My dear, I've brought you a light snack. On Sundays we always have a big Sunday lunch and then high tea. Some people call it supper. We don't mind. You must try to eat.' She set the tray on the small table. 'I'll send Penny up later to bring your sweet course and take your empty plate.'

Mrs Cobb was kind, thought Maude, and meant well but how was she supposed to eat anything? Her throat was dry and she felt slightly sick. She said, 'Thank you. I will try but . . .'

'I know, dear. You've lost your appetite but you need to keep up your strength. You don't want your husband to come back to a wilting flower!' She laughed to show this was a small joke. 'At moments of crisis you should always eat something to help the body's defences. They need to rally against the shock, you see. And I've decided to go ahead with our little *soirée* after supper. We owe it to our other guests and—'

'Oh yes! You mustn't let us spoil things for everyone else.'

'Of course not but I hope you'll come down if you feel up to it. Everyone is wishing you well and you'd be very welcome. It might be easier than sitting here alone.'

Maude nodded without committing herself and looked at the tray.

Mrs Cobb said quickly, 'A slice of my own home-made

onion tart with salad and thin brown bread and butter. And then we have strawberry sponge with cream. I'll send some up in ten minutes. I'll leave you to it, Mrs Brent and . . .' She held up crossed fingers. 'Don't give up hope. I feel sure fate will be kind.' She closed the door carefully and Maude listened to her departing footsteps.

A kind fate. Was that was she was hoping for? Maude picked up a piece of lettuce and put it back on the plate. In a kind of daze she spread the serviette across her lap and picked up the knife and fork. She shook her head, put the knife and fork down and picked up a small triangle of brown bread. Somehow she chewed it up and swallowed it. Then she picked the onion tart up in her fingers and took a large bite. It was delicious. She swallowed, almost choking with eagerness, and bit into it again as though she had not eaten for a week. Still using her fingers, she stuffed salad in to her mouth, chewed, swallowed, then more tart and more salad, forcing it all down.

Before long the plate was empty and she sat back exhausted, but yes, she must be honest, she did feel a little better. She had helped the body's defences. *Thank you, Mrs Cobb*, she thought. She sat back as unexpected tears streamed down her face. Struggling to defeat a growing feeling of hysteria, Maude waited numbly for the strawberry sponge to appear.

Constable Wickens left the Romilees and returned to the Hastings police station. He stood in front of his superior's desk, trying as usual to look older than he was, and hoping to make sense of his handwritten notes.

'Er . . . The Hursts passed the missing man going out as they came back. He said he was going to–to buy his wife something which he described as "a surprise" but wife claims there was no birthday due and no other special date.'

'Special date? Like what?'

'Er . . . like a wedding anniversary or the anniversary of the first day they met . . .'

'First day they . . . Heaven help us!'

Constable Wickens continued, 'Or anything of that kind. Mrs Cobb is the co-owner with her brother and says the missing man is, quote, "quite charming and they are obviously very fond of each other", close quote.'

'So he hasn't done a runner with another woman?'

'No, Guv. Not very likely. Mrs Cobb's brother, Derek Jayson, says he hardly saw Brent except to say, quote, "How do and have a nice stay," close quote. Miss Penelope Trew, maid, says missing man was, quote, "a bit of a dish and spoke quite la-de-dah and must . . . no, might give them a decent tip," unqu—'

'For Christ's sake, Wickens, forget the ruddy quote-unquotes! Just get on with it. I've got a home to go to.'

'Right, sir. Sorry, Guv. A young boy, Billy Hurst, and his father—'

'The Hursts? You've already said them.'

'Have I? Oh, right then . . . The wife, Maude Brent, says it's out of character for him to go missing, never done anything like it before, can't think of any reason for his disappearance and plumps for possible amnesia . . .'

The sergeant yawned. 'Any known enemies? Money troubles?'

'No enemies; she's got money from her family, he works in her smart art gallery in London where she is part-owner. The Barlowe Gallery. She wants to go home to Folkestone.'

'Anyone left at their home in Folkestone?'

'An aunt and a paid companion.'

He looked at the wall clock. 'Hurry it up, Wickens.'

'Mrs Brent says there was an odd chap hanging about. Might get more from the Folkestone follow-up. Jem, his name was, this odd chap.'

'Jem. Right. We'll see what Folkestone have found out. I'll give them a call. Probably all a waste of time. Storm in a blasted teapot! Probably got drunk and fallen asleep somewhere and scared to come back to the missus! Let's face it – he hasn't been gone twenty-four hours yet. Anyway, get off home, Wickens, and tomorrow be in on time. You were late yesterday and twice last month. It's not good enough. You've had your last warning!'

'Yes, Guv. I will.' He made his escape.

* * *

The following morning Maude was asked to attend the police station as there was still no sign of Lionel and they were now taking more interest in the case. She had spent a wretched evening downstairs, attending the amateur *soirée* and trying to appear composed. People were too kind to her and her longing to be at home with Aunt Biddy and Alice was almost a physical pain. She was, however, tempted to stay on in the area where her husband had disappeared and where all the efforts to trace him would be undertaken.

Fear for his safety ate into her like a disease, crippling her mind and making it impossible to sleep. Mrs Cobb had called in a doctor who wanted to sedate her but the idea terrified her and he gave up. Instead he offered a soothing syrup, which she took dutifully at intervals but which did absolutely nothing – or so she imagined. After a sleepless night she felt dull and exhausted but she ate a little breakfast and just before midday she allowed herself to be taken to the police station in Derek Jayson's new Ford motor. He went in with her, on his sister's instructions, and promised to be waiting for her when the interview was over.

Maude found herself seated in a small airless room, sitting on an uncomfortable straight-backed chair, sipping a cup of over-sweet tea.

Constable Wickens was nowhere to be seen but an older man entered the room, smiled and introduced himself as Detective Constable Fleet. He had a world-weary manner but he inspired more confidence in Maude than his younger colleague had. He read silently through a sheet of notes and then looked up.

'We'll find him, Mrs Brent. Don't worry. It's just a matter of time. I'm going to run through what we have so far and you must add anything you think relevant or correct anything you think is wrong.'

Maude nodded without speaking. She had promised herself she would not cry. She would hold herself together and would not invite pity or compassion. Finding Lionel was all important and breaking down would help no-one. She sipped her tea and listened attentively.

'Your husband, Lionel Brent, failed to return from a

shopping expedition yesterday and this is totally out of character so you are naturally worried. He hasn't yet been absent for twenty-four hours but if he doesn't return shortly we will have to take further steps.'

He looked up and she nodded.

'So far the only possible clue to his disappearance is a young man by the name of Jem who came to your house – that is *Fairways*, in Folkestone. Can you tell me anything else about him?'

Maude sat back and clasped her hands to prevent them from trembling. 'He said he had something for Lionel and wouldn't give it to anyone else. We sent him away because my husband was at work in London—'

'The Barlowe Gallery?'

'Yes. When Lionel came home he said the man had been waiting for him at the railway station and had given the envelope to him.'

'So you saw the contents of the envelope?'

'No. But it was some printed material about events that were taking place in Hastings in August and they were for the wrong dates because we were going now, in June.'

'So you didn't see the enclosures.'

'No, because Lionel had thrown them into the rubbish bin on the station.'

Immediately his expression changed. 'Let's get this straight, Mrs Brent.' He leaned forward and the world-weary manner had sharpened. 'If he threw the contents into the bin on the station platform, then he must have been given the envelope *on* the platform so presumably this Jem character didn't wait for him outside the ticket barrier. And yet your husband said they were simply publicity flyers for entertainment venues in Hastings. Didn't you think that a bit odd?'

Maude stared at him. 'Not at the time but I do now.' Thinking back she tried to recall anything else Lionel had told her.

He went on. 'Your husband thought the contents so important he remained on the platform and opened the envelope! He didn't know they were the wrong dates so I would have expected him to open them when he got home.'

He drummed his fingers on the table and Maude felt a shiver of apprehension. This was so unexpected and yet, at the time, she had never given it a second thought.

He narrowed his eyes. 'Does your husband have any enemies, Mrs Brent, or anyone who dislikes him? A rejected artist, perhaps, who was angry at your husband's decision not to accept his painting? Would he tell you that sort of thing?'

'I don't know,' she admitted. 'He hates me to be worried about anything unpleasant. If he thought he was shielding me from some unpleasantness then I dare say he might have kept it to himself.' Her eyes widened. 'Are you saying . . . Are you suggesting that someone has deliberately hurt my husband?'

'We can't rule anything out. This Jem – if he really did come from the Romilees as you were led to believe, the owners will know about it. We'll check that later and have a word with him. There might have been something else in the envelope – something your husband didn't want you to see. Maybe a threat. Does your husband gamble? Would you know if he does? Could he be in debt?'

Maude felt her heart thudding behind her ribs. Hardly able to speak, she cried, 'You think someone's hurt him! You do!'

'We think it's a possibility. On the other hand, sometimes people want to disappear. They have good reasons. Something in their past maybe catches up with them and they need to get away. Go on the run, as we say.'

With a shaking hand Maude reached for her tea and took a mouthful. It was almost cold but it eased the dryness in her throat. She said, 'You make him sound like a criminal! He isn't. He's a good, honest, gentle man.'

'I'm sure he is but you do understand, I hope, that we have to think of the worst that could have happened. We have to face up to reality and in our opinion there are secrets that everyone hides.'

'Not Lionel! Never! I know him better than you do.'

He regarded her unhappily. 'Mrs Brent, please tell me what *you* imagine may have happened. You must have some inkling.'

'I think he's lost his memory or . . . been in an accident . . . or he's trapped somewhere . . .' A new idea came to her. 'He might have been stranded by the tide somewhere by the cliffs or hurt his ankle in a fall and no-one can hear his calls for help. Something good. I mean, not good exactly, but nothing criminal or bad or . . .'

'Does he swim, Mrs Brent? The tides here can be . . .'

'The tides? Oh, don't say such a thing! He hasn't drowned. No, I won't even think it.' She put a hand to her heart and took a deep breath. *No hysterics. Calm yourself, Maude.* She said, 'No, Lionel doesn't swim . . . as far as I know.'

'Does he suffer from depression? Has he ever suffered from it?'

'No! Quite the opposite.' She regarded him desperately. 'I'm sure he will . . . reappear. He'll make his way home and that's where I want to be. Can't I go back to Folkestone, Mr – I mean—'

'DC Fleet, and if you want to help us to find him, you'll stay here for a while longer. If we find this Jem I shall need you to identify him as the man who entered your garden. Then we'll interview him and that may be the starting point that leads us to your husband.' He leaned forward. 'You're booked in here for a week. This is where he expects you to be. Stay another day or two, Mrs Brent. It won't be easy but it might help us to discover the truth. Will you do that?'

She nodded.

He smiled suddenly and she saw a softer side of him. His expression was warmer and his eyes had lost their hard glint.

'Please understand that we will do everything we can and we always hope for a very rational ending, but we wouldn't be doing our duty if we didn't look on the dark side. If we delay, the leads dry up and we can't solve the crime – if there is a crime.' She nodded earnestly and he continued. 'At present this Jem might be the man we need. He can tell us who gave him the envelope that seems to be somehow relevant to your husband's disappearance. Trust us, Mrs Brent. We are on your side.'

He smiled and Maude felt herself relax marginally. She wanted to trust him and she longed to believe that Lionel would be returned to her. Her life – that is her *real* life – had somehow been snatched away from her and minutes later as she left the police station, she was clinging to the idea that DC Fleet would be the man to restore it to her.

Biddy sat up in bed at close to midnight with her diary open on her knees and a pencil in her hand. Earlier in the day Maude had phoned and had explained what was happening and why, at the moment, she felt unable to come home. Biddy and Alice had talked of nothing else all day but neither had been able to think of anything useful to add to the investigation. Now, forgetting her Ovaltine on the bedside table, Biddy wrote in her diary.

'*Monday, June 12th. Our lives are turned upside down by the tragedy of Lionel's disappearance. How can a grown man vanish leaving no trace? It's impossible and yet it's happened. Poor dear Maude. My heart aches for her. She is trying to be so brave and to keep up her hopes but I have this terrible feeling that things will get worse not better. I've tried praying but it seems to have gone unnoticed by Him.*

Even Primmy is affected by the mystery and mopes about the house, not a bit like her usual excitable self. Poor little dog. She cannot possibly understand what is going on and we can't explain it to her. All she knows is that Lionel and Maude are both gone.

I made a huge chocolate cake to cheer me and Alice up but we both ate too much and felt sick afterwards.

Last night we forgot the croquet set and left it on the lawn and it rained hard and it all got wet so we shall have to bring it into the kitchen to dry it off before Maude comes back.

I just keep hoping that in the morning Lionel will turn up and this will all have been a dreadful nightmare and we can go back to the way we were. Please God let it happen that way. If anything has happened to Lionel it will break Maude's heart forever . . .'

Biddy closed the book and slid it under the pillow. Discovering that her forgotten Ovaltine was now stone cold she uttered a word not suitable in decent company and slid down under the sheets.

FOUR

The following morning, Tuesday, Penny and Meg arrived at the Romilees Hotel within minutes of each other and were soon together in the Bluebell Room, comparing notes about the event that was taking centre stage in everyone's life. The local newspapers were full of the mystery and various people had been interviewed for their insights into the disappearance of one of the guests from the well-known hotel.

Meg was wide-eyed with excitement as Penny described what had happened when the police tried to talk to Jem.

'They only knew where he lived because of me,' she told her friend as they began to strip the bed. Penny was trying hard not to feel superior. 'When they asked if any of us knew of anyone called Jem I told them about the chap next door to Tom because it could have been the same man. I mean Jem's about my age although he looks younger but it could be him. Tom says this constable turned up on the doorstep and Jem's mother, that's Mrs Rider, made out he wasn't there and said they were victimizing him just because he was a bit wayward . . . or was it backward?'

'Well, he is! Both.'

'But she's a funny woman. Tom reckoned she's a bit like a witch only fatter and if you cross her she'll give you the evil eye! Like a spell. Not that she's got black hair – hers is a bit gingery – but she's got piercing eyes.'

Together they began to clean the bathroom. Penny threw damp towels out of the door into the basket on the landing, gave the bath mat a shake, draped it over the sill of the open window and began to rub Vim around the bath with a damp cloth. Meg cleaned the basin and polished the mirror above the sink.

Penny went on. 'She refused to let him in – the policeman I mean – so they went away but Tom had seen Jem looking out his bedroom window, so he got on his bike and went after the police to tell them but when they got back, Jem had gone. Run off somewhere. So Tom thinks he must know something or why would he run off like that? Made him look guilty.' She straightened up from the bath. 'That'll have to do. I'll start on the bed.'

Meg said, 'That poor Mrs Brent. She looks so pale and her eyes are all red from crying. If I were her I'd go home.'

Just then the door of the room opened and, as if somehow summoned, Mrs Brent came nervously into the room. Both young women stared at her.

She said, 'I understand one of you knows this Jem. Mrs Cobb told me.'

Meg said,'It's her. Penny. She knows him.'

Penny said, 'It's not me exactly. My young man lives next door to him.'

'Please tell me anything you know about him. I understand the police were going to interview him.'

Penny and Meg exchanged startled looks.

'I'm sorry, Mrs Brent,' Penny said, 'but I've never even seen him. I only hear about him from Tom. He says Jem's a bit of a tearaway and often in trouble with the police but that's all I know . . . except his mother's a bit sort of scary. Tom saw the policeman arrive and Jem was in the house but his mother said he wasn't and as soon as they'd gone away Jem went out.' She shrugged.

'Oh!' Mrs Brent's face fell. 'So he hasn't been interviewed.'

'Not yet.'

She hesitated. 'Would you say this Jem was . . . violent? I'm wondering if he might have . . . done something to my husband.' Her voice was shaking. 'Whether he might have . . . hurt him. I saw him, you see, when he came to my house, but only briefly and I didn't look at him seriously. I had no idea . . .' She pulled a handkerchief from her pocket and pressed it to her eyes.

She looked, thought Meg, as though she might faint at any moment. 'I don't think he'd hurt anyone,' she said quickly. 'Not violent. No. Not Jem Rider. Just up to no good. Pinching things off doorsteps and name-calling and . . . and throwing stones at cats. He was in my class at school and when he turned up he was always getting the cane but no, I don't think he'd do anybody any real harm. Would he, Penny?'

'Not from what I hear.'

Mrs Brent uncovered her eyes and took a deep breath. To Penny she said, 'If you do hear anything else, would you let me know? I'm staying here for another night but I may go home tomorrow.'

'I will, yes. Try not to worry. The detective is really good at his job. You're lucky to have him on the case. He's got a wonderful reputation.' She smiled reassuringly.

'That's good news. Thank you. You've really helped me. I must let you get on with your work.'

When she'd gone Meg looked at Penny with raised eyebrows. 'The detective is wonderful? Good at his job? What do you know about him?'

'Nothing,' Penny admitted, 'but she's in such a state. I just wanted to cheer her up.'

Emily Rider heard the front-door bell and swore under her breath. She went into the front room, looked out through the thick net curtain and swore again. The man on the doorstep wasn't in uniform but she knew the type. A detective. They were back.

'I knew it! I just knew it!' She put a hand to her heart and tried to compose her features. Never let the police think you're scared. Her husband had said that more times than she cared to remember before he took himself off four years earlier – and good riddance to him! In and out of prison like a blasted yo-yo!

On the way to the front door she pushed back her lank hair, which was now a faded auburn, and smoothed her floral pinafore over plump hips. She also struggled to forget her anger with Jem. Must keep calm in front of the police. They were like bloodhounds. If they thought she had anything to hide they'd be on her like a pack of wolves.

Opening the front door she said, 'You lot again?'

'Mrs Rider?'

She gave an exaggerated groan. 'Whatever you're selling, the answer's "No".' She smiled and hoped she sounded perky and carefree.

'I'm Detective Constable Fleet and I'm investigating the—'

'I'm not interested. I've got a load of ironing to do so . . .' She began to close the door but the DC put his foot in the way. 'What?' she demanded.

'I'd like a word with your son Jem, Mrs Rider. We think he may be able to help us in our enquiries. Is he in?'

'No and if he was he couldn't help you. He doesn't know anything, that's why. We know your lot. You'll twist his words, trip him up over everything he says and try and pin the blame on him.'

'Blame? Blame for what? What do you think your son has done, Mrs Rider?'

She was silent for a moment, weighing up what she could and couldn't say. She found herself wishing that she had taken off the pinafore. He was a decent-looking chap, for a policeman.

He said, 'Do you want us to have this conversation on the doorstep, Mrs Rider?' and jerked his head in the direction of the woman next door, who was pretending to polish her already gleaming brass knocker.

'Nosy cow!' Reluctantly Emily held the door open and they moved inside and into the front room. 'She thinks herself so much better than the rest of us, next door, but her Tom's a troublemaker. He tries to wind Jem up. Knows he's got a short fuse, as they say. You can sit down if you want to.' Without waiting for an answer she seized a tortoiseshell cat from the only armchair and tossed it none too gently into the hallway.

'I won't sit down, thank you, Mrs Rider. I mustn't get too comfortable because I have a lot of work to do. We're investigating the disappearance of one of the guests at the Romilees Hotel – you may have heard about it – and we believe Jem met him recently and might give us a clue to his whereabouts. That's the only reason we want to talk to him.'

The relief was enormous. So Jem was not in any trouble. She allowed herself another smile. 'Maybe he can help but he's not here at the moment. If you want to call round again—'

'I need to speak to him now, Mrs Rider. If he *is* in I'd—'

'I just told you, he isn't here!'

'Then if you can tell me where he is . . .'

'No, I can't. I don't know where he is. Very independent, my son. Always off, here and there.' She shrugged. 'Kids, eh! They worry you to death.'

'Are you worried about him?'

Emily cursed her careless tongue. Of course she was worried about him. He hadn't come home the previous night and she had no idea where he was or when he would come home. 'Worried about Jem? No more than any mother worries about her kids. You got a family?'

'Not yet.'

'My advice is to think about it, long and hard. It's not all it's cracked up to be.' She glanced at the only framed photograph she owned, which showed her and her husband outside a church. She said, 'I'm the one in the wedding dress!' and tried to laugh but something caught in her throat and the laugh was choked off.

The detective said, 'Maybe I could speak to your husband.'

'You'll be lucky. He packed his bags years ago, silly sod!'

'So there's just you and your son?'

'My daughter's married with three kids. Jem was a late arrival, as they say. He's a good kid. A bit young for his age but that's no bad thing. He'll get himself a job before long and that'll give him something to do. Keep him out of mischief.'

'I'll call back later then, Mrs Rider, but if Jem comes back, please tell him to come down to the police station as he might be able to help us with this missing person enquiry.'

She nodded and showed him out. So this chap who'd

gone missing was staying at the Romilees Hotel. A bit posh, then. She found it impossible to care about people like that. Rich people. 'Fat cats' her husband had called them. They had too much. Too much luck. Too much money. Too much everything. Served the blighters right if they got burgled now and again. They could afford it.

As she closed the front door the cat slipped back into the front room and leaped on to the armchair. Emily went back into the kitchen and stared round sightlessly. Where the hell was Jem, she wondered, and what had he done – if anything? It wasn't like him to stay out all night. He liked his home comforts, did Jem. Please God he wasn't going to turn out like his father.

Her anger was turning into anxiety.

Biddy and Alice were eating their lunch when they heard a car draw up outside.

Alice said, 'Oh no! Not the police, please! But it might be Lionel!'

Biddy almost choked on her cold sausage and salad while Alice sprang to her feet and rushed to the front door. It was not the police, nor was it Lionel. Instead it was Maude, who stood on the front step waving to two people who drove off in their car.

'Maude!' cried Alice. 'Oh, let me look at you! How thin you look!'

As Maude stepped into the hallway, Alice threw her arms around her neck and hugged her. Biddy arrived and Primmy went mad, dancing round Maude's feet and whining hysterically until Maude disentangled herself from Biddy's arms and bent to make a fuss of the dog.

Biddy cried, 'Oh, Maudie love! Thank goodness you're back. You're much better off here than stuck in a hotel with a lot of strangers.'

'I'm going back later today,' Maude told her as she sank on to a chair in the kitchen and looked round the familiar room with pleasure. 'I began to feel that I'd never see my home again,' she confessed. 'I know that sounds melodramatic but . . .'

Biddy stared. 'Going back? But why?'

Alice put the kettle on and prepared cups and saucers, and then she and Biddy finished what was left of their lunch while Maude explained her situation.

'Mrs Cobb, the hotel's owner, is in Folkestone for a few hours to visit her mother who's rather unwell. Derek Jayson, Mrs Cobb's brother, has driven us over and will take us back some time this evening. The police insist that I stay nearby in case of – of what they call developments. If Lionel had gone missing from here the Folkestone police would handle it but as we were in Sussex the Hastings police have to deal with it.'

'Which makes sense,' Biddy said, 'although I'd feel happier if you came home.'

'I can't, I'm afraid. They feel I should be on the spot. I did wonder whether to ask one of you to stay with me in the hotel but it wouldn't work.'

'I'd come,' said Alice.

'That's kind of you but then Aunt Biddy would be here on her own and that would worry me.'

Biddy muttered something about 'not liking hotels' and Maude said, 'I know how you feel. And there's no way round it. You two are here – safety in numbers. I'm being looked after in Hastings.'

Primmy rushed up with an old slipper and laid it at Maude's feet. 'Oh, Primmy! Just what I wanted!' cried Maude, patting the excited dog. 'Now *sit*, please, Primmy. You're making me dizzy!'

She told Alice she had eaten a substantial breakfast just before ten and didn't need any lunch. Then she explained what had been happening in Hastings.

Alice listened mainly in silence and then said, 'If Mr Brent lost his memory for any reason and then ended up in hospital he couldn't tell them who he is. Maybe you should tour the hospitals . . .'

'I think I would if anyone had been admitted without a name but they haven't. The police are monitoring the hospitals. There's a Detective Constable Fleet who is on the case and everyone thinks highly of him. He's very nice and reassuring and he does give me hope. '

Biddy shook her head. 'If you ask me, that Jem character is somehow responsible for whatever has happened to Lionel. Have they questioned him yet?'

'They're trying to find him.'

The three of them exchanged suspicious glances.

Biddy said, 'Don't tell me he's also disappeared. That would be a bit of a coincidence.'

Maude spread her hands in a helpless gesture. 'I have no idea. It goes round and round in my mind. I can't switch off.' She took the cup of tea gratefully. 'I even wondered whether Jem had done something to Lionel and then –' she swallowed hard – 'made his getaway.'

'Killed him, you mean?' Biddy was horrified. 'Don't even *think* such terrible things, Maude. I refuse to believe that God would allow such a thing to happen!'

Alice leaned forward. 'I've had another thought. Suppose he's been mistaken for someone else – someone by the same name. Mistaken identity.'

'But why?' Maude asked. 'Why would anyone want the other Mr Brent to disappear? Unless it's to do with the gallery! Could that be it? I can't see how or why, but then the whole thing is a mystery.' She took a long shuddering breath. 'This is all so unreal. I keep telling myself I shall wake up and find it was a nightmare!'

There was a long silence.

Biddy said, 'You should keep your eyes open, Maude, at all times. How do we know that *you* aren't going to be snatched?'

Maude stared at her. 'Snatched how?'

'You know – kidnapped.'

'Is that what you think has happened to Lionel? That he's been kidnapped?' Maude's face had paled.

'Look,' said Biddy. 'I wasn't going to say anything but last night I lay awake for hours and eventually I thought . . . someone could want something Lionel has – like the keys to the gallery or to this house. Maybe someone wants to steal some of your father's pictures so they captured Lionel – lured him somehow – so they could take his keys. I think it might be to do with robbery. Do you think, Maude, that the police have checked with the gallery?'

Maude frowned. 'I don't think they've mentioned it. I don't think *I've* mentioned it, come to that, but it sounds reasonable. Really, Aunt Biddy, it sounds a possibility.' Her frown vanished to be replaced by a broad smile. 'How clever you are! When I next speak to DC Fleet I'll tell him about it.' She was suddenly buoyed up with hope that the episode would end happily.

Alice was nodding enthusiastically. 'At least it's plausible. And then, after the robbery, they let Lionel go free. Have they ever had a robbery at the gallery?'

'Not to my knowledge but I don't care about a few pictures if it means I get Lionel back, safe and well. I'm sure my father would consider it a good exchange!' She looked from one to the other. 'I suggest we take Primmy for a walk to the beach, the way we always do. I just want to feel normal, for an hour or so. I'll have to face up to it when I get back to the hotel but the sea air will do me good.'

Alice said, 'I second that!'

Biddy agreed.

'And Primmy looks pleased,' said Maude, as the dog scrambled to her feet and regarded them expectantly. 'I swear she understands every word we say!'

Minutes later they were on their way and Maude allowed herself to believe that the worst was probably over. Fortunately she had no idea of the news she would receive when she returned to the hotel.

While Maude, Biddy and Alice were walking on the beach, Jane Dyer was leading DC Fleet into the gallery's office. He wanted to speak to the co-owner but Frederick Barlowe was in Letchworth in Hertfordshire, in search of new artistic talent. She didn't ask the detective to sit down because she didn't want to be out of the gallery for more than a minute or two. Mr Barlowe had told her never to trust the public. They might deface a painting or scratch graffiti on the wall. They might even steal one of the pictures by cutting it out of its frame or removing the whole painting.

'I don't suppose I can help you very much,' Jane told him. 'Mr Barlowe travels quite a lot, like Mr Brent, visiting art galleries in search of new artists whose work he can buy or commission. I'm doing the best I can on my own. Is there any news about poor Mr Brent?'

'No news as yet,' he replied. 'I really need to ask you a few questions about the gallery – for instance, who actually owns it?'

'They both do – that is Mrs Brent and Mr Barlowe. It was originally Mr Barlowe's, hence the name, but he needed investment and he and Arnold Cope joined forces. When Arnold Cope died he left everything to his daughter, who was then Miss Maude Cope, and she decided to carry on as a partner in the gallery.'

'So they co-own it.'

'Yes, they do. When Miss Cope met Mr Brent and they married, he became what I like to think of as a sort of ambassador for the gallery.' Her eyes shone. 'He helps Mr Barlowe whenever there's going to be an exhibition and things like that – and he also travels about the country finding new work. He does it all for the love of it, he told me.' She smiled at the thought. 'He's wonderful. He really is.'

'And you have been here how long?'

'Soon after they were married and Mr Brent started here, the previous secretary retired and I got the job. Well, actually I'm a receptionist-cum-secretary. I love it here.' Her eyes darkened. 'Naturally it's not so good at the moment with all the worries about poor Mr Brent. I keep praying that nothing too bad has happened to him. He's a fine man.'

'And you haven't seen him since he went missing?'

'No. Although I did think I saw him, yesterday when I came to work. There was a man standing outside the gallery when I arrived first thing and I only saw him from the back and I thought it was Mr Brent. I could hardly breathe, I was so relieved, but then he turned towards me and raised his hat . . .' Her face fell. 'It wasn't him. He had dark hair and spectacles and no moustache. But his voice . . . He even sounded like him.' She blinked hard as though to forestall tears.

'He spoke to you? What did he say?'

'Just "Good morning"!'

'And you're sure it wasn't him?'

'How could it be?' She stared at him, bewildered by the question. 'Mr Brent has fair hair.'

'He could easily disguise himself.'

'Disguise himself? But why would he?'

The detective shrugged. 'And there has been no word from him? No telephone calls or letters. Would Mr Barlowe tell you if he had been in contact?'

'Yes. He promised me he would. Mr Barlowe knows how upset I am. I go to church every evening to pray for him. Mr Brent, that is.'

The detective drew in his breath and started another line of questioning. 'Have you noticed anything different here since Mr Brent disappeared? Any odd strangers around? Any new faces? Any familiar people behaving oddly?'

She frowned, thinking, then shook her head.

'Would you know if there were any financial problems with the gallery? Would you be told?'

'I doubt it.' She smiled faintly. 'Mr Brent said my job is to look pretty and charm the clients!' She blushed. 'It was only a joke. I deal with the telephone, set out the leaflets, open the post and type the answers. Oh – and make the tea! Sometimes we have a launch for a new artist and I arrange for the canapés and pour the wine. I open up the doors if either of the men are late. I did study art history but I don't really need it. I wish I could do more here, to be honest.'

A bell tinkled as the gallery door was opened and Jane excused herself and went out of the room. DC Fleet took the opportunity to look round the office. It could have been tidier, he reflected, but it couldn't be called a mess. There were shelves full of books, papers and files. There was a cupboard and a safe and, as expected, a few paintings still in their wrappings, propped against one wall.

He would come back when Barlowe was around, he decided. Also the 'man-who-wasn't-Brent' intrigued him. For the very first time he thought about Brent not as a victim but as a perpetrator of some crime. Was he planning to rob the gallery? It didn't make a lot of sense but DC Fleet knew all about insurance fraud . . . He thought about the enchanting Miss Dyer, who was obviously carrying a torch for Brent. Praying in church every evening? God! That was devotion . . .

Could Brent and Barlowe be in cahoots? Suddenly everything seemed possible but nothing seemed likely. If Brent was planning to steal from the gallery he would be stealing from his wife, but he might intend to defraud the insurance company . . .

Jane returned and offered him a cup of tea but he had seen enough for the present and declined. He caught a train back to Hastings and spent the journey scribbling notes in his book and planning his report. There was no way he could rule out the possibility of fraud but would he be able to convince his superiors that it was a worthwhile lead, he wondered. They wouldn't want the action to be passed to London. Hastings was a quiet town and the present mystery was exciting. Fights between fishermen, burglaries and a few road accidents were the usual matters that had to be dealt with and, if he were honest, he was not averse to something more challenging.

As soon as he returned to Hastings he became aware that something had happened in his absence. People stood on the platform in small groups, talking with some agitation. He jumped down from the train and made straight for the porter.

'What's up, Mr Statton?' he asked.

'What's up? You may well ask! There's a rumour going round that they've found a body on the beach. A *dead* body, Mr Fleet!' His eyes rolled as he relished both the news itself and the telling of it. 'A very dead body, Mr Fleet! That's what's up!'

* * *

Mrs Cobb, her brother and Maude arrived back at the hotel just as the evening meal was beginning. Mrs Cobb pulled off her jacket and hung up her hat. It was only then that she turned to see Penny rushing towards her.

'Oh, Mrs Cobb! It's terrible news! They've found a body on the beach, near the fish market! Everyone's talking about it and there's dozens of people down there and the police are there and everything!'

Maude, standing just behind Mrs Cobb, gave a groan and before anyone could intervene, collapsed on to the floor. Mrs Cobb almost tripped over her and clutched at her brother, nearly bringing him to his knees. He shouted, 'God dammit, Alison!' and then glared at Penny who, realizing that she had caused the confusion, fled back to the dining room in disgrace.

Mrs Cobb regained her feet and promptly sent her brother for the sal volatile while they carried Maude into the sitting room and laid her on the sofa.

Maude struggled back to consciousness with the pungent whiff of sal volatile still in her nostrils. With consciousness came memory and her colour fled as she gripped Mrs Cobb's arm and tried to ask the dreadful question through trembling lips and a dry throat. 'Is it . . . is it Lionel?' she whispered hoarsely. 'Please God, it isn't Lionel!'

Mrs Cobb and her brother exchanged worried looks. 'No dear,' said Mrs Cobb resolutely. 'That is, we don't know yet, but I'm sure it isn't Mr Brent.'

There was a knock on the front door followed by a long ring and Derek went to answer it. A man in his thirties stood on the doorstep, beaming at him. 'Bit of a scoop this!' he said cheerfully. 'Just come from the beach. Plenty going on down there. Thought we could help each other out here, if you see what I mean. You give me something and I'll see that you come out looking good!'

Derek hesitated and then, remembering his conversation with his sister, he opened the door to admit the visitor. 'I'll tell Mrs Cobb. Please wait here.'

He went into the sitting room, announced, 'Ben Hemmings from the *Gazette*!' and raised his eyebrows.

Disobeying his instructions, Hemmings followed him in. He was a thin, beady-eyed man with the look of a predatory bird. His nose was thin and his cheekbones were a little too prominent. His clothes appeared random and his shoes had seen no polish for weeks but his expression was at odds with his appearance.

'Ah! The lady herself!' he cried cheerfully. 'Mrs Brent, I bring you glad tidings of great joy! The body on the beach is believed to be that of Jem Rider, late of this parish!' He laughed, unaware of the disapproving look Mrs Cobb was giving him.

Maude sat up, her eyes wide with hope. 'It isn't my husband? It *isn't*? Are you sure? Certain sure?'

'Indeed I am, madam.' He gave a small mock bow. 'No need to shoot the messenger on this occasion. Your husband is not lying on the beach dead. We know not where he is, but we know where he ain't!' He turned to wink at Mrs Cobb, who turned back to Maude.

'My dear Mrs Brent!' she said warmly. 'I am so happy for you. We all are! Your husband is alive and well. Splendid news!'

Maude moved her feet from the end of the sofa and sat up. Hemmings at once sat down next to her.

Maude said, 'You are quite, *quite* sure about him?'

Hemmings dropped his humorous manner and nodded. 'Quite sure, Mrs Brent. I've come across Jem Rider on several occasions and he is instantly recognizable. The police say he was killed by a couple of blows to the back of his head. Poor lad.' He smiled at her. 'I'm so glad to be able to set your mind at rest for a while. There's still hope.'

Maude looked into small but friendly brown eyes and no longer saw the rest of his poorly assembled features. This man had saved her sanity for the moment, she told herself. She was aware that the agony was far from over and that the final outcome need not be a good one, but for the present, she had been rescued from the darkest scenario. Lionel was not dead and she was spared the plunge into deepest misery. She must take what little she was offered and be thankful. And she was.

She resisted the urge to hug him. 'Thank you, Mr Hemmings. I can't tell you how grateful I am to hear that.'

She was so grateful that she agreed to grant him a five-minute interview, during which he asked her a series of questions that were easily answered. Mrs Cobb insisted on staying with them throughout the interview, allegedly to support Maude and make sure that Ben Hemmings didn't bully her in any way. Maude went out of her way to praise Mrs Cobb, Derek Jayson and the staff and other guests. Everyone, she declared, had been wonderfully kind and helpful. 'I consider myself fortunate that, in this dreadful predicament, I am surrounded by caring people,' she told him.

When Hemmings left her to go to the bar for a whisky on the house, Maude retired to her room and supper was sent up on a tray.

Later she telephoned Aunt Biddy and brought her up to date on the latest developments, but it was not until she hung up the receiver that she took time to consider the victim on the beach. Was it possible, she wondered, that Jem Rider's death was connected in any way with Lionel's disappearance, or was it just a coincidence? As she climbed into bed, utterly exhausted both physically and mentally, she made up her mind to talk to Detective Constable Fleet and ask for his opinion.

Next morning Maude hugged her jacket against the unexpectedly cool breeze and hunched herself down into the collar. With her free hand she checked that her hatpins were holding fast. She felt rather guilty in case she was doing something of which Detective Constable Fleet would not approve but she had decided that she must see Emily Rider. It was nearly ten and she had eaten a hasty breakfast before informing Mrs Cobb that she was 'going for a walk to clear her head'. Lying made her feel bad, because everyone at the hotel was trying to mother her. Still, it was only a part lie, she told herself. She *was* going for a walk and the blustery wind was certainly clearing her head.

As she walked along the front she saw that some people

were already on the beach, mostly young families whose children were busy collecting seashells or, regardless of the weather, splashing in and out of the shallow water. A few gentlemen armed with walking sticks were giving their dogs a morning run and an elderly couple tottered along arm in arm. Were they demonstrating affection, Maude wondered, or simply propping each other up? She had never found it easy to walk on shingle.

At the eastern end of the beach she regained the road, turned left, and made her way through the old town. At last she found a baker's van and the driver, who was adjusting his horse's nosebag. She asked him if he knew where Mrs Rider lived.

'Emily Rider? Course I know.' He regarded her curiously. 'What d'you want with Emily?'

'I need to speak with her, that's all.'

'Everyone knows Emily. Lived here for years, her lot and his. Sid Rider. Fisherman he was, the husband, when he wasn't in jail. Then he ups and leaves with a woman from Pett Level.'

He gave her the necessary directions and she followed them until she ended up outside a house and rang the bell. After a few minutes she rang again. Waiting longer than seemed likely, she wondered again about the wisdom of this visit but, just as she decided to forget all about it and leave while she could, there were footsteps in the passage, a security chain rattled and the door opened.

'Stop ringing the sodding bell! I've got a blinding headache!'

The woman was red-eyed, her face was flushed and she clung to the door for support. Drunk, thought Maude with a flash of compassion, and who could blame her? This unfortunate woman had just lost her son. She said gently, 'I'm sorry. Maybe I should come back some other—'

'Or not at all!' Mrs Rider swayed and instinctively Maude put out a hand to steady her.

'I'm Mrs Brent. Your son went missing and so has my husband. I'm wondering if there's a connection.'

Mrs Rider put a shaking hand to her head and groaned.

She was still in rumpled nightclothes and her hair was a tangled mess. Maude thought with a shudder that she might herself have sunk into such a pitiful state if Lionel had been the one found dead on the beach. She said, ‘You don’t look at all well, Mrs Rider. Maybe I could come in and make you some tea.’

‘What?’ She swayed again, squinting up at Maude.

The smell of dust, damp and cat’s pee drifted forward from the passage and Maude regretted her offer. She thought it unlikely that she would get any sense from Jem’s mother and was already phrasing a sentence that would herald a change of plan when the woman turned, and stumbled away down the passage, leaving the door wide open. Maude took a deep breath of clean air and stepped inside. She closed the door and headed along the narrow passage into the kitchen where Mrs Rider was slumped in a chair. Her elbows were on the table and her head rested in her hands.

A tortoiseshell cat slept beside the cold stove but there was also a gas cooker that had seen better days and the kettle was already full so Maude found matches, lit the gas and placed the kettle on the hob. She sat down facing Tom’s mother.

Mrs Rider looked up. ‘They was always on to my Jem but he was a good lad. He didn’t deserve nothing bad to happen to him. Nothing like this.’ She raised her head. ‘So what if he did get in trouble now and again? Not surprising with his dad in and out of the nick all the time.’

‘I’m truly sorry.’

‘Yeah!’

Maude pulled her chair closer to the table. ‘Mrs Rider, do you think someone kidnapped your son and then killed him?’

Mrs Rider shrugged. ‘Who cares? He’s dead now. It’s too late.’

‘But do you have any idea who killed him? I’m wondering if the same man has taken my husband and . . . and he might be next. He might also be killed.’

Mrs Rider looked up suddenly, her eyes narrowed. ‘*He* might have done it. Ever think of that?’

'Who might have done it? I don't understand.'

'Your husband might have killed my son!'

Maude's mouth fell open with shock at this outrageous suggestion. 'But that's ridiculous! How dare you even suggest such a thing! Of course he didn't. Lionel would never kill anybody!' Her voice rose slightly. 'Don't you ever say such a thing again! D'you hear me?'

The woman shrugged again. 'Might have. Someone did it. They knew each other.'

'They did not! What on earth are you talking about? Your son was asked to deliver an envelope to Mr Brent. By somebody. We don't know who.'

'By him. By your husband.'

Maude shook her head, confused. 'You're not making any sense, Mrs Rider. Please try to think what you're saying. Lionel did not know your son. I'm trying to discover if the man who killed your—' She stopped abruptly, jerking back in alarm as Mrs Rider's fist crashed down on to the table.

'Jem said the man knew his name. Said he called him Jem and asked him to deliver the envelope, only Jem didn't know that . . . I mean, it was later that he realized . . .'

'That's nonsense!' Maude blinked rapidly, growing nervous. 'Why should Lionel ask someone else to deliver an envelope to himself? Can't you see it doesn't make any sense?' She sighed, ashamed that she was badgering the poor woman at such a time. 'I'll make you a pot of tea,' she began but Mrs Rider was becoming annoyed.

'I can make me own tea, thank you. If you've said your piece you can get out!'

She glared at Maude who, equally irritated, realized she should never have bothered Jem's mother at such a difficult time. She rose to go but as she did so her eye caught a curling photograph on the mantelpiece. It showed a toddler sitting on the step. He was clutching a small wooden horse and smiling broadly.

'Yes, that's my Jem, bless his heart!'

Maude wanted to say something but she had the feeling that the best thing she could do was to leave the distraught woman in peace.

She said, 'He was a bonny baby.'

No answer.

'Is anyone coming to help you? The Salvation Army are very good. They're used to dealing with—'

'My daughter's coming at twelve. Just go. I don't want your help and I don't want no sodding do-gooders snooping round my house.'

Maude cursed her own stupidity. Quietly she let herself out and closed the front door behind her. Walking rapidly away she returned to the seafront and, badly shaken by Mrs Rider's accusation, stopped in a small café for a cup of tea and a biscuit. *Leave well alone, Maude*, she told herself resignedly. *Leave it to the experts. Somewhere Lionel is alive and well*, she told herself. *DC Fleet will find him.*

FIVE

The Hastings pier theatre was like most pier theatres, perched over the sea, its outside walls plastered with programmes of shows past and present, a jumble of posters containing sketches of the various artists and a separate sheet enclosed in a glass-fronted panel, showing the times of each performance and the prices for various seats. Hundreds of pairs of feet clattered past each day, their steps echoing above the waves twenty feet below. When a performance was due, some of the feet stopped at the theatre and carried their owners inside, through the darkened auditorium or, in some cases, round backstage to the dressing room.

Today, the men's dressing room was thick with steam as Wahoo, the Wonderful Wizard, bent over the ironing board, trying to press a crease into each leg of the black trousers that were part of his stage costume. The previous evening, Alfie Parks had spilled half his beer down them and Wahoo (known to his friends, family and fellow artists as Sydney) had been forced to sponge them down today to get rid of the smell and remove the stain.

'You should be doing this,' Sydney grumbled, sending a malevolent look towards the comedian who now sat in front of the large mirror, a glass of ale hidden on the shelf below, applying his make-up with an unsteady hand.

'Stop moaning, Sydney,' he replied. 'Think yourself lucky I didn't volunteer to do it. I've scorched more clothes than you've had hot dinners!'

Alfie Parks, the show's comedian, was a tubby man with what he called a 'dodgy ticker' who, on stage, made himself appear more round than he was by means of a quilted stomach, which he wore concealed under his clothes. He wore shoes that were three sizes too large in the hope that this subtle combination hinted at 'clown' and encouraged the audience to find him humorous. He also wore a small black bowler hat and started every sentence of his patter with 'I say, I say!' His jokes were tried and true but the evening crowd were very tolerant and usually laughed in the right places. The matinee audiences, however, were always the least receptive to the show and this afternoon would be no different.

The small room had beige walls and along one of these there was a row of coat hooks on which the performers hung their clothes. Above the coat hooks there was a shelf for hats and wigs. Six chairs were lined up in front of the mirror, which stretched the length of the wall. The long counter beneath the mirror was crammed with make-up of all shapes, sizes and colours, along with a variety of old rags and flannels and pots of cheap grease for removing the make-up at the end of each performance.

Sydney put the iron down, inspected his newly creased trousers and was satisfied. There was a knock on the door and one of the Sunshine Dancers put her head round the door.

'Can we borrow your iron? Ours is kaput.' She was tall with smooth dark hair and her face already glowed with scarlet lipstick, black-rimmed eyes and false eyelashes.

'You can have it for ten minutes and mind you bring it back – and watch yourself. It's hot.' Sydney handed it over and asked, 'What's the house like?'

'Not many. Mostly old fogeys but there's a class of children booked, coming from Eastbourne on a charabanc. Don't ask me why they're coming here. They've got theatres in Eastbourne.'

Alfie grinned. 'They haven't got us!'

She rolled her eyes. 'Oh yes! I forgot. We're the best!' She disappeared and her high-heeled shoes echoed in the passageway.

The Wonderful Wizard pulled on his newly pressed trousers with a grunt of satisfaction.

Alfie said, 'They look good as new. Better, even.'

'No thanks to you, chum!'

Alfie tried to remember the jokes that would make the

kids laugh and those that would be too risqué and had to be omitted. He knew that if the punters complained, the manager would be laying down the law with a trowel.

Arturio Loreto arrived, carrying his cycle clips, which he tossed on to the make-up counter. He gave the other two men his usual grin.

'Great goings-on at the Romilees!' he said. 'I wonder where the fellow is – the one that's gone missing. Lionel Somebody. It's all my wife can talk about! She's convinced herself that there's a killing spree starting and she's very nervous. I've told her not to frighten the girls.'

Arturio was a singer and a reasonably good one. His speciality was opera and he sang in what passed for Italian to further impress the audience. He believed that his act lent the pier performance a touch of class and secretly no-one would argue with that. He went on. 'Not to mention a body on the beach! If that doesn't put Hastings on the map, nothing will.'

Sydney said, 'Let's hope it doesn't scare off the day trippers.'

'It won't. More likely to draw the crowds. You know how people are. It's sure to be in the local paper this weekend. Our very own thriller! They'll all stand around the spot where the body was found, gawping and chewing sticks of rock!' He began to change into his outfit – black trousers, red cummerbund, not-so-crisp white shirt, black bow tie on a piece of elastic. 'Oh God! Where's the iron?'

'One of the girls borrowed it.'

Sighing, he went off to retrieve it. Arturio's real name was Arthur Law and he was slim and almost elegant and somehow girlish, with a soft mouth and gentle eyes. He was older than he looked.

'Jessie's bringing the children to the matinee,' he announced when he returned. 'It's Dora's birthday treat and the two girls are each bringing a school friend. We're all having an ice cream in the interval and afterwards Jessie's taking the four children home to tea.'

'Very cosy!' said Sydney.

Young Bill put his head round the door. 'Five minutes to curtain! All present and correct?'

They nodded.

'What's the house like?' Arthur asked, fastening his cummerbund.

'First seven rows of the stalls full and the first two in the circle. Not much else.' He hurried away to alert the girls in their dressing room.

Five minutes passed. It was the moment they longed for – and the one they dreaded. The show must go on.

The three o'clock meeting at the Hastings police station was a gloomy affair on the surface, although privately each member of the team was enjoying the novelty of an investigation into a double-edge case – at once a disappearance and a probable murder. They sat back in their chairs as Detective Constable Fleet ran through the information they had accumulated, and racked their brains for something intelligent to offer or an insightful question to ask when their turn came.

'So, Brent goes missing on Sunday eleventh, p.m. Why then? Anything significant about the time of his disappearance? Anybody?'

Feet shifted uncomfortably.

Sergeant Owen said, 'Broad daylight, holiday season.'

'So?

'Easy to disappear in a crowd, maybe. Easier to find a reason to leave the hotel.'

'Very good, Owen. That assumes what?'

'That he wanted to disappear!'

'Right. So question number one . . .' He grabbed a piece of chalk and wrote on the blackboard as he spoke. '*Was disapearance intentional / accidental / malicious*?' He surveyed his handiwork.

PC Adams put his hand up. 'There's two "p"s in disappearance, Guv.'

All heads swivelled in his direction.

DC Fleet snapped, 'You want to do this?' and threw him the chalk.

Adams blushed furiously, mumbled, 'No, Guv. Sorry,' and threw it back.

The detective gave him a baleful glance. 'So . . . Motive? Anyone? Come on! We haven't got all day.'

'He's gone off with another woman!'

'He wants people to think he's dead so he can do something – a crime or something.'

'Quite possible.' The chalk squeaked on the blackboard.

Sergeant Owen said, 'Could be an art theft. He might be going to steal his wife's pictures from the gallery in London!'

'Also possible. Good. Anyone else?'

'The murderer might have got him, Guv. He might be the next body to turn up on the beach.'

'Which murderer would that be, Reed?'

Reed was the youngest and newest constable. 'Might be a mass murderer. There was a murder in Brighton a couple of months ago.'

'True . . .' DC Fleet paused, recalling the details. 'Not very likely. That was a domestic, if I remember rightly. Man killed his father-in-law.'

Taylor said, 'And he's been arrested.'

'So . . . that's a non-starter then.' DC Fleet stared hopefully at his group. They were mostly young and inexperienced but they were willing. His mind moved on, sifting the available evidence, which was slight, and trying to broaden the scope of the investigation. 'It could be an insurance scam involving the gallery. There are two owners and they might both be involved . . . But if so, why draw attention to one of them? No . . . that wouldn't work.'

The youngest constable put his hand up. 'The wife might have killed him.'

There was a moment's silence and then a clamour – everyone had something to say about that but DC Fleet put up his hand. 'Not a goer, I'm afraid. She was asleep in the hotel and he was seen leaving, very much alive.' He wrote *Jem Rider* on the board and said, 'My gut instinct is that there's a connection. Sergeant Owen, you can do some digging into that. See the boy's mother. Talk to his friends.'

'Right.'

Another hand went up. 'If it's a family thing, could the lad's mother be at risk?'

'Emily Rider? Let's hope not but we'll bear it in mind.'

'Guv, the wife could have had Brent killed even if she didn't actually do it.' Reed looked round triumphantly, having added something original. 'She could have paid a professional killer. Maybe he was playing away, as they say.'

The team looked at him with new respect.

Someone said, 'But we don't know that Brent's dead. So far he's only missing.'

'True.' DC Fleet nodded. 'But good thinking, Reed. We mustn't rule anything out at this stage.' He thought about Maude Brent and couldn't believe it of her. She would have needed to be a very good liar and he was sure she wasn't capable of anything mean and certainly not vicious. No, not Maude Brent . . .

'Guv!'

Reed's voice jerked him back to the uncomfortable knowledge that he had been allowing his personal admiration of the victim's wife to colour his judgement. 'Yes, Reed.'

'It might have been suicide.'

'We don't think he's dead, Reed.'

'But he might be, sir. He might have killed Jem Rider in a fit of temper or something and then done himself in.'

'But he went missing before Jem's body was found.'

A ripple of laughter convinced Reed that he had not thought that particular theory through, and DC Fleet was still trying to restore order when there was a knock on the door and a note was handed to him. He read it aloud and whistled with astonishment.

'Well, lads, there's been a ransom demand!' he told them. 'We're looking at a kidnapping!'

Maude sat on a sofa in the hotel owner's private sitting room, away from curious eyes. She held the ransom note in her hand and stared at it sightlessly, waiting for the dark mist to clear so that she could read it again. Alison Cobb had made her drink a nip of brandy as a restorative and her brother was on the telephone to the police.

'No, we don't know how it was delivered,' he repeated,

exasperated. 'One of our guests found the envelope on the mat inside the front door less than five minutes ago . . . Well, of course it's been handled. Someone picked it up and Mrs Brent has opened it . . . She has a perfect right to open any letters addressed to her . . . Yes, I do know what it says but she has asked us not to disclose it until DC Fleet arrives . . . What's that? Because DC Fleet is on the case and Mrs Brent trusts him. She has a lot of confidence in . . . Someone must have told him by now. He's probably on his way . . . Who am I speaking to exactly? The desk sergeant? Good grief! Well then I can assure you that Mrs Brent is in no state to speak to you . . . And don't take that tone with me! We've got enough to deal with already . . . We'll wait for the DC to arrive.'

He hung up, muttering under his breath, and came back into the sitting room, bristling with indignation.

'Uppity young man on the desk asking for a few words with you, Mrs Brent. Who does he think he is? I told him you were waiting for DC Fleet. You drink the rest of that brandy. Do you good.'

Maude said, 'The handwriting – it's disguised, isn't it? They write with the left hand to make it unrecognizable.' Forcing herself, she opened the crumpled sheet of paper and read it again, silently. It was stark and to the point and it terrified her.

> *We have your husband. If you want to see him alive send a thousand pounds in used notes. Await instructions.*

A thousand pounds. It was a lot of money but if it would bring Lionel back to her she would find it somehow. She would talk to the bank manager and arrange a loan of half the amount and then sell ten or twelve of her father's paintings. As many as it took, she decided. She didn't care about the money. If it brought her husband back it was worth every penny. *If you want to see him alive* . . . The question struck dread into her heart.

DC Fleet was shown in to the sitting room as soon as

he arrived and Maude handed him the note and the envelope.

Mrs Cobb said, 'I'll leave you in good hands, then, Mrs Brent. If you need me I'll be in the kitchen or the dining room – and I'll send Meg in with a tray of tea and cakes.' She smiled at the detective. 'In my experience a policeman never refuses either!'

He smiled and thanked her then sat down and faced Maude. His expression was grave and Maude felt a frisson of unease. In silence he read the note, held it up to the light, sniffed it and felt it with his fingers. In spite of the circumstances Maude noticed that he had nice hands – slim fingers like Lionel's.

He sat with his eyes cast down, staring into space and thinking deeply. The longer he thought, the more worried Maude became.

At last she could bear it no longer. 'Isn't it good news? We've heard from them. We know he's still alive. We know we can get him back! I can see the bank manager first thing in the morning and I . . .'

Meg came in with the tray, her eyes like saucers. She set it down on the coffee table and said, 'I do hope everything goes all right, Mrs Brent.'

'Thank you, Meg.'

When she had gone, he looked up. 'I don't want to crush your hopes, Mrs Brent, but it isn't as easy as you think.'

Maude poured the tea before speaking again. 'But the paintings are . . . that is, my father's work is highly thought of . . . I can sell them all if need be.' Her heart was thumping uncomfortably. Maude was fighting a growing consternation. DC Fleet had been the man she trusted to bring back Lionel – so why was he now being so cautious?

'You mustn't make assumptions,' he warned gently. 'Firstly, we don't know for sure that this note is genuine. Anyone could have sent it. Someone who knows nothing about your husband's whereabouts.'

'Oh no! What are you saying?'

'I'm trying to help you understand the situation. If you send the money to whoever wrote the note it may disappear forever but you may not get your husband back. If he *has* been kidnapped and if this *is* genuine then we can be a little hopeful. I'm so sorry. I don't want to take away any hopes you have but you must face facts.'

Maude fell back in the armchair, suddenly breathless with disappointment. He was right, she could see that, but surely there was something that could be done to verify the sender's intentions.

He went on. 'We might learn more when he telephones. If he does. He may send another note. We don't know how he will communicate.'

Maude put a hand to her head. 'But I could take out the money, couldn't I? I could be ready in case it is genuine. I must get him back, DC Fleet. I just want to get him back and to return to my everyday life. Our life, that is!'

'I can't stop you, Mrs Brent, but there is another factor. We need proof that your husband is still alive.'

'Oh!' she gasped. 'But he is. I know it!'

'Do you want to give a thousand pounds to someone who may have – nothing is clear yet – who may have already killed your husband? 'He held up a hand to forestall her next comment. 'I'm not saying he is dead, Mrs Brent, but it's my job to consider the possibilities and not encourage you to rush headlong into a possible trap.' He folded the letter, handling it as little as possible and slid it back into the envelope. 'I'll get a handwriting expert to study this and then try and trace the paper.'

She stared at him despairingly. 'So what are we going to do? What are *you* going to do? Nothing?'

'No. I'll stay here throughout the night in case he rings or sends another note. He may insist on speaking to you – that's quite common – so keep your slippers and dressing gown handy. Try to sleep but be prepared to be woken up at any time.'

'But won't he wonder who you are? He might guess that you're the police.'

He nodded, frowning. 'That's something that's puzzling me. Kidnappers normally say "Don't tell the police" but they haven't. It's almost as if they know that you'll insist on paying up. There's another factor, Mrs Brent. It does happen sometimes that after the payment the hostage is not released and a second payment is demanded.'

Maude drew a long breath and let it out slowly. 'Have you been involved in many cases like this?'

'Just one but we do study all kinds of criminal behaviour and *modus operandi* – that's the way they work.' He smiled faintly. 'I'm not a novice, Mrs Brent, I promise you that. We'll do everything possible to bring about a good result.'

As he stood up, Maude almost panicked. 'You're not going?'

'No. I need to use the telephone to fetch one of our lads to ride over here and collect the ransom note.'

'Then I could buy you supper, DC Fleet, here in the hotel. That way we might both manage to eat something. No!' She held up her hand. 'Please don't refuse to be my guest. It's the least I can do. Mrs Cobb might allow us to eat in here, away from the curious stares.'

He nodded with the briefest of smiles and Maude hurried out of the room in search of Alison Cobb, grateful to have something to do – anything to take her mind off the situation. If she allowed herself to think about the difficulties ahead, she knew she would break down.

Biddy tried to concentrate on the job in hand in an attempt to keep darker thoughts at bay. Enveloped in a large pinafore, she stood at the kitchen table, surrounded by various jars and bags – currants, sultanas and a handful of dried figs waited to her left for her attention but she was chopping dates with unusual vigour. To her right was a selection of flour, a sugar cone, a tin of black treacle, eggs, a lump of butter, a paper screw of cinnamon and another of mixed spice.

Maude had telephoned the bad news that Lionel had been kidnapped and a ransom was demanded. Biddy knew that Maude would do anything to bring her husband home safely. When Maude told her the official police policy on kidnaps, she sympathized with her niece but advised her to be guided by DC Fleet. Now she worried in case Lionel was never seen again and Maude would blame her. Biddy couldn't quite convince herself that the police were right but neither could she risk confusing the issue by persuading Maude to defy them.

She glanced up as Alice entered the kitchen with Primmy by way of the back door, and stopped chopping long enough to remove the dog's lead.

'Let's hope the walk has tired her out!' said Biddy, straightening her back with a sigh.

Alice was staring at the table. 'What on earth are you doing?'

'What does it look like?' Biddy spoke sharply. She wasn't in the mood to answer stupid questions.

'It looks as if . . . Are you making a Christmas pudding?'

'I am indeed.' Biddy poured herself a glass of water and drank it all. It was a warm day and close and the kitchen still smelled of the ironing Alice had done earlier.

Alice looked bewildered. 'But Biddy, it's only June. You told me last year that you always make the pudding in September.'

Primmy rushed to her water bowl and drank thirstily.

Biddy's expression hardened. 'If I want to make the Christmas pudding in June it's my business.' She scooped the chopped dates into the large mixing bowl, sprinkled a handful of flour over them and reached for the figs.

Alice sat down. 'Sorry, Biddy. You're right. It's not my business.'

'You thought I'd mixed up the months, didn't you?' Biddy looked at her accusingly. 'You thought I was getting vague – just because I sometimes forget things. Well, Alice Crewe, for your information I'm not losing my mind. I'm just under a lot of strain because of all this kidnap and police and–and I felt like doing a bit of cooking to take my mind off things.' Despite her expression, her voice shook. She dropped the knife, snatched a handkerchief from her pocket, turned away and blew her nose loudly.

Then she said, 'Not that I can imagine us ever having a normal Christmas again. I don't dare think about the future without Lionel. And what it will do to Maude . . . It will be the end of her if he doesn't come back – or if he dies.'

Alice said, 'I'll make some tea. And stop thinking like that. Of course he won't die. Everything will be all right, Biddy. Trust me. It will. I promise you.'

'Promise me? Don't talk so daft, Alice! What do you know about anything? I don't mean to be rude but what makes you so sure? It's not some kind of game, you know. Not some story that is bound to have a happy ending. Kidnaps go wrong sometimes and the person dies. That's what the policeman told Maude. That's why I said she should be guided by him.'

'Maybe she should follow her own instincts. Pay up and get it over with. That's what I'd do in her shoes.'

'Well, you're not in her shoes and if you were you might feel very differently.'

Alice shrugged. 'Maybe I'm an optimist. Maybe I don't ever expect the worst. You're a pessimist, Biddy. You can't help it. That's the way you're made.' She hesitated. 'D'you want some help with the pudding? I can chop things for you, if you like.'

Biddy made an effort to relax. 'No. I want to do it. I'm using a different recipe today. My grandmother's. She always used black treacle but my mother didn't like it. She thought it made it bitter so I'm going to use the treacle and add some extra sugar.' Feeling more collected, Biddy went on, 'A thousand pounds! Where will Maude find all that money?'

'She can afford it. She's got all those pictures and a part share in the gallery. A bank manager would lend her the money.'

'Well, you know a lot more than I do then . . .' She frowned. 'Someone knows a lot about her. It must be someone who knows about pictures and also the gallery. I wonder if the police have checked on Mr Barlowe. What do we know about him?'

Alice busied herself with the kettle and teapot.

Biddy went on slowly, knife poised over the figs, the pudding forgotten. 'Frederick Barlowe . . . He would also know where they are – in Hastings on holiday – because Lionel will have told him. Or if it's not Barlowe, it might be someone who knows him . . . Alice, what do you think?' When there was no reply she said sharply, 'Alice! What do you think?'

Alice rolled her eyes. 'I think you're clutching at straws and I'm sick of talking about it.' She set the cup of tea in front of Biddy and flounced out of the room.

Hurt by the sharp words, Biddy stared after her. 'We have to clutch at something!' she said.

The clock in the nearby church had just struck midnight but Biddy lay awake trying to work out a way to get Maude home. She hated the idea that her niece was alone in the hotel without a friend or a family member to support her during these agonizing times. Of course the hotel owners were being very kind and understanding but Maude needed someone closer to her. Unless . . . Maybe she, Biddy, could go and stay at the hotel to be with her. But that would mean leaving Alice alone in the house and she might not feel very safe. The visit from Jem had left them all a little nervous and they would never forgive themselves if anything happened to Alice.

She heaved herself over on to the other side, pulled the pillow into her neck and decided to sound Maude out on the subject.

Click.

Biddy froze. 'What on earth . . .?' She sat up, peering round in the darkened room. There were a lot of clouds and very little moonlight.

Click. Click.

The sound came from the window. Something was tapping at the glass!

'Dear God, help me!' she whispered. Was someone throwing stones at the window?

Gathering all her courage she clambered out of bed and tiptoed across the bare boards. When she reached the window she stood to one side, eased back the edge of the curtain and tried to see out without being seen.

'Can't see a blooming thing!' she grumbled. Below her the lawn was cloaked in sinister shadows and for a moment nothing could be seen, but then she thought she caught a movement just below the window and a sudden break in the clouds revealed what she thought was a man. It was only a glimpse but she saw him quite clearly. He wore a long duster coat and a broad-brimmed hat that hid his face. Then it was dark again and Biddy's heart was racing so fast that she dared not move from the spot for fear she might faint. She clung to the window sill until she recovered and then made her way unsteadily to the room next door and opened it.

'Alice! Wake up!' She crossed to the bed and shook the sleeping woman, who sat up in alarm.

'What?' cried Alice. 'What's happening?'

'There's someone in the garden. Get up quickly and look. He's been throwing stones up to my window.'

'But who would . . .?'

'Get up and see for yourself! Hurry! He's wearing very strange clothes – a long coat and . . .' She followed Alice to her window and they looked out together on to the gloom of the garden.

'I can't see anyone,' Alice said.

'He was there, Alice! I saw him. His clothes were . . . Look! There he is – running away into the shrubbery. You must be able to see him.'

'Well, I can't.'

She sounded shaken, thought Biddy. There was something odd about her voice. 'Are you all right?' she asked. 'I had to wake you. I'm sorry if I frightened you but . . . Who could it be? Not Jem, because he's dead.'

Alice said, 'You imagined it, Biddy. There was no man in the garden. I'd have seen him and I didn't. I didn't see anything.' She climbed back into bed while Biddy stood indecisively by the window.

'Alice, you *must* have seen him.'

'Go back to bed! It was too dark for anyone to see anything.'

'But I *saw* him. I know I did.'

'You thought you did, Biddy. Maybe you were having a nightmare and got out of bed and imagined it all. Maybe you were sleepwalking. Just go back to your own room and get into bed.'

'It may have been the man who killed Jem!' Although they were her own words, they sent a shiver down Biddy's spine. 'I'm going to telephone Maude and tell her to tell DC Fleet.'

Alice glared at her. 'If you do I shall telephone her and say you were having a funny turn and there was no-one there.'

'*A funny turn!* You wouldn't dare!' Biddy was shocked. 'You're in no position to tell me what I can and can't do, Alice Crewe! And I don't have funny turns! What's got into you?' Her chest heaved with indignation. The words 'only a paid companion' hovered on her lips but common sense prevailed and they remained unsaid. Instead she said again, 'I'm sometimes forgetful but I do not have funny turns! I know exactly what I saw and someone ought to be told.'

Alice sighed loudly. 'Very well, Biddy. I take back what I said but look at it this way. I think poor Maude has got enough to worry about without you making it worse. If you tell her what you *think* you saw she'll start worrying about us as well. She knows we're unprotected here and she'll imagine us being murdered in our beds. Leave the poor soul in ignorance – and let me go back to sleep.'

Biddy left without another word, too confused to argue further and half persuaded by Alice's point about Maude's other problems. She went back to bed but didn't lie down. Instead she sat up, trying to focus her mind and trying to convince herself that she *had* seen a man in the garden and he *had* been throwing stones up at her window for some unknown reason. Either to frighten or to wake her or to warn her about something . . . Suppose he had been a friend instead of an enemy . . . But if he had been a friend he would never have run off.

'Too late now!' she told herself. 'And I did see something and it looked like a man in a long coat with a hat with a wide brim. A bit like a highwayman!' Which made no sense.

'Unless . . .' Her eyes widened suddenly. 'Unless he was trying to awaken Alice and chose the wrong window.' No, that was impossible. If Alice had a young man she had kept him very quiet all this time for no good reason. Maude had teased her once or twice about finding a nice young man to marry but Alice had always laughed it off, saying she found men conceited and self-centred, and she had no intention of marrying.

'So . . . did she recognize him? No, surely not!' No self-respecting suitor would come dressed like that, Biddy assured herself.

She got out of bed again and crossed to the window to see if the intruder was still out there. Peering into the darkness she could see very little, and nothing that moved or resembled the figure she had seen earlier, yet the memory of what she had seen remained stubbornly clear in her mind. Suddenly she came to a decision. She would face Alice with the question once and for all. If Alice convinced her that she had imagined it then where did that leave her, Biddy? She did not want to believe that her mind was beginning to play tricks on her. Senility was a word she feared because she had seen her mother slip into that confused state that robs people of their personality.

'And all their memories!' she murmured. Biddy's mother had ceased to recognize her own daughter, had existed in a world that she no longer understood, and for that reason Biddy had been glad when she died.

'But I'm not like that – I'm just a little forgetful!' she declared.

Acting on impulse, she went back along the passage and knocked on Alice's door. When no-one answered she turned the handle and went in. 'Alice! I have to talk to you.'

There was no reply and, moving closer, Biddy realized that the bed was empty. So where had she gone? Down to the kitchen, perhaps, to heat a cup of milk.

The kitchen was empty too, but the back door was open. Primmy was fast asleep in her basket, which was odd. Hastily Biddy stepped back from the doorway. So Alice *did* have a young man! Biddy was engulfed by a feeling of deep disappointment. Alice, lying to them. Alice of all people! She sat down on a stool and waited, trying to decide what exactly she would say when Alice returned.

A moment later she heard footsteps and Alice appeared in the doorway. She looked shocked when she saw Biddy – as well she might, thought Biddy grimly.

'So I was right!' said Biddy. 'I did see someone in the garden. Your young man!'

Alice hesitated, disconcerted.

Biddy said, 'You could have told us. We're not ogres. Why did you lie to us, Alice?'

Alice closed the door quietly then turned to face Biddy. 'I went out to make sure there really was no-one there. I didn't want to frighten you so I went out on my own with this.' She held up a torch. 'I wanted to reassure us both. There was no-one out there, Biddy. There was no man in a long coat with a big hat. So please, don't alarm Maude. I'm sorry, but it was all in your imagination – or else it was a nightmare and it was very real to you.'

Biddy's mind whirled. She was relieved that Alice had not lied to them about a young man but now she worried about her own confusion. She said contritely, 'I'm sorry, Alice, but what else was I to think? You should never have gone out into the garden alone. If it *had* been someone you might have been attacked! You might have been killed! At least you should have taken Primmy with you. Her mad barking would have scared him off.'

'I called her but she didn't want to leave her basket. She just wasn't interested. She seems to be very tired tonight.'

'Tired? That doesn't sound like Primmy. She usually has too much energy! I hope she's not ill.' She crossed to the basket and patted the dog. 'Primmy! Wake up!'

The dog made a muffled sound then slowly opened her eyes. Her tail flopped twice by way of a greeting but she didn't even lift her head. The two women exchanged worried looks.

Alice said, 'She ate all her dinner. She can't be ill.'

'Maybe she's eaten something that's upset her.' Biddy sighed heavily and got to her feet. 'If she's like that in the morning I'll call the vet. We can't let anything happen to Primmy. That would be the last straw.'

Leaving Primmy to recover, Biddy and Alice turned off the kitchen light and made their way up the stairs. As they parted company on the landing Alice said, 'If we don't get some sleep soon it will be time to get up!'

And face another day, thought Biddy, and wondered what news that would bring. Nothing good, she thought unhappily and sighed deeply. She was beginning to doubt that there would be a happy resolution to their troubles.

SIX

It was almost four o'clock the next morning when the call finally came. DC Fleet held up a warning finger and then beckoned Maude outside to the telephone, which was in the hall on the reception desk. Maude had decided against retiring to her room. Knowing she was hardly likely to sleep in the circumstances, she had dozed on and off in an armchair in the lounge. The detective had sat opposite her, lost in thought as he studied his notes.

Maude's hand shook as she picked up the receiver and held it to her ear. 'Yes. Who is this?'

'Mrs Brent?'

'Yes.' She frowned. The voice was tinny, unlike a real voice, she thought, but the words were clear enough.

'The money must be in used notes. Place it in a carpet bag or similar—'

'Used notes in a carpet bag. Yes . . . Whoever you are, I want to speak to my husband. I want to hear his voice. How do I know you have my husband? You could be anybody.'

As though she had not spoken, the tinny voice continued. 'At ten minutes after two tomorrow night leave the bag tied to the hand rail at the entrance to the pier – left-hand side—'

'Ten past two tomorrow on the hand rail, entrance to the pier, on the left,' she repeated. 'Now may I speak to my husband? Please!' She tried to keep the desperation from her voice but already tears were pressing against her eyes and her lashes were wet.

At last she heard his voice. He sounded strained but the words were clear enough. 'Maude, do what he says!'

'Oh God! It's you, Lionel!' She turned to DC Fleet. 'It's him. I know his voice. He's still alive! Oh God! Thank you!'

The tinny voice resumed. 'Satisfied?'

'Yes!' she cried between sobs.

'Now I must speak to the policeman.'

She stared at the receiver in surprise. How did he know DC Fleet was with her?

As if reading her thoughts the kidnapper said, 'Credit me with some sense, Mrs Brent. The affair is plastered all over the *Hastings Gazette*. Of course the police are involved.'

Wordlessly, Maude handed the receiver to the detective. As he listened carefully Maude tried to pull herself together. She told herself that Lionel was alive and before too long they might, God willing, be reunited. The end was in sight.

DC Fleet said, 'But when will we see Lionel Brent? Will he be . . . No! That's most unsatisfactory. If the money is delivered . . . Forged money? Certainly not. Mrs Brent is determined to give you the full amount and . . . No! First we have to know when and how Mr Brent will be returned. That's not open for discussion . . . Hello? Hello . . . Damnation!' DC Fleet replaced the receiver. 'He's hung up. *You* have to deliver it,' he told Maude. 'You have to take a taxi to the pier, fasten the bag to the railings, walk back and get into the taxi and be driven away. If anyone is with you the kidnapper won't collect the money.'

'And Lionel?' She almost held her breath.

'You'll never see him again. But that's simply a threat, Mrs Brent. To frighten you into complying.'

'They've succeeded, DC Fleet. I'm very frightened indeed.' Maude put a hand to her heart, which was beating painfully fast. 'You must allow me to collect the money and deliver it as instructed. I've spoken to the bank manager. It's all arranged. I know you don't want me to hand it over but you don't understand how I feel. How can you? I *have* to have Lionel back or my life as I know it is over. He means everything to me. Please don't fight me on this.'

His expression was unhappy in the extreme. 'The kidnapper won't say how or when your husband will be released, Mrs Brent. I find that extremely worrying. That's why I—'

'But he's alive! I heard his voice. There were times when

I thought . . . when I suspected that he was already dead. But I spoke to him. It was Lionel!'

'It's suspicious. You have to understand, Mrs Brent. He might take the money and kill your husband anyway. Such things are not unknown, believe me. He could make utter fools of us. Will you at least think—?'

Maude interrupted him. 'Forgive me but I don't want to discuss it, DC Fleet. I just have to hope. I can't go on like this. I simply want us to bring things to a close. I want my husband and my well-ordered life back.'

He shrugged. 'My superiors won't like it but it's up to you. If you do insist on going through with it I would ask you not to raise your hopes too high. I'll be delighted if all goes smoothly but please be prepared for possible . . . disappointment.'

Maude, however, was determined not to be discouraged. 'I have a good feeling about it,' she told him. 'Hearing his voice . . . It's going to be all right.'

'How did he sound? Distraught? Angry? Frightened?'

She thought about it. 'None of those – but then he's not the type to panic. Tired maybe. I would say he's facing up to the ordeal very well. He's a strong personality. He'll come through.'

Unconvinced, DC Fleet announced that he would go back to the police station to consult with his immediate superior. 'Detective Inspector Merrit won't be too pleased about your decision but we'll have a look at the site and see if we can place some of our people in and around – incognito, of course. We might be able to follow the taxi . . .' He gave her a wan smile. 'We'll do our best, Mrs Brent. Everything in our power, in fact.'

'I have faith in you, DC Fleet.' She smiled. 'I can't wait for tomorrow night.'

Friday morning surgery started at nine o'clock and Biddy was there in good time. She hated to sit among too many other patients in case she caught something from one of them. She had chosen a seat in the corner and anyone who ventured near was rewarded with an unflinching glare that persuaded them to sit elsewhere. Biddy was the second person to be called and she settled herself nervously on the upright chair as the doctor glanced at her file.

'What can I do for you, Miss Cope?' he asked. 'I don't see you very often.' Doctor Courtney was a small bespectacled man who, in Biddy's infrequent meetings, came across as calm and reliable to the point of blandness. His expression of friendly interest rarely wavered. Now he regarded her with slightly raised eyebrows as she tried to recall the speech she had prepared. As she struggled for her opening line, he waited patiently.

At last she said, 'I'm sixty-nine, Doctor Courtney. Would you expect me to be . . . a little forgetful?'

'It would be fairly normal. Yes.'

'What about sleepwalking?'

He hesitated. 'Not as a new phenomenon. If you have done this before then not surprising.'

'I've never done it. Not to my knowledge.'

He nodded.

Biddy swallowed. 'Suppose I . . . I started to imagine things . . . things that weren't there?' She clasped and unclasped her hands.

He gave a little shrug. 'Imagining things? That might worry you a little but it would depend on the circumstances.'

'What would they be – the circumstances?'

He rolled his eyes thoughtfully. 'In times of great stress the mind can play tricks. It could well be a temporary aberration. Nothing to suggest a serious problem.' He sat back and steepled his fingers. 'I'm sixty-five, Miss Cope. I forget things. I don't think I sleepwalk but since my wife died I wouldn't really know. Who would tell me?' He smiled. 'I might wander back to bed and know nothing about it in the morning.'

Biddy took a deep breath. 'Last night I clearly saw a man in our garden. I *saw* him, Doctor Courtney. It wasn't a vision or . . . or a mirage. It certainly wasn't a ghost. An odd-looking man in a long coat with a big wide hat. But . . . Alice Crewe was with me and she saw nothing. Nothing at all! How could that be unless . . . Was it a hallucination,

Doctor Courtney?' She closed her eyes. 'I'm afraid . . . that is, I think I may be . . . losing my mind!'

'Ah! I see your problem, Miss Cope, but let me try and set your mind at ease. A hallucination is most unlikely but the moon throws strange shadows. Did this strange man speak?'

'No. Or if he did I didn't hear him.'

'Do you know anyone who might wear an outfit like the one you've described? To me it sounds rather like a poacher. Do you know any poachers who might sneak through your garden?'

'A poacher? Certainly not!'

'Is it possible?'

'Anything's possible, I suppose, but . . .' She fell silent. She had come for a straight answer but was obviously not going to get one – which meant that she would not go home reassured, but neither would she feel confident to pass on what she had seen to the police for fear they laughed at her.

The doctor studied her thoughtfully. 'I know the problems you have at the moment – the kidnapping. It was in the paper, of course, but there are always rumours. All extremely upsetting for you. I speak for the whole village when I say we sympathize with you all. Poor Mrs Brent! My heart bleeds for her.'

'Then you don't think I . . .'

'You and Miss Crewe must be under a great deal of pressure, Miss Cope, and that is affecting you. Your mind is playing tricks, perhaps, but I suggest that is a temporary problem and that as soon as the police have solved the crime, you will once again be restored to your normal cheerful self.'

Biddy found this bland assessment irritating. 'But I can't sleep, Doctor Courtney, and I can't think straight. I–I made a Christmas pudding a few days ago. Miss Crewe thought I was quite mad!'

'Forgive me, Miss Cope, but Miss Crewe is not a doctor and doesn't understand the workings of the mind. Can you tell me today's date?'

'The date? It's the sixteenth.'

'And is Queen Victoria on the throne?'

'No. She died a long time ago.'

He smiled faintly. 'There you are then. I rest my case. If you failed to answer either question correctly I would worry about you. But you didn't fail!'

She opened her mouth to add something but he held up his hand to silence her. 'I am going to give you a sedative. Not only to help you sleep at night but to calm your nerves and help you through the next few days. A few spoonfuls of medicine, Miss Cope, and I guarantee you will see no more strange men.'

Around the same time Maude sat down opposite the bank manager with a comparatively light heart. The end was near. She told herself so at intervals and was beginning to believe it. All she had to do was deliver the money and Lionel would be released and they would go back to *Fairways* together. Time would pass and they would forget all about it.

She smiled at Mr Franks. She had always liked him. He had managed their affairs for as long as she could remember and must be due to retire soon.

He greeted her rather nervously, she thought, but grasped his plump outstretched hand as warmly as usual.

'So sorry to keep you waiting, Mrs Brent.'

'I've only been here a few minutes.'

He lowered himself into his chair, avoiding her gaze.

Maude felt the first frisson of doubt as she watched him assemble the papers he had brought with him. She said, 'It should soon be over, Mr Franks, with your help. As I told you on the telephone . . .'

He glanced up unhappily. 'I shall do all I can, of course, but I have to be guided by Head Office. I have explained exactly what we need – a loan – but they are still deliberating.'

'Deliberating?' It was little more than a whisper.

'Considering how best to deal with the . . . the difficulties. It is a most unusual request, Mrs Brent, and we do have a responsibility to our shareholders . . .'

'I am one of them!'

'Ah! Yes, you are indeed but . . . these things take time, Mrs Brent. A thousand pounds is a very large sum and one you do not have in your account.'

'But you know we are able to afford the ransom. You know I have my father's pictures, which are possibly worth twice that amount. We are not paupers, Mr Franks! We have goods to a value far above the loan I am asking for. I don't have to tell you that. You have the file in front of you. Look at it!'

To her dismay he shook his head. 'It's not as simple as you imagine, Mrs Brent. We also owe a duty of care to you, as one of our clients, to give you sound advice and, in this instance, Head Office feels that we should all step back and take a deep breath before we rush into something we might—'

'I shan't regret it, Mr Franks, if that's what you're implying. I want my husband home safe and well. I can't begin to imagine what he is going through with his life hanging by a thread. He is relying on me and the police and you, Mr Franks, to save his life. Who is this nameless man at Head Office? Let me speak to him. I'll tell him what I think about a man in his position who dithers at a time like this!' Breathless, she pressed a hand to her heart. 'I wonder just how different his reply would be if his wife had been kidnapped! Very different, Mr Franks, and you know it.' She glared at him, her chest heaving with anger.

'Really, Mrs Brent, you must calm yourself!' he begged, taken aback by her uncharacteristic attack. 'We only have your best interests at heart. The police believe, they have told me, they fear it will not be the last payment you have to make. They also think you should delay the—'

'Oh, I see it now! You've been in touch with the police behind my back! That's despicable, Mr Franks! What happened to client confidentiality? You have betrayed me!' She leaned across the desk, stabbing her finger at him so violently that he drew back in his chair in alarm.

'Mrs Brent! You are beside yourself!' he gasped.

'And you are the reason, Mr Franks, for my anger. You and Head Office are driving me to the point of hysteria! Every minute wasted is a minute nearer to my husband's death!' She flung herself back in the chair, almost choking with fear and anger. She took several deep breaths in an attempt to compose herself. This, she told herself, was not the way to win them over. Tears might have been the best option but she was far from tearful. She steadied her voice with an effort. 'Please allow me to speak directly to someone at Head Office.'

'I'm afraid that won't be possible.'

'Please try, Mr Franks.' She pointed at the telephone.

For a moment they stared at each other, both refusing to give ground, but then the manager shrugged. Without another word to her, he reached for the telephone and asked the operator to connect him to his Head Office. They waited in silence for the connection. When he was put through, Mr Franks said, 'I have one of my clients with me. A Mrs Lionel Brent . . . Yes. That Mrs Brent. She is insisting on speaking to someone . . . I see. Perhaps you would tell her that.' He handed the telephone to her.

A young male voice said, 'I'm sorry, Mrs Brent. There is nobody available to speak with you. They are all in a meeting. I'm so—'

'I don't believe you.'

'I beg your pardon!'

'I think no-one wants to speak to me so you have been told to tell me they are all in a meeting!'

Mr Franks rolled his eyes and then shook his head.

The voice continued but there was now a distinct edge of irritation to it. 'I'm sure Mr Franks can help you. You can trust him to give you good advice and the police have briefed him. That's all I can say at this point.' The line went dead.

Slowly she handed back the telephone.

'Everyone is "in a meeting"! You really think, Mr Franks, that I am convinced by that?' She eyed him coldly. 'They are ashamed of the line they are taking and nobody will speak to me.'

'Really, Mrs Brent, that's . . . I'm sure that's quite untrue.'

She stood up. 'I shall have to take the pictures instead of the money. I shall hand them all over to the kidnappers – and you should be prepared for my husband's response when he learns how narrowly he escaped death – and no thanks to your bank. We shall be closing our account. Rest assured of that!'

Ignoring his protests, she jumped to her feet and stormed out of the room, slamming the door behind her as loudly as she could.

As all the heads in the public area turned to stare she shouted, 'Don't ever rely on this bank to help you in an emergency! Take my word for it – they won't!' Aware of the shocked and puzzled glances that followed her to the door, Maude pushed blindly past the doorman, ran outside and into the taxi. She pulled the door shut and burst into tears of rage and frustration.

Utterly betrayed by the bank manager's reluctance to provide the money she needed, Maude finally dried her tears, scrubbed at her eyes with a handkerchief and set off for the nearest telephone box to contact the police.

'I need to speak with Detective Constable Fleet,' she told them. 'Is that possible?'

The reply was not helpful. 'I'm afraid not. I dare not interrupt them, Mrs Brent. DC Fleet's in with DI Merrit. Detective Inspector Merrit. He's the big man here. They've decided the two crimes are linked, you see – the murder and the kidnap. They just don't know how exactly. Seems Jem sort of knew the hostage.'

'Knew him?' Distracted from her immediate purpose, Maude blinked in surprise. 'Lionel knew Jem Rider? What makes them think that?'

'His mother turned up, first thing this morning. Wanted to know when she could have her son back. Her son's body, I should say. Wants to bury him, poor soul! Who'd be in her shoes, eh?' He tutted. 'She saw a photograph of your husband stuck up here on the wall.'

'Oh that. It's not one of his best,' she protested. 'I was

in rather a hurry when they asked for one. He looks quite ordinary.'

'It's good enough because she said she recognized him when he came to the house looking for Jem. Anyway the two big noises are "in conference" and not to be disturbed.'

For a moment Maude fumed helplessly but then she snapped, 'Tell him Mrs Brent will deliver the paintings instead of the money. He'll know what that means.' Simmering with anger, she pushed open the door of the telephone box and climbed back into the taxi. 'Drive me to Folkestone. I'll give you directions when we get nearer.'

'Whatever you say, missus. You're the guv'nor!'

The guv'nor? Maude rolled her eyes. Little did he know just how helpless she felt in the face of the police's unyielding attitude towards her preferred options. Lionel was her husband and she genuinely believed that she knew what was best for him. Now that she was being prevented from delivering the ransom, she would offer the pictures instead.

When Maude returned to Fairways she paid her fare and dismissed the taxi. 'Home!' she murmured gratefully. She would make the most of it. If possible she would take time out for a quick walk to the beach with Primmy. Anything to bring back a sense of normality into her fractured life, and the fresh air would do her good.

It would take a long time to collect and prepare all the pictures, but then she would call for another taxi. She would not contact the police again, she told herself. DC Fleet had betrayed her by persuading the bank not to make the money available. From now on she was going to deal with the kidnappers herself.

Biddy met her at the door and for a moment they clung to each other in silence, both fighting back tears, each trying to comfort the other.

Maude said, 'The bank won't help so I'm giving the kidnappers the pictures. It's as broad as it's long. Alice must help me because some of them are too heavy for one person and we have to carry some of them up from the cellar.'

Biddy said, 'Alice is in a funny mood this morning. She

won't get out of bed. We had a bit of a fright in the middle of the night and–and a few sharp words.' She led the way into the sitting room and they both sat down.

'Won't get out of bed? Is she ill?'

'Maybe. She won't say very much – just keeps telling me to leave her alone.'

With an effort Maude dragged her thoughts from the pictures and tried to make sense of Biddy's disturbing news. 'What happened in the night?'

She listened in growing dismay to her aunt's account of the events of the previous night.

'And so today,' Biddy continued, 'I went straight round to see Doctor Courtney and asked him for the truth and he was very reassuring.' She tossed her head triumphantly. 'I'm not going senile at all; I'm just becoming forgetful. And I was not sleepwalking and it's nothing a few spoonfuls of medicine won't cure. It's all because of the strain we're under with Lionel being kidnapped and everything. So I did see a man in the garden, even if he was a poacher, and so why did Alice insist I was imagining things? She's upset me dreadfully, Maude – and why shouldn't I make a Christmas pudding in June? I live here. It's my home. She can't tell me what to do.' Her voice shook.

Maude said, 'Of course you can make a pudding, Aunt Biddy, whenever you like – and I'm sure it will be delicious. It will have longer to–to mature. Try to forget all about it and, since I'm here, I'll have a word with Alice.' Seeing that her aunt was about to continue, Maude said quickly, 'What have we got to eat? I shall be starving by midday.'

Her aunt's expression changed. 'We've got a bit of beef. I could make some rissoles with a bit of onions and some herbs . . . or we could have the sausages I was keeping for tomorrow and take them out of their skins and layer them with slices of potato under a pastry lid . . . Have I got enough lard? I think so . . . Yes, sausage and potato pie sounds nice and filling. You've lost weight, Maudie love, but that's to be expected . . . I noticed some early courgettes in the vegetable patch . . .'

Having found her aunt something purposeful to do, Maude

hesitated. She would have to talk to Alice but first she wanted to discuss the pictures with Lionel's partner. Standing in the hallway she waited for the operator to connect them and was relieved to learn that Frederick Barlowe was in the gallery that day and not away following up new artistic talent.

She listened in silence for a moment or two as he commiserated with her on the situation and then she explained what had happened at the bank and how angry she was. 'I feel it's a sort of conspiracy to prevent me from saving Lionel. First the police and then the bank manager! So I'm going to take some of my father's work in lieu of the money. He can sell them – the kidnapper – and get the money that way.'

Frederick Barlowe interrupted her. 'Not in this country, surely! The name is very recognizable and the kidnap has been reported in the newspapers. Who would buy stolen paintings?'

'They wouldn't be stolen, Mr Barlowe. Not if I give them to the kidnapper.'

'They would be "obtained under duress"!'

'Oh! For heaven's sake! The wretch can sell them abroad. I don't care where they go and I know my father would approve of what I'm going to do. All I need from you, Mr Barlowe, is an idea of each picture's proper value. You have a list, I know, somewhere in the office in the gallery. The pictures are numbered and some you have already sold. You will be able to see at a glance which ones are still here in our cellar. If I can find enough works to add up to a thousand pounds I can—'

'Please, Mrs Brent!' His voice was rising. 'This is not a good idea! I do think you should let the police advise you on this.'

Maude bit back a sharp retort and counted to ten. No point in antagonizing him. She needed his help. 'If you can't guide me in this I shall just have to make a wild guess at their value.' She waited. In the kitchen she could hear Aunt Biddy clattering spoons and crockery and the occasional thump of the rolling pin as the sausage and potato pie took shape.

She heard Frederick Barlowe sigh. 'Very well. I will find the list and ring back when I have worked out a few prices, but I shall write a letter to my solicitor, spelling out my reluctance in case there are problems later that rebound against me. I don't want to be blamed for something that is against the law.'

'Thank you so much, Mr Barlowe,' she said sarcastically. 'You must do as you see fit. I'm sure Lionel will be grateful later when he learns later of your "assistance".'

'There's no need to take that tone. I think you are misguided, Mrs Brent, and I think you may live to regret your hasty actions.'

'I would regret it more if Lionel dies, Mr Barlowe! I love my husband. If your wife would not do anything, in similar circumstances, to save *your* life, then I'm sorry for you!' She hung up, breathing hard and fighting back doubts as she set off up the stairs to see if she could get any sense out of Alice.

She knocked on the bedroom door and Alice called out in a muffled voice, 'Come in!' To Maude's surprise, Alice was still in bed, huddled under the bedclothes.

'Alice! What's the matter? Are you ill?'

'Please just go away. I want to be on my own for a while.'

'But why? You're not usually like this. Something must have happened. Are you upset?' She moved to stand beside the bed. 'Talk to me, Alice! How can anyone help you if you hide away under there?'

'I don't want to talk to anyone. I don't need help. I need to be on my own – to think about things.'

Maude tugged at the bedclothes. 'Sit up, for heaven's sake! I don't have time for all this nonsense. Is it because of what happened in the night . . . or because Aunt Biddy went to see the doctor?' There was no answer. 'Alice!' she shouted, losing patience. 'Sit up and talk to me.'

At last there was a reluctant movement and slowly Alice's head emerged from the bedclothes. She pulled herself to a sitting position and glared at Maude. She looked very pale and had been crying.

An unwelcome thought entered Maude's mind and she

had to hold back a groan. Was Alice expecting a child? Was it possible that she had been keeping secrets about her relationships? An unwanted pregnancy would certainly be enough to bring about this extreme reaction. If it were true, would Alice know? Would she recognize the symptoms of a pregnancy? Maude decided, rather than ask an outright question on such a delicate subject, that she would try a roundabout route to the truth.

'Are you ill, Alice? Feverish, maybe or . . . sick?'

Alice shook her head.

'Has anyone . . . upset you? A man, perhaps.' Maude's thoughts flew to the man Aunt Biddy insisted she had seen the night before. This was obviously why Alice had denied seeing him in the garden. Her heart sank at the prospect of more worries – as if she didn't have enough. 'You can tell me, Alice. I'll do my best to understand. Don't we know each other well enough by now?'

'No! We don't! That's the whole point!'

Maude reached out to take Alice's hands in hers but the girl snatched them away.

'Don't touch me! Don't talk to me. Don't try to help me, Maude, because you can't. Nobody can, so just let me sort it out for myself.'

Maude glanced at the small clock on Alice's bedside table. She had to go down to the cellar and look through the pictures so she could decide which ones to give to the kidnappers. Or kidnapper. Was there only one or two – or maybe a gang? Thank heavens she didn't have to hand the pictures over in person. That would have terrified her. And thank heavens she had to leave them at the entrance to the pier and not the end of it. She would have had to struggle to carry the pictures all that way and dare not let anyone accompany her.

Alice said, 'You might as well give up on me, Maude. I can't tell you what's troubling me and . . . there's really nothing anyone can do.'

She sounded more subdued and less sullen, Maude thought with a glimmer of hope. She wondered whether she dare ask a direct question about the man . . . or about a child. Suppose she didn't ask and Alice was pregnant and the man had refused to marry her. She might kill herself. She wouldn't be the first troubled young woman to do so.

'Are you with child, Alice?' She blurted the words out before she could change her mind.

Alice's expression turned to one of amazement. 'With child? Of course not.'

'That's a relief, then.' Maude gave her a weak smile. Alice's reply sounded totally genuine. 'I thought that might explain your mood.'

'A baby?' Alice sounded wistful. 'That would be so much easier to deal with. I'd quite like a baby! No, Maude, you're quite wrong. Barking up the wrong tree, as they say!'

Maude said, 'You've upset Aunt Biddy. She was so worried she went to the doctor. You made her think she was losing her mind. That was very unkind.'

'I know. I couldn't think what else to do or say. Don't ask me to explain because I can't. I just need time.'

'And whatever happened to Primmy? Do you know what made her so dopey? Aunt Biddy said she wouldn't wake up.'

'She was all right this morning. She must have swallowed something poisonous. Some poisons make you sleepy before you actually die. Anyway, it's no good asking me.' Abruptly, she slid back below the bedclothes.

Maude, baffled and rapidly losing patience, shook her head. 'Aunt Biddy's making a sausage and potato pie so if you're hungry, get up. No-one is going to wait on you. Now, I have things to do so you'll—' The telephone rang. 'I must go. Try and pull yourself together!'

She ran downstairs and snatched up the telephone. As soon as she spoke, however, the line went dead. Maude redialled the operator. 'Operator, the line went dead.'

'I'm sorry, ma'am. The caller hung up.'

'Thank you.' She frowned. 'Was it a man or a woman?'

'A man.'

Baffled, Maude made her way into the kitchen where Aunt Biddy was humming cheerfully under her breath as she arranged a fancy edging around the edge of the pastry lid.

Biddy said, 'That was a short phone call.'

'This day started badly and it's getting worse!' was Maude's only reply.

SEVEN

It was nearly two o'clock and the gallery was empty except for the staff. Jane Dyer and Frederick Barlowe faced each other over the desk at reception. Looking up from her chair, flushed with anxiety, Jane stammered as she spoke.

'I really don't . . . I wish you wouldn't ask this, Mr Barlowe, because . . . because I don't want to do anything that might hurt poor Mr Brent.'

'For heaven's sake, girl, be reasonable. No-one is trying to hurt him. It's more a matter of protecting the gallery as well as preventing thieves from succeeding. If Mrs Brent goes ahead with this foolish plan of hers—'

'But she's trying to save her husband's life!' Jane stared at him, bewildered that he could not see the matter through her eyes. To her it was writ large. The kidnappers would kill Mr Brent if they did not get what they wanted and Jane knew it would break her heart to lose him from her life. Not that she owned even the smallest part of him, for he was well and truly married to Maude, but she loved him nonetheless and would never do anything to hurt him or the wife he adored. 'You're asking me to risk his life for the sake of a few pictures!' she cried. 'I think that's truly wicked!'

Colour drained from his face and his expression grew thunderous. Jane drew back defensively. She had seen her employer angry before but never as furious as he was now.

'I never took you for a fool, Miss Dyer!' he cried. 'We are not talking about a few pictures. We are talking about an artist's inheritance! His reputation. The best of Cope's paintings!'

Jane tried to interrupt him but he shouted over her.

'Hell and damnation! Surely after all this time in the art world, you understand that much.' He paused briefly to catch his breath and went on. 'The police think it unwise but Mrs Brent seems determined to flout their advice so they ask us for help. We are trying to prevent a major robbery. All I am asking you to do is tell a small white lie. Just tell her I have been called away suddenly and you cannot find the list of paintings. Is that really too much to ask?'

Jane swallowed. Her throat hurt with the effort of holding back tears of fright and misery. It was all she could do, earlier in the morning, to come into the gallery at all. Sick at heart, she had been unable to eat anything and her mother had tried to keep her at home, 'away from all the nastiness'. Now she wished she had allowed herself to be persuaded. It was becoming much nastier than she had expected.

'Think, Jane!' he urged, finally making an obvious effort to control his anger. 'When it's all over and Mr Brent is back safe and sound we can forget all about it – and he'll be immensely grateful that we haven't squandered a thousand pounds' worth of valuable paintings, which, in case you hadn't realized, have, over the last year or so, made this gallery famous. When he comes back he'll have you to thank.'

'If he does come back.' She regarded him fearfully. 'Suppose they kill him. Suppose we never see him again and never know what happened to him. How is Mrs Brent going to feel then, knowing that I helped to kill him? How shall *I* feel? Surely his wife knows better than we do, and if she wants to hand over the pictures—'

'She's not thinking straight, can't you see that? Maude Brent is half mad with worry. How can she know what's best?' He waved his hands in a gesture of helplessness. 'She can't step back and see the whole picture – no pun intended.'

He smiled faintly and Jane longed to slap his face. Lionel's life was on the line and Frederick Barlowe thought it funny! He was making stupid jokes. She regarded him with sudden loathing, wondering how she had ever thought him a decent man with principles.

Just at that moment the phone rang, cutting through the tense atmosphere.

They froze.

'Answer it, Jane!'

'I can't!' She sprang from her chair and retreated a few feet from the telephone. 'No!'

R-r-ring! R-r-ring!

'Jane! Do as you're told!'

She shook her head.

Barlowe grabbed her arm, pulled her closer, snatched up the receiver and thrust it into her hand. He forced her fingers to close around it then forced it to her ear. His face was very close to hers and she was terrified. The operator said, 'I have a call for you,' and there was a click as the connection was made.

A woman said, 'This is Mrs Maitland. I'm wondering if my picture is ready for collection. You told me to telephone either today or tomorrow. It's *The Old Mill* by Andrew Lotts . . . Hello? Is anyone there? Hello . . .?'

The receiver dropped from Jane's hand and she followed it on to the floor in a dead faint.

After lunch Aunt Biddy stood at the top of the cellar stairs and watched Maude's careful descent into the gloom, where about thirty pictures lay propped against purpose-built wooden racks. Each painting had been carefully wrapped in brown paper and lengths of sacking, and tied with string. Each one carried a large white label, which in turn bore a number and details of the painting – the date it was painted and the subject matter. Arnold Cope had become fashionable in his mid-thirties and had been fortunate to find an experienced agent who taught him what he knew about storing works of art and controlling the rate of sales so that his income rose steadily and the supply of paintings for sale remained steady throughout his life.

In her pocket Maude carried a list that she had found after a prolonged search earlier – a list of the works that had remained when her father died, but which she knew was out of date. The price allotted to each picture was also unreliable but at least she would know which were the most valuable and could select those. Fewer valuable works would be easier to handle than a large number of the lower-priced items.

She paused to study the list, frowning in the dim light. Possibly half a dozen had been sold recently but they had not necessarily been the best and therefore not the most valuable. Maude thought carefully. There was really no need for her to make a varied selection of subject matter – all she wanted were paintings that would total one thousand pounds when sold. There were possibly a few paintings in reserve at the gallery itself, kept with those by other artists in the room over the gallery.

Maude was also at a disadvantage because, after her marriage to Lionel, she had spent very little time in the gallery, relying on Frederick Barlowe and Lionel to deal with the business side of the enterprise. Lionel was determined she should have no worries and she had easily been persuaded to hand over most of the day-to-day management to him.

Before Barlowe rang her back, Maude wanted to acquaint herself with the available paintings so that she would waste no time in making her selection when the time came.

'Go steady down there, Maudie love!'

'I am. My eyes are getting used to it.' The overhead light bulb had failed and, unable to find a replacement, Maude was making the best of a powerful torch, stepping carefully over the uneven bricked floor and ducking her head to miss the worst of the cobwebs. As a child she had often sneaked down to the cellar to frighten herself with thoughts of ghosts and witches, enjoying the frisson of fear as she allowed her imagination to run riot. The rows of blind packages had assumed subhuman forms, lying in wait for the unwary to turn their backs . . . Spiders, too, had given her the shudders until eventually she had taken fright and scrambled frantically back up the creaking steps to the safety of the light.

Today, however, she had no time to reminisce and no desire to relive her childhood traumas. She had plenty of her own terrors to deal with and she forced herself to take a few deep breaths before she made her rounds. She checked each numbered package against her outdated list, trying to recall each painting but failing most of the time. With a pencil stub she marked the pictures that still remained. Later, Barlowe would advise her on the best ones to choose.

Time passed. Something scratched in a corner of the wall and she resisted the urge to run back up the steps. A mouse, perhaps. Definitely not a rat. Please God!

'I should have brought Primmy down here,' she muttered, although she knew that the excitable dog would be more trouble than she was worth.

As though reading her thoughts, Primmy suddenly appeared at the top of the steps and began to bark.

'All right, Primmy! I've just about finished.'

Aunt Biddy called down. 'I'm going to shut her outside in the garden.'

At last, reasonably satisfied with her findings, Maude went back up the steps and closed the door behind her. A fresh tray of jam tarts waited on the kitchen table but Maude had eaten too much pie at lunch and for the moment was satisfied with a cup of strong sweet tea.

Good for my nerves, she told herself, only too aware of the task that would face her at two ten a.m. when she delivered the pictures.

Facing her aunt across the table, she tried to smile. 'This time tomorrow it will all be over!' she said firmly.

Biddy said, 'God willing!' and held up her hands. She had crossed the fingers of both.

Maude said slowly, 'About Alice. I have a nasty feeling that she might be . . .'

'With child?' Aunt Biddy nodded. 'I was trying not to think it, but now that you've said that . . . Well, it would explain her funny mood and what happened last night. But how on earth did she manage to carry on that sort of . . . behaviour without us noticing? When did she see this man? How did they meet? And, worst of all, who is he? Because if he was a decent type, she wouldn't need to hide the friendship. We wouldn't object.'

'Unless she thought we'd disapprove.'

'Or unless . . .' Biddy screwed up her face in distaste.

'Oh no! Don't even think it!'

They were both silent, each trying to find a reason why Alice should have been spared the ultimate disgrace of rape.

Maude rubbed her eyes wearily. 'If someone . . . If some wretch has assaulted her . . . we would have known, surely! She trusts us, doesn't she?'

'We could ask her, but would she admit it?' Biddy regarded her niece helplessly. 'As if we don't have enough troubles with poor Lionel . . .'

Maude drew a long breath. She had lost her faith in Detective Constable Fleet and had spurned his advice, but now she felt the need to seek his help again. They couldn't ignore Alice's problem simply because they had other things to worry about. But had she been assaulted? If so she might refuse to speak of it to the police for fear of the embarrassment of discussing the details with a man.

She said, 'It's always seen as such a shameful thing . . . Most young women would feel their lives had been ruined. Oh no! I can't believe it . . . But maybe we should ask her outright. She'd need to see a doctor and we'd need to notify the police.'

Biddy helped herself to another jam tart. She had already eaten two. Now she pushed the plate towards Maude and, to please her, Maude took one.

'Look, Maude, you have enough to think about. Let me deal with Alice. I'll take her up some tarts and a cup of tea and try to talk to her. You concentrate on Lionel.'

By way of thanks Maude hugged her. 'I shall have to telephone the gallery,' she said. 'I thought Barlowe would have rung by now.

Ben Hemmings stood on the doorstep of the Romilees Hotel. He almost bounced on the soles of his feet and his blue eyes shone with anticipation.

Derek eyed him suspiciously. 'If you're here to speak with Mrs Brent, you're out of luck,' he told him. 'She's gone back to her place in Folkestone for a few hours.'

The reporter appeared undismayed by this news. 'Mrs Brent is only one of the people I want to talk to,' he explained.

'I've been commissioned, as in *commissioned* – by a national magazine, no less – to do an in-depth article about kidnapping with this current case in particular. But I have to get it in as soon as possible in case the mystery is suddenly solved. You see my problem? If I get it in to them quickly I can leave the article with unanswered questions and then, with luck, I get to write a second, shorter, more specific piece which crosses the "t's" and dots the "i's"!' He tapped his nose. 'I get paid twice!'

Remembering that his sister had nominated her brother to deal with Hemmings, Derek opened the door for him and led him into their own private sitting room. 'My sister is also out of the building,' he said as Hemmings settled himself comfortably on the sofa and produced his notebook and pencil.

'Aha! Is Mrs Cobb on a mission connected with the case?'

'Hardly. We've had an unexpected booking for seven for supper tonight so she's rushed out for a few more ingredients. Our dining room is fairly small, as you've seen, and seven extra means a bit of jiggling of the furniture and padding out of the menu. Ali wants to offer a third dessert and—'

'Nice-looking woman, Mrs Brent. I sometimes think I married too young!' Hemmings laughed.

'Mrs Brent? I've never really looked at her.' He frowned. 'I suppose she is, although she's not at her best with all this trouble.'

Hemmings scratched his head with the blunt end of his pencil. 'Give me a quote. Anything. Maybe she said she was "desperate"?'

'Not that I recall.'

'I bet she did. I bet she is desperate even if she didn't say it aloud.' He wrote busily. 'She might have said she couldn't go on without him. Or she would die if anything happened to him.'

'She didn't.' He thought back. 'She's been crying some of the time.' Now he wished he had taken more notice of her, maybe said something sympathetic or offered to help in some way. What a heartless beast he'd been. He felt a sharp pang of remorse.

'Sobbing . . . her . . . heart . . . out.' Hemmings spoke the words as he jotted in shorthand. 'Beautiful . . . even when, er . . . when grief-stricken.' He narrowed his eyes. 'Her . . . young . . . life . . . shattered.' Looking up, he grinned with satisfaction. 'It's coming together in my head! What colour are her eyes? You must have noticed that. I always notice the colour of a woman's eyes.'

'I'm afraid I don't know.' Had he ever even looked at them? He was beginning to wonder what sort of man he was.

Hemmings wrote aloud. 'Tossing her luxuriant hair . . .'

'Sounds more like a novel than a newspaper article!'

'. . . her eyelashes wet with tears.' He glanced up happily. 'Yes. I might interview her again. Women often warm to me. Don't know why.'

Neither do I, thought Derek. He said, 'Anyway, she's married, remember?' For some reason, he was starting to feel defensive on her behalf. 'You must have noticed,' he added with a touch of sarcasm. 'Her *husband's* been kidnapped. Isn't that a bit of a clue?'

Hemmings said, 'Too late then. Story of my life. But to get down to business: if I'm interviewing you, you might as well sit down.'

'Didn't know you were . . .' But he sat down, intrigued in spite of himself.

'I smell a rat,' the reporter announced. 'There's something about this story that smells fishy – and it's not only the body that was washed up on the beach.' He tapped his nose. 'The police are keeping schtum, as in silent, if you know what I mean. Not letting on. Either that or they don't have a clue what's going on and don't want to admit it. Won't answer some of the questions I've asked them. Won't admit that the body is connected to the kidnap, but it stands to reason, doesn't it? What d'you think, Mr Jayson? You're right here in the thick of it. Must have an opinion.'

Derek hesitated. Did he want his opinion splashed all over the newspapers? If he was wrong he'd look foolish. Did his sister want him to air his opinion? Was she going to air hers? To delay his answer he said, 'Don't forget Ali's offer. Bed, breakfast and evening meal for two.'

'Except in July and August. Yes, thanks. My wife was thrilled. Her mother will look after the little 'uns.' He glanced up, pencil poised.

'I dare say it is a bit strange,' Derek began. 'I've always thought it was a bit of a coincidence, he goes missing the very day they arrive here. No, the second day they're here. They must have been watching the family or they wouldn't have known they were going to be here and not at their home in Folkestone.' He frowned. He had not given it too much thought before.

'Precisely my point!' Hemmings' excited pencil flew across the page. 'So who knew they would be here? I take it you knew!'

'Naturally. It's my job to know.' Derek felt slighted somehow. 'We couldn't run a hotel without having some idea when guests are due.'

'Right . . .' Hemmings glared at his pencil. 'Got a pencil sharpener?'

'Not handy, no.'

'Never mind . . . it'll do. Now, his partner in the gallery. Name of Barlowe. That's where I'd be looking. He knows them. He knew Mrs Brent when she was Maude Cope . . . before she *was* Mrs Brent.' He leaned forward earnestly. 'My article is going to be divided into three areas. One – general facts about kidnappings; two – the facts so far about this case, and the people involved or possibly involved; three – the different theories about this case.' He glanced up, smiling broadly, obviously delighted by the opportunity. 'That's what I mean by "in depth", Mr Jayson.'

He looked pleased with himself, thought Derek, and wished for the first time that he hadn't taken his sister up on her offer of a share in the hotel. It had seemed an easy option and she had needed someone but, in fact, it was not much of a challenge and he was beginning to envy Ben Hemmings his interesting lifestyle. Derek had been a professional piano player and had frequently accompanied well-known singers when they took to the concert platform in major cities around the country. It had paid well and he had enjoyed it. It had paid for his tiny bachelor flat in north

London and although now he was very comfortable at the Romilees, he often missed his independence.

'But Mr Brent would recognize Barlowe if he turned kidnapper,' Derek protested. 'They must know each other well.'

'He might keep his head covered. A mask or something.'

'He'd recognize his voice!'

Hemmings hesitated. 'He might simply mastermind it from a discreet distance. Use an intermediary. You should go up there, to London, to look round the gallery. Nice receptionist.' He winked.

'You mean Miss Dyer.'

'Yes. Very pretty girl, Jane Dyer. Now there's another twist, you see. Might be something going on there between Brent and the girl!' He tapped his nose again. 'So what do you think of that idea? This is your interview, remember. I need quotes from you.'

Derek shrugged. 'Look, Mr Hemmings, I don't have any answers,' he admitted, 'or even any theories, but you can quote me on Mrs Brent. She's quite a heroine, if you ask me, the way she's bearing up. Someone is putting her through absolute hell and she doesn't deserve it. My sister and I are full of admiration for her . . . and the sooner they arrest the swine who kidnapped her husband, the better.'

Beaming, Hemmings put his shorthand to further good use and by the time he had finished Alison had returned.

'It's disturbing the day-to-day routine of Romilees,' she told the reporter when asked for a quote. 'When one of the guests is kidnapped everything else pales into insignificance.' She smiled as she waited for his shorthand to catch up. 'But we are not at all concerned on that count. The Brents are our guests and, as first-class hoteliers, we believe it is our duty to help them as much as possible.' Before Hemmings raised his head she gave Derek a quick glance. 'Mrs Brent has gone back to Folkestone for a few hours and my brother volunteered immediately to go and bring her back when she's ready. You see, nothing is too much trouble.'

Derek took his cue promptly. 'Er . . . yes! Of course I did.

The least I could do.' He felt rather ashamed that he had not thought of making the offer himself but was suddenly rather looking forward to it. 'Yes,' he elaborated, glancing at the clock. 'I'll telephone her in a moment and see when she's ready. No trouble at all.'

The reporter looked up at them. 'Be terrible if he's dead!'

Alison drew herself up. 'We don't even *think* such a thing here, Mr Hemmings. All our guests do their utmost to keep Mrs Brent's hopes alive. We pray for her – and for his safe return. If people choose to holiday with us at the Romilees Hotel, they can rely on a hundred per cent of our attention. No challenge is too great – is it, Derek?'

Another of those looks of hers, he noticed. Maybe he wasn't contributing enough to this article, although he had been grilled by the reporter before his sister returned. 'Certainly not!' he replied. 'While you are under our roof, we are your family!' Hmm. Maybe that was a step too far, but Hemmings was writing it down. Derek said quickly, 'I'd better make that call to Mrs Brent.'

Alison said, 'She'll be relying on you, Derek.'

Out in the hall, he breathed out slowly and made his way to the telephone. He was beginning to feel like a knight on a white horse.

Maude, dusty and dishevelled from her work in the cellar, waited impatiently for the telephone to be answered. She had waited long enough for Barlowe's call and was now ringing him. To her surprise it rang and rang and no-one answered. The operator came on the line and said, 'It's not engaged but no-one is answering. Maybe no-one is there.'

'There most certainly *is* someone there, Operator. It's an art gallery and it's open at this time and is never unattended. Do you think there is a fault on the line? Please try again.'

While she waited Maude had a sudden image of Frederick Barlowe lying on the floor injured or dying and Miss Dyer rushing out in search of help.

'Nonsense!' she muttered. 'Don't be ridiculous, Maude!'

But the idea persisted. After all, Jem had been murdered and no-one was certain that Lionel was still alive.

At last a voice said, 'Yes. Who is it?'

Maude frowned. If that was Miss Dyer she didn't sound very confident or welcoming. She was supposed to say, 'Good morning. The Barlowe Gallery. How may I help you?' She always said that.

Maude said, 'Miss Dyer? Is that you?' A long pause followed. 'This is Mrs Brent. Who am I speaking to?'

'It's me.'

'Miss Dyer? It doesn't sound like you. Is something wrong?' The image of Frederick Barlowe rushed back into her mind. 'Has something happened? Are you all right?'

'Yes. I suppose so. It's just that . . .'

'Maybe I should speak with Mr Barlowe.' What was wrong with everybody today, she wondered, trying to curb her impatience.

'It's just that . . . Well, Mr Barlowe can't come to the phone.'

'Why not? I spoke to him earlier. He was there. He must be around somewhere and is expecting a call. In fact *I* was expecting one from *him*. Have you looked upstairs in the stock room?'

'Yes . . . That is, he . . .'

Maude had the feeling that she was not being told everything. 'Is he ill or something? Has something happened to him?' Her irritation was giving way to alarm.

'No. No. Not exactly, but he . . . he had to go out somewhere . . . in a bit of a hurry.'

'Oh dear. That sounds very worrying. I was expecting an important call from him. When will he be back?'

'I don't really know. Mrs Brent, I'm truly sorry but—'

'He was making a list for me. My father's pictures and their value. Maybe you could read it out to me.'

After a silence Miss Dyer said, 'A list. No, no! There's no list, Mrs Brent. Oh, I'm so sorry. I can't . . .' Her voice had risen and now it shook and Maude heard what sounded like a muffled sob.

Maude's anxiety increased. Suppose they were both in

some kind of danger. There might be a third person in the gallery making sure they did not help her with the information she needed about the paintings. Suppose one or both of them disappeared . . .

'Is this a police matter, Miss Dyer?' she asked rashly.

'A police matter? No. It's just that I cannot . . . Mrs Brent . . . Oh! If anything happens to Mr Brent . . .'

The line went dead.

Maude stared at the silent receiver and slowly hung up. There seemed to be a giant conspiracy that included everyone else but left her in the dark. Perhaps the strain was getting to Jane Dyer, she thought.

'And maybe I will be next!' she muttered. Aunt Biddy wasn't the only person who wondered if she was losing her mind. But Miss Dyer had said it was not a police matter, so could she accept that as the truth? She told herself that her imagination was getting the better of her and decided to put that particular conversation at the back of her mind.

She was about to return to the kitchen when the telephone rang. This time it was Derek Jayson offering to come and collect her whenever she was ready to return to Hastings.

Maude smiled at him across the dividing miles. Here was someone who wanted to help and was not putting obstacles in her way. 'That's so kind, Mr Jayson. So very thoughtful of you. Yes, I accept your offer. I'll be ready to be collected by the time you arrive.'

He insisted that it was no problem and agreed to set off immediately.

When Derek Jayson arrived, Maude showed him the paintings propped outside the front door and explained that they had to be transported to Hastings to be given to the kidnappers instead of the money. With some difficulty they managed to pack them into the rear of the car and were then ready to set off.

Before she left, Maude made a last appeal to Alice to come out of her bedroom and tell them what was troubling her. She spoke through the locked door, heard nothing in reply, and gave up, feeling extremely angry.

Biddy shrugged. 'She won't speak to anyone,' she told Maude. 'She won't even open the door. I've been traipsing up and down these stairs with cups of tea and jam tarts but to no avail. To tell you the truth I'm getting really angry. After all we've done for her since she came, taking her into our home and treating her like one of our own!'

Maude agreed reluctantly. 'I'll have to talk to her again when all this is over – which should be shortly. Maybe when Lionel comes home she'll decide to come out for him. She's always respected him.'

Biddy snorted in disapproval. 'I never saw Alice as wayward. We're seeing a new side to her.' She sighed heavily. 'Whatever you say, Maude, I still think it's most ungrateful. As far as I'm concerned I've done all I'm going to do. She can come out of her room when she's good and ready. I wash my hands of her.'

Maude closed her eyes to her aunt's cross face and turned back to Derek Jayson, trying to compose her thoughts. Hopefully the walk had done her good and poor little Primmy had enjoyed it. Now, Maude told herself, she needed to put everything else out of her mind and concentrate on the ordeal ahead. She was not looking forward to her adventure in the early hours of the morning but she would not allow anyone to know how terrified she was. She felt herself to be on the verge of collapse but told herself repeatedly, albeit with growing hysteria, that she needed to stay strong only until Lionel was back. Then he would once more take control. She could then relax, she promised herself, and they could gradually pick up the pieces of their broken lives.

She hugged Biddy, then smiled gratefully at Derek Jayson. 'Let's go,' she said simply.

Meanwhile, in the basement of the local hospital, Detective Constable Fleet had been standing in the morgue for less than twenty minutes but he felt it was already too long. He had had to force himself through the door into the cool atmosphere and had tried not to breathe in the unpleasant smell – cold flesh, stale blood and strong disinfectants.

There was also a distinct lack of fresh air. No doubt the pathologist was used to the combination but the detective found it unpleasantly cloying.

He averted his eyes from a large tray in which various instruments had been laid out but was immediately confronted by a row of larger instruments hanging along the wall on hooks – knives, a hammer, three saws of varying sizes, and something that looked like a suction pump. There were several white-painted cupboards and a basket containing discarded bloodstained aprons waiting, presumably, to be sent to the laundry. How, he wondered, could anyone spend their entire working hours in such a depressing place?

He began to feel slightly sick as Samuel Wetton, the pathologist, continued to describe and assess his findings about Jem Rider's body.

'Definitely dead before he went into the sea,' he announced. He had a pompous manner and DC Fleet had never taken to him although he respected his work. Samuel Wetton was a professional who took pride in his work and demanded respect. 'No salt water in the lungs. He'd already stopped breathing.' He glanced up. 'If you would step a little closer, DC Fleet, I can show you what killed this young man.'

Reluctantly, the detective stepped closer and forced himself to watch as the pathologist turned the body on to its side so that he could show the back of the head.

'One blow might have been an accident,' he said. 'But two indentations, just slightly overlapping – much more likely to have been deliberately inflicted.'

The skull was certainly crushed, thought the detective. 'So it was murder. Not an accident.'

'I would say it was deliberate. Yes.'

'And you would stand up in court and say so?'

'I would – without hesitation. Someone wanted to kill this young man. Might have used a piece of driftwood – assuming it happened on the beach – or possibly a heavy stone. A large pebble, maybe. There are no wood fibres, however, so I would think a heavy pebble. A small rock, I suppose . . . And he wasn't in the water long. A few hours at most. Do you see, DC Fleet, the skin is hardly affected.'

DC Fleet nodded and quickly stepped back and turned away from the table, pretending to find more light by the window by which to write up his notes. He tried not to think about how sick he felt, and wrote: 'Large pebble or small rock, two overlap indents'. His insides churned and he longed to get away from the smell and unpleasant sights.

Wetton went on relentlessly. 'If you look closely at the fingernails, DC Fleet, you'll notice there is nothing under them, so I doubt he put up a struggle. Most likely didn't expect the attack.'

'So maybe knew the attacker?' He wrote 'fingernails – nothing'.

The pathologist shrugged. 'Quite possible. Just unfortunate the rock found the weakest spot. The victim might already have been on the ground, face down. Still, he wouldn't have felt anything for more than a few—'

A commotion outside in the corridor interrupted Wetton.

A voice cried, 'You can't go in there, Mrs Rider! It's not allowed. Not yet!'

'But he's my son. I'm entitled to see my son and you can't stop me!'

Wetton said wearily, 'Oh dear! Another hysterical woman. The government ought to ban them!'

The door burst open and as it did so the pathologist snatched up a rubber sheet and hastily draped the young man's body.

Mrs Rider came in, her face contorted with a mixture of grief and anger. A young attendant followed her in, red-faced and full of apologies for the intrusion. The woman's face was blotched, her hair dishevelled. Seeing someone she recognized she stabbed a finger into DC Fleet's chest.

'I want to see my son. My murdered son – and I can tell you lot who did for him. That Mr Brent. He's the murderer! When you find him, arrest him!'

'Mrs Rider, you must come with me,' DC Fleet told her, taking hold of her arm. 'Please. We can't talk here. This is most irregular.' He had recognized the intrusion as his opportunity to get out of the room with dignity.

'Is that Jem?' Transfixed, she stared at the covered body on the table.

'No.' Both men spoke as one.

Wetton said, 'If you must know, it's an elderly lady. Now please go with the detective. You have no right to burst in here.'

Wide-eyed, she looked round. 'Does he . . . How does he look? Jem.'

Wetton said, 'Very much as normal, Mrs Rider. Now, please . . .'

DC Fleet guided her firmly from the room and into the corridor. 'We'll find you a cup of tea,' he promised rashly. 'And you can talk to me.'

She allowed herself to be led along the corridor and up some stairs to a small canteen. Finally overawed by her surroundings, she waited silently for the tea.

'I've brought you a currant bun,' he told her. 'Not much choice, I'm afraid.'

'I can't eat. It sticks in me gullet. So when will I see him?'

'Probably tomorrow. I'll see what I can do to hurry them up.'

She sipped the scalding tea carefully. 'My Jem had a friend – Robbie his name is. Robbie Johnson. He came round this morning wanting his comics and magazines back. They used to swap. "Take the horrible things," I told him. "Can't think why you have to look at stuff like that." All monsters and ghosts and everyone killing everyone else!'

'Boys will be boys!' He smiled. 'It's in their nature. Well, some of them.'

She shrugged. 'Robbie says he reckoned this Mr Brent done it. Killed our Jem. Maybe because they had words over something and Jem told Robbie about it – although he can't recall properly what it was because he wasn't that interested – and this Brent wouldn't give him what he said he would – money-wise, I mean.' She looked at him anxiously. 'So Jem said he'd split on him, and then he stormed off – Brent I mean – but course Jem wasn't really going to the police. My Jem was brought up to stay as far away from the police as possible . . . So Robbie reckons it was Brent that killed him.' Her lips trembled. 'So when can I see him? I just have to see him one more time before his funeral. To say goodbye. You can't say I'm not entitled.' Tears trickled down her cheeks.

Briefly, DC Fleet laid a comforting hand on her arm. The idea that Brent himself might be more involved had occurred to him once or twice in odd moments but until now he had never seriously considered him as anything other than a victim and Mrs Rider's story was fairly thin . . . Plus it was all hearsay and she would be regarded as an unsatisfactory witness if she ever ended up on the stand. Still, he would bear it in mind. Might even talk to this Robbie.

He frowned, wondering why he had never seriously fingered Brent for the murder. Abruptly, his face cleared. Of course. Brent had been kidnapped before Jem disappeared.

He looked at Mrs Rider. Somehow her frazzled appearance and the tears for her dead son touched him unexpectedly. Poor woman. Would she ever recover from this loss? Impulsively, he pulled a clean, folded handkerchief from the breast pocket of his jacket and handed it to her. Without unfolding it, she dabbed carefully at her face, then put it into her pocket undisturbed. She stood up unsteadily and straightened her clothes. 'I'll be off then, Mr Fleet,' she said, with a belated attempt at dignity.

'I promise to be in touch, Mrs Rider.'

EIGHT

Detective Constable Fleet heard about Maude's outburst in the bank and went round immediately to speak with the bank manager.

'You can't blame me!' cried Franks, the moment they entered his office. 'I was only following your orders. "Hedge", you said. "We have to play for time." Those were your exact words! "She stands to lose a huge amount of money." That's what you advised and that's what I did. She flew into a rage and was nearly hysterical.' He closed the door carefully so they should not be overheard. 'You, Detective Constable Fleet, are certainly out of favour with Mrs Brent – but so are we, and that dreadful Hemmings fellow has been in, as pleased as punch, hoping to have another titbit for his wretched article!'

Franks had decided not to allow the policeman to sit down. That would punish him for the grief he had caused the bank. Head Office had been most censorious when they had received an account of Mrs Brent's behaviour. They had refused to listen to Mr Franks' explanation that he was merely complying with the wishes of the police in an attempt to prevent a crime. He sat down in his chair and shuffled a few papers, refusing to make eye contact.

'I'm sorry, naturally, Mr Franks, that she saw fit to make a scene. Very unpleasant for you and your staff.'

DC Fleet glanced towards a chair but the manager ignored his unspoken request. *Let the blighter stand up*, he thought venomously.

'Unpleasant?' he echoed. 'It certainly was. A shocking outburst. I would describe it as humiliating. Our clients were astonished and no doubt offended by the accusation she made – telling them we refused to support her in an emergency! Can you imagine that? Worse, it will now be repeated all over the town and our reputation will suffer.

Even if they didn't take her seriously it made us all look utter fools!' He blinked rapidly. 'And who is going to be blamed? Me, of course!'

The policeman began to improve on his earlier apology but Franks took his watch from his waistcoat pocket and glared at it. 'I'm a very busy man, DC Fleet,' he said curtly. 'I've plenty to do with my time and I've told you what happened.' He remembered suddenly that he had more to say. 'I do, however, have a suggestion to make. I have talked at length with Head Office since the unpleasantness and they think there may be a way out of the dilemma. They suggested we might release half the money as a show of goodwill. Another meeting could then be arranged which would be an exchange – the rest of the money for the handover of the hostage – when hopefully an arrest could be made.'

Still smarting from the disrespect the manager had shown him, DC Fleet tried to hide his satisfaction. The bank, fearful for its good reputation, was trying to redeem itself. But was it a serious possibility? At this stage he felt willing to clutch at any straw and cursed inwardly for not thinking of it himself. Of course, it would all depend on the kidnappers' patience, but he certainly must raise the suggestion with his superiors and also with Mrs Brent.

'Well,' he said, trying not to sound too excited. 'I'll pass on the suggestion. Please thank your Head Office.'

Franks nodded without much enthusiasm. He had the air of a disillusioned man, thought the detective, but it was understandable in the circumstances.

Without more ado, Franks rang his bell and asked his secretary to show the detective out and, after a moment's hesitation, DC Fleet nodded and followed the young man out of the manager's office.

Turning to the detective he asked excitedly, 'Are you going to get the kidnappers, sir?'

DC Fleet nodded. 'Of course we are! It's our job!' he said but as he returned to the sunlit pavement, he wished he felt as confident as he sounded. The truth was that he felt out of his depth, never having dealt with such a complex case, and terrified that he might put a foot wrong and compromise the investigation. A good result might mean promotion but a failure to apprehend the kidnappers would quite definitely minimize his chances.

Some time later, when Biddy opened the door to DC Fleet, she looked at him with mixed emotions. She accepted that he was doing his job according to police policy and that they had their strategies, but wondered if they were handling Lionel's kidnapping in the best way possible. Obviously Maude did not think so and Biddy, influenced by her niece, also had her doubts.

She said, 'Oh! Not more trouble! If you want Mrs Brent, you've missed her. She's taken some paintings to Hastings for tonight's rendezvous. Mr Jayson from the Romilees took her in his motor car. She was so grateful.' Should she invite him in, she wondered, in Maude's absence? Was it appropriate? 'He's a really kind man, is Mr Jayson.'

'I'll speak to Mrs Brent when I get back to Hastings but now I'd like to speak with Alice Crewe.'

Biddy hesitated. She didn't fancy admitting that Alice was refusing to leave her room and had gone into the mother of all sulks.

'She's resting. She's not at all well.'

'In that case I'd like to talk to you about her. May I come in, please?'

Sensing that he was not likely to take no for an answer, she opened the door reluctantly and led him into the sitting room. Once ensconced in an armchair he said, 'I'd like to know a little more about Miss Crewe. How did you meet her?'

Biddy explained about the surprise interview that Lionel had arranged. She smiled. 'Maude was determined she wasn't going to agree because she has me and didn't need a companion, but when they met they got along like a house on fire. Once she'd moved in, it seemed she'd always belonged here. The three of us get along very well.' *Except for the past day or two*, she thought somewhat guiltily, but there was no need to mention that.

'So where did Mr Brent meet her?'

Biddy leaned back in her chair and stared at the ceiling. She frowned. 'Well, I can't say. Either I never knew or I've forgotten. Funny . . .'

'But Mrs Brent saw her references, I take it.'

'Oh yes! At least, I suppose so.' Her memory was playing tricks again, she thought nervously. At the time it hadn't seemed important for Biddy to know everything that happened before Alice had been with the old lady. 'I'm sure Lionel would have checked references.'

'I wonder . . . Perhaps I could see one or two.' He looked at her hopefully. 'Just to satisfy my curiosity.'

'We–ell, you can if I can find them. It means looking through Lionel's desk and I don't really care to do that.'

He said firmly, 'I'm afraid it's necessary.'

'But why?'

'We can't ignore any possible leads, Miss Cope. You see, someone from Miss Crewe's past might have traced her here and decided there was money to be made from kidnapping her current employer.' Seeing her expression change, he went on hurriedly. 'I'm not suggesting Miss Crewe is involved in any way. I'm sure she isn't, but if we could contact some of her earlier employers . . . She may have had a young man, a male admirer, perhaps, who was taking advantage of the situation.'

'Oh dear! She wouldn't like that!' Biddy hesitated. 'I'll look in Lionel's desk, then. It's in a good cause, isn't it?'

'Certainly. It might lead to his release.'

She returned five minutes later looking uneasy. 'I can't find anything, but maybe he returned the references to her after he'd read them.' She sat down. 'I'm sure we must know all about her.'

'She has a family, I take it?'

'Er . . . yes, she must have family.' Had she ever mentioned them?

'Does she get many letters?'

Biddy's anxiety increased with a jolt. 'Not really. No.'

'But she goes away sometimes to visit them?'

'No, but . . .'

'Is she an orphan? Does she have a young man?'

Before the kidnap, Biddy would have flown to Alice's defence, but the last few days had thrown up doubts on another aspect of her life and now, the more she thought about it, the more she became uncomfortably aware that they knew very little about Alice Crewe's background.

She came to a sudden decision. 'You must ask her these things yourself. I'll go and wake her up. Or perhaps you'd come up with me. She seems unwilling to come downstairs today and won't tell me why – but she would have to talk to you if you tell her you're the police.'

Ignoring his confusion, she led him upstairs and Biddy knocked on the door. 'Alice, DC Fleet is here and wants a word or two with you. DC Fleet from the police in Hastings. I think you'd better come out now and talk to him . . . Please, Alice.' She waited but they heard nothing.

DC Fleet narrowed his eyes. 'Alice Crewe, this is Detective Constable Fleet. I need to talk to you. There is no point in refusing to come out. If you do you might be charged with refusing to cooperate with the police and that is a felony.'

Silence. Biddy waited, unaware that she was holding her breath. Surely Alice was not going to defy the police. 'Alice love, you're not in any trouble,' she said loudly. 'The policeman wants you to help him, that's all!'

DC Fleet said, 'I don't like the sound of this. It's *too* quiet. Is she the type who might take her own life?'

Biddy's mouth fell open. 'Take her own . . .? Good Lord! I should think not! At least, I hope not. *Take her own life?*' She banged on the door with her clenched fist. 'Alice. Come out this minute!'

Another silence.

'I may have to break into the room.' The policeman looked at her grimly.

'No! Wait!' cried Biddy. 'There's a ladder we bought when the painters did the windows!'

Five minutes later, after a short search, the ladder was found propped against the back of the garden shed, which made the detective shake his head.

'The number of people who do that! An open invitation to any passing burglar looking for an easy entry!'

'Don't blame me!' Biddy replied indignantly. 'I didn't leave it there.'

They carried it to the house and propped it against the wall below Alice's bedroom and Biddy leaned against the bottom of it to hold it securely in place. DC Fleet climbed up while Biddy prayed that Alice was still alive. Her heart was thumping and she felt weak with dread.

He stared in for a moment or two then turned. 'I don't see her and the window is slightly open at the bottom. I think Miss Crewe has gone!'

He pushed up the window and climbed in while Biddy returned to the house and hurried upstairs. He unlocked the bedroom door and together they surveyed the room. To Biddy's eyes it was neater than usual. The bed had been made and there were no odd clothes draped over chairs and no shoes tucked under the bed. There was an unnatural stillness about it, which further affected Biddy's heart.

The detective looked in the wardrobe and found it half empty. 'Ah! She couldn't carry everything!' he said. 'My guess is she put the ladder in place when no-one was looking, packed her things, threw out her bag, climbed out . . .'

'And then she must have returned the ladder to the shed!'

They regarded each other speechlessly.

Biddy said, 'Her clock's missing from the bedside table and her dressing gown gone from the back of the door. She *has* gone!' Still only half convinced, she searched for another reason for her disappearance. 'She can't be gone unless . . . She wouldn't just leave like this.' She turned to the policeman. 'D'you think they've kidnapped her, too?'

DC Fleet hesitated for a moment but then shook his head. 'Hardly. I can't imagine kidnappers allowing her to tidy the room and choose a few clothes and personal objects . . . nor can I imagine how they could force her to climb out of the window.'

Biddy noted his expression and realized that this was a blow to him personally. He was in charge of the case and now it appeared that he had misread the signs. Or rather he had been too willing to take matters at face value. He would be hauled over the coals, she thought, and that would do his career no good at all. She felt a moment's pity for him but then reminded herself that if he had been clev-erer, maybe . . . But no. She shook her head, unable to work it out. Thank heavens women were not allowed to become detectives, she thought. Solving crimes must be a nightmare.

He said slowly, 'I think she ran while she still could. I think she was involved. In other words, Miss Cope, Alice Crewe was a co-conspirator!' He sighed heavily – a sigh of failure, of helplessness.

'Alice . . . *involved*? That's nonsense.' Biddy, totally bewildered, refused even to consider the idea. All she could think of was poor Alice alone and desperate. 'But where has she gone? This is her home.'

'She's gone to him. To Lionel Brent.' Slowly he sat down on the edge of the bed and looked up at Biddy who had one hand to her heart, her face pale, her body trembling. 'I'm afraid, Miss Cope, that from Mrs Brent's viewpoint this is even worse than we imagined. Mrs Brent may never see her husband again. I'm beginning to think she's been the victim of a well-planned fraud.'

Biddy's legs chose this moment to give way and she half fell on to the bedside chair. DC Fleet put his hands to steady her and she sat up gingerly.

'This is quite beyond me . . . quite out of my league,' she whispered, as though talking to herself. 'Maude . . . I mean Alice, wouldn't . . . No! She's not that sort of girl. Why should she, after all we've meant to one another? There must be some other explanation.' Her eyes widened abruptly. 'Oh! What will Maude think if you're right about all this? She'll be devastated when she knows.' Clapping a hand over her mouth as if to prevent any more awful truths from escaping, she looked at DC Fleet but found no comfort there.

He said, 'So if what I think is true then there's no actual kidnap. If they are together they can fade into the landscape – but they won't have the money they wanted!' He frowned, trying to assess the changed situation. 'And Mrs Brent will never see her husband again – if he really *is* her husband.' His eyes narrowed. 'Maybe it was a bigamous marriage . . . set up to swindle your niece from a large amount of money!'

'A bigamous marriage? How dare you suggest such a thing!' Biddy sat up straight, fired up with indignation. 'Maude would never do such a thing . . . and I was there! I was at the wedding. It was lovely. A wedding with rose petals and–and the bells were rung and everything. You can ask the vicar. He was real and so was the church!' For a moment she frowned but then a smile lit up her face. 'I made the wedding cake! That proves it, doesn't it? Rich fruit but without the candied peel. Maude doesn't care for candied peel, bless her, so I substituted a few dates chopped very small.' She didn't like the expression on his face. 'It was a proper marriage!' she insisted.

'What do you know about Lionel Brent, Miss Cope? How did he and Mrs Brent meet? Where did he live before he married her?'

Biddy hesitated. 'I don't know where he lived but he did have some letters. What I mean is someone wrote to him, because letters came occasionally. I do remember that. But his parents had moved to somewhere miles away – it might have been Scotland. I forget why exactly, but they were too old to travel any great distance. He did say that.'

'But they came to the wedding, surely?'

'No. I've just explained that they were too old.'

'But somebody came? Friends, other relatives?'

'No–o, but they all had reasons why they . . . couldn't be with us.' Biddy swallowed hard.

They regarded each other soberly until the detective straightened his shoulders. 'We'd better go downstairs. There's nothing we can do here.'

Downstairs, in the sitting room, he tried to think it through. 'I should have seen through it! I should have suspected there was more to it! Nothing in police work is ever straightforward so there must have been clues . . . I should have recognized them. But . . .' He gave her a look of pure misery. 'But it's not too late! Maybe I can still catch him. And her . . .'

Biddy gasped with horror. He meant to arrest them both. Was he mad?

Ignoring her reaction, DC Fleet went on, talking aloud to himself. 'The question is, what will Brent do now if Alice Crewe has run out before the swindle has been completed? Is she in any danger? If Brent killed Jem Rider then he might kill again . . . God in Heaven!' He glanced at Biddy. 'I could do with a stiff drink!'

But Biddy's mind was spinning, unable to hold any thought for more than a second or two. She felt totally adrift, as if the real world had been replaced with something unfamiliar and darkly threatening. She wanted to cry but her eyes remained dry.

'Not Alice!' she muttered. 'I can't believe it . . . And Lionel? No, he's a good man. You must have got it wrong. Not Lionel. Certainly not.' She peered at him as though through a mist. 'A stiff drink? Is that all you can think about? Alice is in trouble and Lionel has been kidnapped – or maybe not – and all you can think about is a stiff drink!' She closed her eyes. 'I think I'm going to be sick!' Struggling to her feet she stumbled towards the door and along the passage towards the kitchen. Primmy barked, sensing excitement, and the two of them went out into the garden.

DC Fleet followed them out and when Biddy re-entered the kitchen he offered her a damp towel. While she sobbed and shivered with shock he filled the kettle and set it on the stove and while he waited for it to boil, he telephoned to the Romilees Hotel and asked for Maude Brent to telephone him as soon as she and Derek Jayson arrived with the paintings.

'Friday 16th June. Ten past eight and he's gone. DC Fleet. Wretched man. I was glad to see the back of him in the end. Telling me all those dreadful things about Alice and Lionel. How am I to make head or tail of it? Saying poor Maude is a bigamist – or was it Lionel? He got me so

confused my head is splitting so I've made myself some barley water, which is always soothing. Lord only knows what's going to happen next.

He was all for taking me to Hastings with him – DC Fleet I mean – so that I won't have to be here all alone, but I said, No! You're not getting me mixed up with all that nonsense. And my mother warned me against sleeping on hotel mattresses because you never know who slept there the night before and they might have had fleas or there might be bed bugs.'

Biddy was sitting up in bed, having decided that that is where she would feel safest. She had locked herself in, just in case anyone broke in to the house. If they did, they were welcome to take anything at all as long as they left her in peace. She sipped her barley water, imagining it slipping down to soothe her stomach, which was in a bit of a state. Not surprising with all the shocks she'd had earlier. Primmy was downstairs in the kitchen and she would bark if anyone broke in.

'I can't get over Lionel, or Alice, come to that. I keep thinking I shall wake up in the morning and everything will be back to normal. I shall pray very hard tonight and hope that DC Fleet has got it all wrong. Of course I don't want Lionel to still be kidnapped but it would be better than being a bigamist and him being married to Alice and it all being a dreadful trick . . .'

Her stomach rumbled and she said, 'Stop that silly noise!' A good thing no-one was around to hear it. She wondered about Primmy all alone in the kitchen. Maybe she should bring her up to the bedroom just this once because it was a strict rule that Lionel had made: no dogs in the bedrooms. She smiled, recalling how Maude had pleaded with him to let the dog sleep on the landing, but Lionel had been adamant. She frowned. They had all been so fond of him and poor Maude had adored him. How could he be a *different* Lionel? Could they really have been so wrong about him?

Suddenly Primmy started barking and that set Biddy's heart to fluttering – a nasty feeling that she had suffered on and off for some months now without telling anyone. Old age, she had assured herself. Nothing to fuss about.

'Now what are you barking at, Primmy?' she asked. Probably a hedgehog in the garden. They snorted and wheezed like miniature hogs. She climbed out of bed and listened at the door. No footsteps on the stairs. Cautiously she opened the door but heard nothing. Slowly, one step at a time, she went downstairs, along the passage and into the kitchen. Nothing out of the ordinary, she thought thankfully. No mysterious men in long coats and big hats. Primmy rushed to greet her, wagging her tail ecstatically.

'Come on then, silly old girl!' said Biddy, patting her. 'Just this once you can come up into my room but you have to be good and not fidget. I don't want to be awake half the night.

'I've brought Primmy upstairs. I think she was frightened by something. She rushed to me and almost jumped into my arms. Poor thing. I expect she wonders where everyone is with Lionel and Alice and Maude missing. She's only got me now. And I've only got her . . .'

The seafront was becoming chilly by ten to eleven but there were still a few late-night strollers – mostly people with dogs, Alice noted, although there was a rowdy group of young men on the beach, laughing a lot and swearing and trying to push each other into the water.

'Go on!' Alice muttered. 'Drown yourselves, why don't you! It would be a good riddance!'

Huddled in a shelter, staring out across the sea, she saw the pier outlined against the moonlight, which sent a glistening beam of sparkling silver across the placid surface of the water. She was waiting for the clock to strike the hour and then she would go to Lionel and confront him. She had strict instructions on how to carry out her part of the deception but running away from *Fairways* was not one of them. Turning up uninvited on Lionel's doorstep before the agreed time was also not one of them, but she was desperate.

She shivered in her thin skirt and jacket, trying to plan

what she would say to Lionel and to imagine what he might say in return.

'Mind you,' she whispered, 'you haven't kept to the plan either. You killed Jem Rider and that was never part of it.'

Her love for him had been changed by his actions and now she was desperately trying to recover the strength of her earlier feelings for him. But since their meeting in the garden that night, Alice knew he could kill and it had shaken her to the core. All the things she had originally loved most about him – his confidence, his ambition, his sense of humour – had been tainted by his admission. She struggled now to find excuses for the change in him because without him she felt empty and worthless. Somehow they must get through the next few weeks and hope that by some miracle they could survive the crimes they had committed.

The idea of the kidnap had originally frightened her but then Lionel had somehow convinced her that the world was a very unfair place. Her husband made her see the idea in a different light. He made it into a game they would play together, pitting their wits against society. He almost made it into a noble fight – the poor against the rich. No-one would be ruined and she and Lionel would be richer.

'We're not stealing from her,' he had argued. 'Because the paintings were her father's. She didn't paint them so why should she benefit from them? She's done nothing to earn the money.'

It had sounded entirely reasonable at the time. Lionel had explained that once they had the money they could go anywhere in the world and make a new life for themselves. 'It's only money, Alice!' he had insisted and she knew that was true. Rashly, she had put aside her doubts and entered into the spirit of the adventure. The best bit had been the interview because afterwards she had felt so proud of herself. She had acted so well and answered all their questions. They had been totally deceived. She had even wondered whether she had missed her vocation and might still earn a living on the stage.

Later, as she grew fond of Maude and Biddy, it was too late to undo the wrong. She was Lionel's wife and couldn't betray him. Nor could she disappear from the household without a convincing explanation and without infuriating Lionel.

Tears came into her eyes as she thought of Maude and Biddy and the hurt she had caused them. Poor old Biddy was confused and fearful, and Maude was terrified that she was going to lose the man she loved – and she was. She, Alice, had ruined their peaceful lives. Worse, she had abused their trust. Weighed down with guilt, Alice sighed deeply.

The clock struck eleven and on the last stroke she rose slowly to her feet. Now she was going to confront her husband and beg him to give up the whole scheme. She wanted them to forget all about the paintings and the money, and slip away in the night before it was too late. Deep inside, however, she felt intuitively that time was running out for them and that the police might be cleverer than they expected.

She felt in her pocket for the slip of paper on which he had written his address but it was not there. Never mind. She knew it by heart. He had told her it was an attic above a cobbler's shop in George Street at the eastern end of the town. He wouldn't be pleased to see her but she had made up her mind. They had to give up the whole thing and make their getaway.

She set off briskly, her head held high. Halfway along the seafront a middle-aged man suddenly lurched into her path. She smelled alcohol on his breath and his words were so slurred that at first she couldn't understand what he was saying. She tried to ignore him but he caught hold of her arm and wouldn't let go. Finally she translated something.

'Come with me, little lady!'

'No I won't! And let go of my arm!'

'Don't be like that!' he wheedled. 'Just for a few minutes. Just for a bit of . . . you know!'

'Not for one second!' she told him. She jerked herself free but in doing so, stumbled and almost fell and he once again had hold of her arm in a painful grip.

She opened her mouth to scream for the police but abruptly shut it again. She was now on the wrong side of the law, and possibly also a wanted person. Calling for the police might not be a very good idea.

Sobered by the hard reality of her changed status, she kicked him hard in the shin and then stamped on his foot. He let out a roar of pain and relaxed his grip on her arm. As she took her chance and ran off he shouted after her and this time Alice heard every word clearly.

'Bloody good riddance to you – you cheap little whore!'

No-one had ever spoken to her like that before and Alice felt her cheeks burn with embarrassment and shame. She had reached a new low, she reflected unhappily.

She didn't stop running until she found a shop in George Street that had shoes in the window. The cobbler's shop. Holding a hand to her side she stood panting outside a door that evidently led up to the accommodation above the shop where there was a light on in the window. Taking a deep, nervous breath, she rang the bell. She wasn't looking forward to the conversation with Lionel but she was longing to be with him again. Since the night in the garden she had had terrible doubts but surely somehow they could be reconciled. He would forgive her for her harsh words on that occasion if she forgave him for killing Jem.

'Please God!' she whispered.

After a long wait a woman opened the door about three inches. Suspiciously, she peered out at Alice.

'What is it? It's gone eleven. Waking decent folks in the middle of the night!'

'I'm sorry,' said Alice, taken aback. 'It's late I know but it's . . . it's an emergency. I have to speak to Mr Bre . . . that is . . .' Just in time! He would obviously be using a false name. 'I need to see your lodger. It's really urgent.'

'Well, since we don't have a lodger, that's not going to be easy. Who are you, coming round at this time? What sort of emergency?'

Alice was wondering whether she dare use Lionel's first name but decided that too would be risky. If the woman reported her visit to the police they might make the connection. 'He's a friend of a friend,' she offered. 'I–I forget his name but this er . . . this friend of mine needs to see him and I've got a message for him and . . .' She stopped. Even to her own ears she sounded slightly crazed.

'Friend of a friend?' The woman opened the door a little wider and examined Alice through narrowed eyes. 'Are you drunk?'

'No! I just . . . This is difficult,' she stammered. What could she say without giving her husband away? Her mind began to race with possible explanations for the confusion. None of them were good. Maybe Lionel *was* inside the building but was still angry with her and had told the landlady to deny his existence. Maybe this woman was involved somehow in the kidnap and she, Alice, had been used. Was she now going to be cast aside? She felt cold and her stomach churned with fright.

'Well, we don't have any lodgers so you've come to the wrong place.'

'No! This is the place. Over a cobbler's shop, he said.' She thrust her foot into the gap as the woman tried to close the door.

'And I say we don't have any lodgers so sling your hook, whoever you are.'

'Maybe I could speak to your husband? He might know where I might find my . . . my friend.'

'He doesn't know anything about any friends or any lodgers. There's just him and me and he's poorly and won't thank me for waking him up so stop arguing and leave us in peace.'

Before Alice could guess her intention, the woman kicked her foot from the step and slammed the door in her face.

Alice stood there, stunned, her heart racing, sick with disbelief. After a few moments a window above her opened and the woman poked her head out. 'You still there?' she demanded crossly. 'You've got one minute before I fetch a policeman!'

Alice mumbled an apology and began to retrace her steps. Passing a pie shop and a draper's she came to a fishmonger's. Then, as her legs still felt as weak as water, she stopped to rest. Slowly a terrible numbness filled her and she felt nothing but the ache in her heart. She slid down until she was sitting on the pavement with her back to the wall. She felt lower than the cat that slipped past her without interest, and as insignificant as the scraps of rubbish that littered the street around her. One truth filled her thoughts.

Lionel had lied to her about his lodgings, which meant he wanted to be rid of her. They had no future together.

Moments later she dragged herself to her feet and began to walk back towards the seafront. She walked slowly with her head down, trying to clear her mind and somehow make sense of the situation. He had deliberately given her the wrong address and had done so before they met in the garden . . . which meant he had been planning all along to finish with her. He meant to take the money and run.

'No! That can't be true,' she whispered. They were man and wife. Nothing could change that. And he loved her – at least he had once loved her. She had loved him in return, enough to agree to the kidnap. She sighed as she turned right and walked in the direction of the pier. Presumably this was the night Maude would hand over the money – unless Lionel had changed the plan.

An elderly man slumped on a seat called to her. 'Over here, me duck! Give an old man a bit of comfort!' He took a gulp of something from a bottle and began to cough and splutter. 'I'll make it worth your while, me duck!'

Alice shied away like a startled horse. 'I'm not your duck!' she muttered. 'I'm nobody's duck!' But what exactly was she? she wondered with a surge of anguish. She had no job, no home, no money – and possibly no husband. She was nothing.

It took a few moments for her to rally. She was still Alice Brent. No. She was Alice Crewe – at least that was her maiden name.

'I'm still Alice!' she reminded herself with a flash of defiance.

Not that she really cared at that moment. She wanted to be Mrs Lionel Brent but he had abandoned her. Her heartache was a physical thing, tearing her apart, and her conscience was pricking her fiercely. 'Stupid little fool!' she told herself. 'You've been duped! You fell for his charm and then his lies and you helped him cheat poor Maude. Too late now to change your mind. Too late to undo the wrong. You're in it as deep as he is – well, almost!'

Seeing two men approaching she didn't wait to be accosted again but hurried down the nearest steps to the beach itself and continued to head for the pier. What was to become of her, she wondered anxiously, a married woman without a husband.

Maybe if she waited for Lionel by the pier she could talk to him and make him change his mind . . . but then she might be arrested with him. The idea of prison brought her up short. Standing stock still, she stared out across the moonlit water and felt herself drawn towards it.

Alice crunched over the pebbles until she stood at the water's edge. Glancing back she could make out the edge of the town, lit by flickering gaslights and her throat contracted with misery. Hastings was her town, the place where she was born. She had gone to school here and vaguely remembered Jem Rider as a snotty-nosed, bare-footed child who never had a handkerchief. He was always getting into mischief and always getting the cane. She had earned her first meagre wages as a young barmaid in the Pig and Flute, which was where she had met Lionel and fallen so disastrously in love.

Turning her back on the town, Alice studied the sea. It looked so peaceful. 'Like a mill pond!' she exclaimed. Wistfully, she imagined herself floating gently on the placid surface, her hair floating out around her head, her eyes closed. She had known the sea in all its moods – from this calm oily motion, which the fishermen call 'swallocky', to the wild crashing waves of a full-scale storm. She had never seen it as a way out before but, with the inner turmoil that now racked her, it was tempting. If she could not see a way out of this trouble she was in, she might dare to think the unthinkable.

It was a few minutes past midnight and the only light in the Romilees Hotel was in the private sitting room where three people conversed in lowered voices. One was DC

Fleet, another was Derek Jayson and the third person was Maude Brent. Ever since the detective's return from Folkestone, Maude had been in a state of utter denial. She refused to listen to his account of what had happened at *Fairways* and was insisting that she would carry out her plan to take the paintings instead of the money. She had angrily rejected the bank manager's last-minute offer of half the money, insisting that the kidnappers might take umbrage and kill Lionel out of spite. 'With the paintings I have selected, they will be amply rewarded. What's the difference between money or goods in lieu of money? If I were a kidnapper I would take the paintings and disappear to the other side of the world.'

Maude also flatly refused to believe a word against Alice, accusing DC Fleet of trying to make a fool out of her with a pack of lies. In a desperate attempt to hold on to her self-control, Maude clung to the previous understanding of the situation and condemned DC Fleet's latest revised reading of it as 'highly implausible'.

'You forget,' she hissed, 'that I know Alice better than you do and I have a very good idea why she has run off. It's nothing to do with my husband or the kidnap. I suspect she has been ill-used by some wretch and doesn't know how to handle the matter. In other words, she is with child. She is simply too embarrassed to tell us what has happened.' She glared at DC Fleet. 'You have jumped to conclusions, DC Fleet. The wrong conclusions. As a policeman, you should know better. As soon as Lionel is home safe and sound I shall make enquiries and find Alice. I shall speak with Doctor Courtney. He may well know something. Whatever her problem, Aunt Biddy and I will see her through it.'

The two men exchanged helpless glances. In her present mood, Maude Brent was implacable.

Lionel and his new friends finally exhausted the pleasures of the beach and, crunching their way across the shingle, made their way unsteadily up the steps to the road level. A small cloud had now covered the moon and there was no reflection from the water so that the whole atmosphere seemed to Lionel to have grown more sombre. He shivered, squinting upward at the dark sky and hoping it was not an omen. He was not normally superstitious but a successful outcome to tonight's adventure was crucial to the rest of his life and he did not want anything to go wrong.

He was killing time with his idiot companions, waiting for the moment when he would get his hands on the money that Maude would bring to the pier. He knew her well. Nothing would deflect her from rescuing him. Poor little Maude. She was besotted with him. He smiled into the darkness. Forgetting that he had shaved off his moustache, he put up a hand to stroke it.

'Damn!' he muttered.

'Wossat?' asked one of the men, clinging to the handrail as he pulled himself up and on to the road.

'Nothing!' Lionel slurred his voice as he slapped him on the back but in fact he was not drunk at all, simply pretending. Thank God it would soon be over. Once away from Hastings he could regrow his moustache, hopefully wash the dye from his hair and part it in the middle again. He was a vain man and preferred his original appearance.

Two of his companions were now spoiling half-heartedly for a fight and another was becoming morose. The latter clung to Lionel's arm, trying to tell him about his unlucky past. The fifth man, younger than the rest, stood on the top step, unbuttoned his trousers and peed down on to the beach. 'Look! A waterfall!' he crowed, hiccuping with laughter. 'Better than that Niagara thing they've got in America!'

Suddenly Lionel longed to be rid of them, despising their inane antics and pathetic schoolboy humour. He had allowed himself to be drawn into their group in the public house, partly because he was lonely and partly because he feared that resisting their invitation might look churlish and draw attention to him. All he could think about was collecting the money but now he needed to be alone to wait for whatever the next few hours would bring. These drunken revellers no longer interested him.

'I'm off then, gentlemen!' he said as he walked swiftly

away eastward, in the direction of his room, praying that they wouldn't decide to accompany him. One of them, he saw as he glanced back, was staggering after him but finally tripped over his own feet and ended up on the ground. Serve the silly blighter right! Lionel certainly didn't want them to follow him, even at a distance. That would never do.

'Oi! Dodger! Where you off to?' another shouted plaintively but Lionel waved an arm without even turning back. He would hole up, until it was time, in his attic room above the barber's at the far end of George Street. There his bag awaited him, already packed, and there was a small pile of coins on the mildewed sideboard in payment for the room. He was taking no chances. If he left without paying the rent the landlord might report him and the police, though hardly the most intelligent of men in his opinion, might just put two and two together and make four.

When he had the money from Maude he would stow it in the bag, sling it over his shoulder and stroll off. He planned to walk along through St Leonards and keep walking through the night until the buses started in the morning. The train would have whisked him away faster, of course, but there was more chance of being spotted once the alarm was raised. It was a pity about Jem. He hadn't intended to kill him, just give him a bit of a beating to guarantee his silence. Jem's mistake was fighting back. Stupid beggar! He shouldn't have done that. Lionel had lost his temper. It just happened. A couple of taps on his head and down Jem went. Must have had a thin skull. It was an accident. Nothing more.

'I'm no thug,' he muttered resentfully. No need for Alice to have made such a fuss about it. Once the boy was dead, of course, he'd had to get rid of him. He should have thought more about the tides and where they would take him. Hadn't expected him to show up again so quickly. Lionel took a few deep breaths and made up his mind to forget all about it.

And poor Maude. She'd assume he was dead, killed by those wicked kidnappers. No doubt she'd weep over his grave . . . Oh no! He grinned suddenly. There wouldn't be a grave! Maybe she'd spend her life in widow's weeds like Queen Victoria. God bless Her Majesty!

He frowned suddenly as he noticed a young woman on the beach, staring out to sea. He smiled grimly. He knew her sort. Do anything for a few coins. Probably had found herself in the family way. She wouldn't be the first and she certainly wouldn't be the last. Was she going to drown herself? Losing interest, Lionel walked on, smiling to himself. Soon he would be rich and he would have the pick of any woman, anywhere in the world!

He glanced back. She was still there. Excited and full of plans for a wonderful future, Lionel didn't give her a second thought.

At ten to two the three people in the sitting room were quietly contemplating what was to come. Maude, her face pale and drawn, looked at the detective writing something in his notebook, and wished she had not needed to flout his wishes on the business of the paintings, which were stacked in readiness in the hall, waiting for the taxi to arrive so that she could take them to the pier entrance and deposit them. She knew he believed he was doing his best but his ultimate aim was to catch the criminal and hers was to bring about her husband's return.

She glanced at Derek Jayson, liking what she saw. He had been very kind to her, trying to act as a go-between for her and DC Fleet and eager to help her in any way he could. If only she had had a brother like him. How much easier it would have been for her to be able to rely on a close family member.

She glanced at the clock. 'Not long now.' She imagined the taxi driver checking his watch and yawning. Still, he had insisted on double pay for the trip so he wouldn't complain.

The policeman nodded without answering. Derek Jayson smiled, leaned across and patted her arm. 'It's going to be all right, Mrs Brent. You'll see.'

The detective rolled his eyes at this blatant oversimplification of the negotiations ahead. 'Let's hope so.'

Maude tried to imagine how Lionel was feeling. She hoped he knew how near he was to being set free. And he would be able to thank her for that. If she had been guided by DC Fleet and the bank manager, things might have looked very different.

'But if he's not there?' she asked again. 'Lionel, I mean. What will we do?'

'He will be, Mrs Brent,' Derek Jayson told her soothingly.

'I've been praying,' Maude told him. 'Perhaps we should pray together.' She bent her head and, after a moment's hesitation, the men joined her. 'Dear Lord,' she began earnestly, but just then there was a timid knock on the sitting-room door. Maude jumped and they looked at each other in surprise.

Derek Jayson said, 'Who on earth . . .?' and then called out, 'Come in!'

Mrs Hurst appeared. She was still in her night clothes and slippers and her head was covered in curling rags. Maude stared at her.

'I'm ever so sorry to intrude, but I was looking out on to the street and I noticed a woman lurking about outside. She kept looking up at the windows and I thought . . . Well, you know, it's rather late!'

Maude jumped to her feet but DC Fleet put up a warning hand. 'I'll check this out,' he told them. 'It may be connected with the kidnap.'

'They may have sent a message!' Maude cried, and a faint wash of colour swept across her face.

The detective shook his head. 'Please don't get your hopes up, Mrs Brent. It may not be good news.'

He left the room and Derek Jayson said, 'We must have faith!'

'It might be Alice.' Maude clasped her hands.

'Would she dare?'

'I'm giving her the benefit of the doubt until we know exactly—' She broke off as footsteps sounded in the hall and DC Fleet came in dragging a reluctant Alice.

'You're hurting me! Let go of my arm!' The young woman looked terrified but the policeman held on to her.

He said, 'She only wants to talk to you, Mrs Brent, but I've told her I have to be present. Time is running out and if there is any—'

Maude cried, 'Alice! Do you know where Lionel is being held? If so you must tell us at once. Everything else can wait.'

They all turned towards Alice, who looked as if she might faint with fright. She looked beseechingly at Maude and burst into tears.

Maude stepped forward. 'Please release her, DC Fleet. She won't run away – will you, Alice?'

She was rewarded with a shake of the head. Reluctantly the policeman relaxed his grip and she snatched back her arm and rubbed it with her hand.

Derek Jayson hesitated. 'Shall I make her a warm drink?' he suggested and Maude suspected that he found it hard to deal with the emotions.

'Thank you, Mr Jayson. That would be helpful.' She turned to Alice and guided her to a chair. 'Now, Alice, sit down there and forget about DC Fleet. And tell us at once if you know anything at all about where Lionel is and whether or not we can expect to have him back safely. What you can tell us may save his life.'

Alice drew a long breath and began to cry again. 'Oh, Maude! How can I . . .? You must forgive me . . . That is, you won't, of course . . . How could you?'

Exasperated by Maude's gentle approach, DC Fleet stepped forward. 'Answer these questions, Miss Crewe,' he snapped. 'Have you been in contact with Lionel Brent in the past twenty-four hours?'

'No. I went to his lodgings but . . . He said it was over a cobbler's shop but the woman . . . Oh God! Forgive me! I don't understand what's happening.'

Maude said, 'Went to his lodgings? But how . . .? He doesn't have . . . What are you talking about?'

He shook Alice's shoulder roughly. 'Miss Crewe, do you know where the suspect is right now?'

'No. But I have to tell you, Maude, that . . .' She scrubbed at her tears with both hands, gasping for breath. 'It's not what you think. He isn't going to be killed. He . . .'

DC Fleet was losing patience with her. 'Stop this nonsense!' he warned. 'You are wasting police time and that is punishable by—'

'He isn't? Oh, thank God!' Maude cried.

DC Fleet, white-faced, stared at Alice. 'You know something! What is it?' He moved closer. 'If you don't—'

Maude pulled him back. 'Stop browbeating her! You won't frighten it out of her!' She crouched beside Alice. 'Please, Alice, we have to understand what is going on. All I want to know now is if my husband is alive. Can you answer that?'

'He's alive. Yes.'

DC Fleet said, 'Ask her how she knows that.'

Maude hesitated, frowning. 'Alice?'

'Because he . . . Maude, we made it all up. I'm so sorry. We didn't mean . . . At least we did . . . but I didn't know about Jem.'

DC Fleet almost pushed Maude aside in his eagerness to obtain the information he needed. 'What happened to Jem Rider? Did Lionel Brent kill him?'

At that moment Derek Jayson arrived with a cup of tea and a sugar bowl but the detective waved him away. He hovered uncertainly in the doorway, confused, staring at Maude as though expecting her to explain what was happening.

DC Fleet now held Alice's shoulder in a fierce grip.

'I don't understand!' cried Maude, turning towards the policeman. 'Lionel hasn't killed anyone. He's been kidnapped. You're not making any sense. Lionel never would do such a thing. He couldn't.' She turned to Alice. 'Tell him! You know Lionel. Butter wouldn't melt in his mouth!'

'He didn't mean to. It was an accident!' Alice covered her face with her hands.

Maude felt the first frisson of fear curling up her spine like ice. She heard the words but didn't understand what she was hearing – although she knew she didn't like it. Nor did she like the fact that Alice seemed to understand what the policeman was talking about. Alice, of all people!

Alice cried, 'Maude, I know you'll never forgive me, but I wish with all my heart that—'

'Forgive you for what?' What on earth had Alice done? What had happened to her? 'Was it a man . . . That is, has someone assaulted you?' If that were so, she could understand and, of course, she would forgive her – there would be nothing to forgive! But how was Lionel involved? He would never assault Alice. He would never assault any woman. In despair, she let the argument roll around her, trying to make sense of the incomprehensible.

DC Fleet asked, 'Is he going to turn up to collect the money, Miss Crewe? Yes or no? Will he be at the pier – in person?'

Alice screamed. 'You mustn't . . . Oh no!' Her voice rose.

'Tell me, Miss Crewe.'

Alice turned her gaze imploringly towards Maude, who could only shake her head.

'Miss Crewe! I shall arrest you for withholding information if you—'

'I . . . I expect he will but he wasn't where I thought he was so I don't know for sure. Oh, do you have to catch him? He's not really a murderer. It was an *accident*! He told me how it happened.'

DC Fleet narrowed his eyes. 'When exactly did he tell you?'

'The night he came into the garden. He said if anyone ever asked I was to tell them it was an accident.'

Maude thought rapidly. Alice was claiming that Lionel was the man who had come into the garden at *Fairways*! If that were true, he had been free to come and go. Finally one of the pieces of the shocking jigsaw had fallen into place. 'You mean while I was here, my husband came to *Fairways*? In the night? How was that possible, Alice?'

DC Fleet snapped. 'It was all lies, Mrs Brent. Now would you please stop interrupting and allow me to question Miss Crewe.'

'But the paintings! Time is short and—'

'They won't be needed. We can catch him without them.'

Alice said, 'Jem sort of tripped and knocked himself out. He was unconscious, that's all.'

DC Fleet flushed angrily. 'You're saying Rider slipped

and fell and banged his head twice in the same place? You see my problem, Miss Crewe? He had *two* overlapping blows to his head! Really, you cannot be so naive as to—'

'But he . . . he said it . . . it was . . .' Alice stammered then fell silent before his withering tone and cold gaze.

He went on. 'And Rider, already unconscious, somehow *threw himself* into the sea?' The policeman regarded her scornfully. 'Don't try to make a fool of me, Miss Crewe. And don't fool yourself. You and Mrs Brent have both been deceived. The man's a wrong 'un!'

Still uncomprehending, Maude turned to Derek Jayson but at that moment the door flew open and Alison Cobb came in.

'For heaven's sake, keep your voices down!' she told them urgently. 'I could hear you upstairs. Do you want to rouse the rest of the guests?' She caught sight of her brother and walked towards him. 'Is that tea? If so I'll have it.'

'It's for Miss Crewe.'

'Who?' She took the tea from him and sipped it. She saw Alice. 'Who's this?'

Maude began to explain, as calmly as she could, that Alice was Miss Crewe and that she was her companion who had come in search of her, but even as she spoke she was uncovering doubts. It seemed more likely that Alice had come to convince them that Lionel was not a murderer. Which made no sense unless someone was accusing Lionel of Jem Rider's death, which they weren't . . . Were they?

Everyone was talking at once and Maude put a hand to her head, which was beginning to ache. The detective had said they didn't need the paintings and he seemed to be expecting Lionel to turn up at the pier and he also seemed determined to arrest him.

Earlier Maude had been full of nervous energy and ready to face the kidnappers with the paintings. Now she felt exhausted by the confusion and momentarily closed her eyes as a great weight settled over her – a weight she recognized. It was fear of the truth. She needed to know what was going on but she dreaded the truth.

She opened her eyes as someone touched her hand, and looked up to see Mrs Cobb's brother leaning over her.

'You look as though you could do with some air,' he suggested. 'Would you like to stand in the garden for a few moments? I'll come with you. You might feel stronger.'

At that moment Maude saw a chance to delay the reality that awaited her and she nodded dumbly. No-one even noticed as he steered her out of the room, through the kitchen and out into the small back yard that he had elevated to a garden. There was nowhere to sit down and gloomy clouds had covered the moon. A cat appeared from behind a display of potted plants and rubbed itself against her ankles, but as she bent to fondle it, it sprang away and disappeared into the shadows.

He said, 'There's nowhere to sit, but if you wouldn't object or misunderstand, I could put an arm round you. You must be feeling very disturbed by everything and I don't want you to faint.'

Touched by his kindness, she said, 'I won't object, Mr Jayson. The fresh air is very welcome.' She trembled a little as his arm went round her then leaned towards him, grateful for the support. 'Rather like an oasis, this little yard,' she said inconsequentially. It was a relief to be out of the fevered atmosphere inside the hotel.

'A sea of calm,' he agreed. 'A chance to catch your breath.'

'Yes.' She sighed. 'It was kind of you to think of me.'

'I'm sorry I can't be more help.'

'You and your sister have been more than kind. I'm afraid I've been an unwanted disruption.'

'Not at all.'

For a few moments they stood in silence while Maude tried to summon her courage for the inevitable question. At last she asked quietly, 'Do you understand what's going on, Mr Jayson?'

He hesitated. 'I think so but perhaps DC Fleet should explain it all.'

'I'd rather hear it from you – if you could bear it.' She smiled faintly. 'I know what they say about shooting the messenger that brings bad news but . . . It's none of your doing and I do need to know.'

He sighed deeply, obviously unhappy with his task. 'I gather that this was not a genuine kidnapping, Mrs Brent,' he began. 'It was a ruse. Your husband thought of a plan to extract money from you and . . . and your companion was part of the plan. I think her part was to win your confidence.'

Maude's head swam but she told herself to hear him out. She had to face up to whatever had happened.

'Go on,' she whispered.

'It seems that they were going to take the money and run away together. Then Jem got involved and presumably knew too much. He must have become some kind of a threat, so your husband . . . It's alleged that your husband killed him. Possibly accidentally.'

At last she was forced to protest. 'My husband is not a murderer, Mr Jayson.' He was silent, leaving her time to think. She went on, 'At least . . . he might have done it accidentally. Alice did say something like that, didn't she?'

He nodded.

Maude continued, 'So Alice is . . . is somehow close to him. I dare say she has fallen in love with him but she . . . It's hard to believe that all this time . . .'

Suddenly DC Fleet stood outlined in the back doorway. 'I'd like you to come back inside,' he told them. 'I'm going down to the station for reinforcements. We'll get the blighter!'

Maude, galvanized into action, stepped forward. 'If he's not going to get any money, why do you have to try and arrest him?' she demanded desperately. 'Let him turn up, find nothing and go away. Just forget everything. I won't bring charges. Please!'

'I'm sorry, Mrs Brent. A crime *has* been committed. A robbery has been planned. A ransom note has been sent. There has been a conspiracy to defraud.'

'But if I choose not to press charges?'

'You forget, Mrs Brent, that he is also wanted for murder.'

Once inside the sitting room, he told Maude to keep Alice at the hotel.

'And if I don't?' she demanded.

To Mrs Cobb he said, 'You hear that. Alice Crewe doesn't leave this building. If we can arrest Brent we'll lock him up overnight pending enquiries and tomorrow we'll be back to interview Miss Crewe.'

Derek Jayson said, 'Hang on a minute! We can't keep the young woman here against her will! I'm sure my sister doesn't want to be held responsible for her.'

'It's either that or I arrest her now for conspiracy. Make up your mind because we've got bigger fish to fry. We have to catch a murderer!'

Hidden under a large sack beside a dustbin, Lionel waited on a darkened corner on the opposite side of the road, about a hundred yards from the entrance to the pier. He needed to discover what the police intended to do. He had stipulated that Maude should come alone in a taxi and leave the money in a bag tied to the pier's rail, but he didn't expect the police to allow this. They might send a policeman disguised as a woman. That had been known. They might try and surround the place. His own plan was to be there early and watch for anything suspicious, and if he spotted an ambush he would melt into the darkness and try again some other time with a different plan.

The church clock struck quarter past two and still the street seemed to be deserted; there was no sign of the taxi. Cautiously Lionel moved the sacks so that he could peer over the edge of them. A quick glance to right and left revealed nothing remotely suspicious and he smiled with satisfaction. There was an unfortunate smell coming from the dustbin and he wrinkled his nose in disgust. If anyone had ever told him he'd be hiding under sacks beside a stinking dustbin he'd have laughed at them but it was a case of playing the police at their own game. They'd sneak along and try to hide but he'd spot them a mile off. 'No flies on me!' his father had frequently claimed and his son was made from the same mould.

The beach in the middle of the night was eerily silent. A world away from the daylight when the day trippers enjoyed their ice creams, toffee apples and the inevitable sticks of rock. An image rose unbidden, of Alice sitting on the beach eating her ice cream, her eyes sparkling with happiness, while the gusty breeze blew her hair around her face. He had told her she looked like a mermaid.

'Oh, happy days!' he murmured. He had enjoyed his short marriage to Alice but it was time to change his life around and there was now no place for her in it. He frowned. 'Stupid wretch!' All that fuss over Jem Rider, who was worth less than a snap of the fingers. She had actually wept for him! No accounting for taste.

He squinted into the darkness. Any minute now. There was no sign of the taxi or the bag of money but surely there was still time. Nothing on the seafront moved until a cat slithered along the road and disappeared down the steps to the beach. No doubt hoping for a mouse that had ventured on to the shingle in search of careless crumbs left by a holidaymaker's picnic.

To dull the agony of waiting he thought about his future. He would go abroad, he promised himself, once he had the money. He would make his way to somewhere where it was always sunny and every day was exciting. Mexico appealed to him. He had discussed it with Alice and they had agreed it would be fun to live somewhere like that. They would rent a hacienda. Correction. *He* would rent a hacienda. Alice, his lawful wedded wife, would not, after all, be travelling with him. He grinned. There would be plenty of *señoritas* in Mexico who would appreciate a handsome man with money to burn . . .

To his right, a movement caught his eye. Damn. An elderly man was shuffling along towards him and Lionel ducked back beneath the sacks, pulled them well over his head and held his breath. The old chap was snorting rheumily – like a sick pig, thought Lionel irritably – probably about to shuffle off this mortal coil. With any luck he would cross over to the beach side of the road. To his dismay, however, the erratic footsteps didn't waver but came closer still and Lionel hunched down as far as he could and pulled the sacks a little closer. He closed his eyes.

'Keep going, old man!' he urged wordlessly but instead he heard the dustbin lid being lifted and there were sounds of a hand rifling through the rubbish. In the darkness, Lionel could see nothing as he tried to peer through the mesh of the sacks but he could hear various items being tossed from the dustbin – an empty bottle that smashed on hitting the ground, a couple of tin cans, one of which rolled, and something that sounded wet, like soggy cardboard.

'Nothing. Sod it!' the old man muttered and, replacing the lid, he shuffled on, fortunately ignoring the shapeless mound beneath the sack.

Lionel breathed a sigh of relief as the footsteps retreated. His first challenge successfully overcome, he told himself triumphantly. He was going to outwit them all – even the coppers when they came, which he knew they would. He had killed Jem Rider and they wanted his scalp! Still, he had always considered himself more than a match for them. Coppers were a joke. They were nothing but a load of pea-brained numbskulls dressed up in fancy uniforms.

Further along the road the old man reached a row of shops and stopped at one that had once sold a variety of seaside souvenirs – framed sketches of the pier or the famous cable car; pottery mugs with the words 'From Hastings' painted round the side; tasselled pencils and small shell-topped boxes and the inevitable saucy postcards. Now awaiting a new owner, the windows were painted with whitewash on the inside and covered with a motley arrangement of bills and posters on the outside.

The old man tapped twice on the door and, when it opened, stepped smartly inside. In the gloom he could see his four colleagues waiting eagerly for the chance of some action. PC Batts pulled off the false beard and greasy old cap, and divested himself of the shabby coat. Then he grinned broadly and gave them a thumbs up.

He turned to DC Fleet. 'You were right! He's under the sacks beside the dustbin.'

Grumbling good-naturedly, the rest of the men handed

over their sixpences. Betting on the suspect's hiding place had helped them through a boring wait.

PC Batts said, 'I doubt he can see anything through the sacks.'

DC Fleet nodded. 'Then we'll send you and you –' he pointed to the chosen constables – 'to make your way along the beach westwards, then cross over and make your way back along the beach. Then come up on him from the other side.' He turned. 'You two do the same going east. When you're within ten yards, whistle and we'll all close on him. We should have him surrounded before he knows what's happening. Everyone clear? Right, get to it. And good luck.'

NINE

Lionel heard the single whistle blast and, taken by surprise, it took him a fateful second or two to understand what it meant. He had seen and heard nothing suspicious, but the sudden sound of pounding feet coming in his direction finally alerted him to his danger. He'd been outwitted! As he hurled aside the sacks and scrambled to his feet, the police were already upon him. They surrounded him and DC Fleet cried, 'Give yourself up, Brent. There are five of us. You have no—'

Lionel's instinct for self-preservation kicked in and adrenalin surged through him. Springing to his left, he snatched up the metal dustbin lid and swung it with all his might at the circle of police who waited with their truncheons raised. Only their teeth showed in the darkness and the grinning policemen reminded Lionel of a pack of animals with bared fangs. But their grins faded abruptly. By the time they saw the impromptu weapon it was too late. It caught DC Fleet full across the forehead and knocked him backwards. He fell with a scream of agony and struck his head on the ground as the vicious sweep continued to scythe through his men. It hit the next man across the neck, causing blood to spurt and then, still arcing downward, caught the third man's upraised arm and broke it. DC Fleet had not moved.

That did it, thought Lionel, with a mixture of regret and satisfaction. Even as he darted forward, pushing the two remaining constables aside, he knew he had gone too far. Assault on three policemen! If he was caught now, he could look forward to charges on multiple offences and hanging might be the kindest sentence he could expect. He had nothing to lose. Whatever it took, he could not allow himself to be taken. Turning only to hurl the dustbin lid at one of his pursuers, he raced across the road and on to the pier. There was no sight of the bag containing the ransom and he swore. His feet echoed on the wooden boardwalk as he forced his legs to a maximum effort, conscious of the footsteps behind him and the frantic whistles of the police who were trying to call up help.

Long before he reached the end of the pier, Lionel was gasping for breath and he sensed that the man behind him was gaining. If he were caught, he could expect a thorough beating on the spot.

'Give yourself up, you swine!' his pursuer shouted breathlessly.

Lionel realized with a sickening feeling in his stomach that he was running out of pier. He couldn't swim but there was only one way to go and that was down into the water. He staggered to the railings, climbed shakily over the rail and turned back to shout a last defiant curse at the policeman.

'See you all in Hell!' he yelled. Then he steadied himself, took a deep breath, pinched his nose and hurled himself into the darkness.

As he fell he heard the constable shout, 'Drown, you bastard!' and then, with a splash and a flurry of gurgling bubbles, the cold sea closed over him.

The following morning found Jane Dyer at the reception desk of the gallery as usual. It was nearly eleven o'clock and raining steadily, a fact that always seemed to deter people from browsing in art galleries. Normally Jane would have been in the small kitchen next to the office, making a pot of tea for herself and Mr Barlowe, but today she was being deliberately awkward.

'Let him ask for it,' she told herself irritably. He shouldn't take her for granted. She was a paid employee, not a slave. He should consider her feelings more than he did. Since their disagreement over Mrs Brent and the list of paintings, Jane had cooled towards her employer. Not that she had ever liked him the way she liked Lionel Brent, but she had always been polite and respectful and ready with a pleasant smile. She enjoyed her job and her mother had advised her to be 'biddable' whenever suitable, but not ingratiating.

Today Jane's pretty face bore the signs of strain as she

turned to see her employer coming down the stairs, his face like thunder.

Now what has upset him? she wondered. If he asked about the pot of tea she would give him an innocent smile and pretend she had forgotten the time.

Glancing round the gallery to satisfy himself that there were no clients to overhear, Barlowe pulled up a spare chair and sat down next to her desk. He looked shocked and Jane prepared herself for bad news.

'There's been some trouble, Miss Dyer. Serious trouble. You'll have to hear it sooner or later.' He rubbed his eyes.

'Oh!' She stared at him fearfully. 'It's not Mrs Brent again, is it?' If he was going to try and involve her again in lies, she would walk right out of the gallery and go home. Then she would write a letter of resignation. Her mother had told her Mr Barlowe's behaviour was unpardonable.

'Not exactly.' He leaned back and stared upwards, his mouth tight. 'It's Mr Brent. He's . . . The police think he's dead.'

Jane felt as though he had punched her. She sucked in air and then let it out again in a long trembling sigh. 'Dead? Oh no! Not Mr Brent. What happened to him? Who killed him? Is he going to be all—?' *Don't be stupid!* She stopped herself just in time. Of course he wasn't going to be all right! He was *dead*. He would never be all right. Lionel Brent would never be anything but dead. Tears filled her eyes.

Barlowe said, 'For heaven's sake, don't give way to tears. Not here. Save them until you get home.' He shook his head. 'I never really believed anything like this would happen. It all seemed so . . . unlikely.'

'But who killed him?' She fumbled for her handkerchief.

Barlowe drew in a long breath and let it out slowly. 'He jumped into the sea and they think he drowned. So nobody actually killed him. It seems he attacked a policeman – several actually. Injured a couple of them.'

Jane wiped away her tears and shook her head vigorously. 'No! Not Mr Brent. He would never do such a thing! Attack the police? Never!'

Her employer shrugged. Briefly he brought her up to date with the case. 'That was them on the phone,' he went on, 'warning me to be on the lookout in case he didn't in fact drown. It was pitch dark and they only saw him jump. They have to assume that he might somehow have survived. If he *has* survived and shows his face here, try not to let him in. He's killed a man, remember. And the one called Fleet, the detective, is injured. Felled by a blow on the temple. Unconscious. Maybe in a coma.' He tutted. 'Brent's very dangerous, Miss Dyer. Remember that.'

'If he's still alive, you mean.' Her voice quivered.

'Let's hope he isn't. Better for everyone.' He pursed his lips, frowning. 'It's all very awkward at the moment. If he is still alive he's definitely on the run and he's still married to Mrs Brent, in which case he might try to take away some of our paintings.' He wagged a finger at Jane who recoiled slightly. '*If* he's alive and you help him in any way, you'll be an accessory to a crime. If he sets foot in here call the police and on no account help him in any way.'

'But . . .'

'I'm only trying to help you, Miss Dyer. If you are foolish enough to help a wanted criminal – a wanted *murderer* – I won't be able to bail you out. In fact, to be brutally honest, I wouldn't want to bail you out if you had been so foolish as to ignore my advice. Just so you understand my position. I have to be seen to be beyond reproof – and so should you.' He sat back in the chair and eyed her severely. 'But I'll tell you this – I shall be staying well away from him if he does turn up again. Lionel Brent is not going to ruin my life. When I think of the way he's behaved and the lies he's told . . .' He leaned forward, his elbows on the desk, and covered his face with his hands.

Jane watched him, wondering what she herself would do if the man she had adored had survived and should ask for her help. If he needed money he might come to her to beg for one of the Cope paintings. Could she refuse him when he needed her most? She had never had a gentleman friend and her ideas about the opposite sex were mostly gleaned from the books she read, which her mother recommended from time to time – mostly the classics, but Jane did sometimes buy magazines, which she read avidly at slack times in the gallery and then threw away. She would never take them home.

Mr Barlowe asked, 'What happened to the tea, Miss Dyer?'

'Oh dear!' She glanced at the clock with feigned surprise. 'I didn't realize it was so late, Mr Barlowe. I'll make it now.' She jumped to her feet but he was also rising.

'I won't have time to drink it now,' he said. 'The phone call has made me late already. I have to catch a train for Canterbury. This Miss Brompton seems promising. We sell quite a few miniatures . . .' He paused to snatch up his hat and umbrella. 'I'll see you tomorrow, Miss Dyer. Try to forget about Lionel Brent and concentrate on your work.'

She watched him go, pleased to see the back of him. She needed time to think about Lionel. Could he really be dead – and could he really have killed somebody? It was ridiculous. Perhaps he was being framed! She gasped. Had the police thought of that, she wondered? The Lionel she knew was a gentle soul. She smiled as his image rose in her mind. He had always treated her with respect, she thought, a faint smile lighting her face. Pushing aside the ugly accusations, she thought over the time she had spent working for the gallery. Mr Barlowe had always been fair, she conceded, but Lionel Brent had made her feel . . . desirable.

The bell jangled and a client came in. She recognized him as Mr Stewart from Hampstead who had bought several works over the past few years. He seemed a nice man and he was always polite to her. He leaned towards sea views, she recalled. Mr Barlowe would appreciate her quick recall, she reflected. All part of the job.

Jumping to her feet she greeted him. 'We have a beautiful study of Loch Ness,' she told him. 'The artist was there on holiday recently. Very serene.' She led him to the painting and they stood together admiring the watercolour. Mr and Mrs Stewart had spent several holidays in the area and Jane knew that Mr Barlowe had bought the Loch Ness painting with them in mind. They would expect her to bring a little pressure to bear on him but her thoughts immediately wandered to more important matters.

If Lionel were to ask for her help, would she be able to give it? How wonderful it would be to offer help. But of course, he would never dare show his face in the gallery. It was too obvious. Nor would he ever dare go back to his home in Folkestone.

She tried to concentrate on the potential purchaser. 'Of course, it's some years since the monster was last sighted,' she said. 'But it will always be a lure for holidaymakers.'

He nodded. 'Last seen from the water in 1908. Last sighting from the shore three years ago. My wife is fascinated by the whole thing. This would have made a perfect birthday present for her except that it was last month and I bought her a bottle of very expensive French perfume.'

'Perhaps you could give it to her for Christmas.' She tried to summon up Lionel Brent's face for a second time but now it refused to materialize and she sighed.

'I like the hint of yellow in the sky!' said Mr Stewart, his head on one side as he scrutinized the painting. 'It is often there when the sun comes up, but for such a short time. Maybe only seconds.'

She nodded, trying to maintain an air of deep interest. She had secretly harboured romantic thoughts about Lionel Brent ever since they had first met and now she was reluctant to surrender them, hoping against hope that he was still alive somewhere. She thought she might be the one person in the whole world who would dare to help him in his hour of need. Her mother, of course, would be horrified if she found out. Jane's face fell at the prospect.

'And the two birds flying from right to left. Almost an afterthought.' Mr Stewart half-closed his eyes. Then he turned. 'Is it true what they're saying – about Mr Brent?'

For a moment she was too shocked to speak. Did everyone know? She stammered, 'I–I'm sure it isn't. I can't believe it. Can you?'

'Lord knows. My wife says you can never tell with people.'

She didn't want to have this discussion so she said, 'The police have told us not to discuss the case.'

'Ah! I suppose they would. Stands to reason.'

'Yes. My mother says we should never speak ill of the dead!'

'Dead? Is he really dead?'

'Er . . . Well, I don't think anyone knows for sure.'

'They say he jumped to his death in the sea. Couldn't swim. But that means very little. He could have clung to the pier supports until the tide went out. That's what I'd have done in his shoes. Wouldn't you?'

Jane felt a glimmer of hope. 'I'm afraid the police said . . .'

'Oh yes! You mustn't talk about it. Well, I'll think about the Loch Ness painting. Might bring my wife in to see it.'

It didn't sound very convincing, thought Jane. He made his way to the door and put on his hat. 'I'll be seeing you, Miss Dyer.'

Jane watched him retreat. What a nasty little man. He just wanted to gossip about Lionel, she realized sadly, and he had almost persuaded her to do just that. With an effort, she returned to her dreams.

Maude stood in the garden at *Fairways*, a blank stare on her face. She was still in a state of shock, and still hardly able to grasp the immensity of what had happened – or rather what might have happened. She had insisted on going home to be with Aunt Biddy in the hope that, in familiar surroundings, her mind might function more satisfactorily. Her gaze travelled slowly across the grass and came to rest on a croquet hoop . . . then another. Aunt Biddy walked towards her.

'It was the first night you were away,' she said in answer to the unasked question. 'We felt odd without you and Lionel, and sort of lost, so we thought we'd play croquet to pass the time.'

'They're not supposed to be left out.' It suddenly seemed important to her.

Biddy said, 'No. Shall we take them in and put them away?'

Maude nodded but didn't move and Aunt Biddy began to collect the pieces. Maude said, 'Where were they?'

'In the cupboard under the stairs.'

'They'd better go back there then.'

Biddy, fifteen yards away, gave her a quick, anxious glance. What on earth did it matter? How could Maude bother about anything as trivial as a croquet set when the entire structure of their lives was crumbling around them? She hoped that her niece was not going to slide into a decline because of this tragedy. Biddy was already severely shaken and drained of energy. Having to care for a depressive invalid would be beyond her.

Maude clasped her hands. 'I wonder what has happened to Alice? It was terrible, seeing them take her away. She conspired, you see.'

'So when did she tell you all this?'

'While the police were trying to catch Lionel. We had to keep her at the hotel until they came back for her. She and I talked. She was desperate for my forgiveness but I–I couldn't give it. Isn't that dreadful?'

'No, it's not dreadful. It's natural. I wouldn't have forgiven her if I'd been in your shoes!'

Maude sighed. 'They're probably going to charge her and . . . and she'll have to stand trial. Poor Alice.'

Biddy, walking back towards her niece, snapped, 'Poor Alice, my eye! You're not thinking straight, Maudie love. She made fools of us. She lied. She pretended to like us and we trusted her. Some friend she turned out to be. Scheming little madam!' As she made her way back to the house, staggering under the weight of the croquet set, Biddy paused. She said, 'I'd like to ring her neck with my bare hands! That's what I'd like to do – God forgive me!'

Maude stared at her impassively and made no effort to help her. Trying to imagine life without Alice made her ineffably sad and thinking of Alice in a police cell was like a cold lump in her heart. She glanced across the lawn to the shrubbery. That was where Jem Rider had appeared with his missive for Lionel. *All part of the plot – a ploy to confuse the issue*. How easy it had been for Jem. A simple way to earn a shilling. And now he was dead – killed by Lionel, according to the police.

She made her way with faltering steps around the side of the house and looked up at her aunt's bedroom window. The very window where Lionel had thrown the small stones, thinking it was Alice's room. She frowned. Was that a mistake on his part or part of the plot? It was all so devious. She didn't know what to believe.

One thing that she found impossible to believe was that she was not Mrs Lionel Brent. That title went to Alice, who had married Lionel a few months after the plan had taken shape in Lionel's head after meeting Maude at home in Folkestone.

Slowly, Maude followed Biddy into the house. Her aunt had already stowed away the croquet set and was washing her hands in the kitchen.

'What do you fancy for tonight, Maudie love?' she asked. 'I was wondering about lentil soup. It's not heavy and I can make some fresh bread. And don't tell me you're not hungry.'

'I couldn't eat anything, Aunt Biddy. It would stick in my throat.'

'Now what did I say? Soup can't stick in your throat. It's not made that way. It just slips down and you can float the bread if you want to. There's no-one to see but you and me.' She held up a hand. 'Don't say a word. I shall make it and, if I have to, I'll feed it to you spoonful by spoonful. We've enough trouble to deal with without you getting run down.'

'Thank you, Aunt Biddy.' Giving in meekly, Maude made her way up the stairs. As she went she thought wistfully how happy the three of them had been together – herself, Aunt Biddy and Alice – and yet it had all been a sham. Fake. If only they could have stayed that way. If only it had been genuine.

She went into Alice's room, sat on the chair next to the bed and stared long and hard at the spot where Alice had lain. Had it been a strain, pretending for every moment of every day? Had it been difficult not to show her true feelings for

Lionel? Had she hated the fact that Lionel was sharing his bed with her, Maude? That must have hurt, surely?

Finding it all impossible to comprehend, she went back into her own bedroom where a photograph took pride of place on the mantelpiece. Lionel and Maude at their wedding, taken outside the church. Lionel looked every inch the sort of man a mother would want her daughter to wed – upright, handsome, healthy and charming. If she met him now, knowing nothing about the events of the last week, she would fall in love with him. No doubt about it.

Her throat was tight as she gazed at the likeness. Fate had stolen the man she thought he was and left her nothing but bitter memories of the man he really was. So should she blame herself for being gullible, for being so easily seduced? He had charmed her into a false relationship with the sole purpose of eventually stealing her wealth and disappearing. He had planned heartache for her, right from the start.

Maude picked up the photograph, deciding that she would never look on him again. Nor did she want to see again that young and hopeful young woman standing beside him with her hand in his. Slowly she dismantled the frame and retrieved the photograph. Carefully, with deliberate and restrained movements, she tore it into small pieces and threw them into the fire-grate. When winter came and the fires were lit, the proof of her undoing would be burned.

As she turned away, another thought struck her. 'How did you manage to trick the vicar?' she asked the absent Lionel. How had he persuaded the vicar that he was a single man? Or . . . Another thought struck her. Was Lionel really married to Alice? Perhaps he had also tricked Alice into believing they were man and wife. Would anyone ever know the whole story, she wondered?

Maybe she should do some investigating. Briefly the idea intrigued her but then she hesitated. Lionel had betrayed her and ruined her life and Alice was in a police cell because she had been cajoled by him into criminal ways. Did she, Maude, really want to know any more about the man who had broken their hearts?

* * *

Biddy wiped her eyes for the third time. They were streaming but that might be the onions she was chopping for the soup, or the tears she was shedding for their cheerful existence that had gone for good. She gripped the knife tightly, considering the idea that she might use it to stab Lionel Brent if by some miracle he suddenly stepped into her kitchen.

'It would serve you right!' she said. 'Give you some of your own medicine. A wolf in sheep's clothing – that's you, Lionel Brent!'

Or *had been* him. She hoped he was dead, although, on the other hand, it would be good to know that he had been hanged for his crimes. Still, maybe drowning took longer, in which case he could recall his wickedness and maybe repent.

She found the right saucepan, tipped in some lentils, added the onions, cloves and salt and pepper. Moments later she smelled hot metal and rushed to the stove.

'Lordy! I've forgotten the water!' Shaken by the mistake, Biddy covered the contents of the pan with cold water, sending up a hiss of reproachful steam.

'Sorry!' she told it and set it on a low heat to simmer for forty minutes.

She stood in the larder and felt comforted by the familiar shelves crammed with the pickles and jams she had made over the year, by the crock of flour, the butter under its net cover and the lump of Cheddar cheese in its china container. Food. That was the answer to everything in Biddy's mind. Now she would make bread – enough to go with the soup and leave a few slices for toast in the morning. Little and often. That would be the way to restore Maude's appetite. Small tempting titbits of this and that at regular intervals, and gradually increasing portions so that whatever happened to Maude's mind and spirit, her body would be nourished.

Eventually they would return to normal eating habits. This thought brought a smile to Biddy's face and she assembled flour, milk and water, yeast and salt, and set about making the bread with her usual enthusiasm.

Forty minutes later she retrieved the softened lentils from

the stove and beat in an ounce of butter. The bread was baked and supper was ready.

'All's right with the world,' she whispered, and although that was far from the truth, it gave her hope for the future.

17th June, 1922. I thought the day would never end. It must have been the longest day of my life. It has all been such a strain I fear my mind is becoming less clear with every hour that passes. Today I made lentil soup and baked some bread and then spoiled everything by laying the table for four the way it used to be and poor Maude took one look at the table and burst into tears. When I tried to comfort her she pushed me away so fiercely that I fell backwards and hit my shoulder on the sideboard as I fell. I was terribly winded and for a while I couldn't get myself up from the floor but by then poor Maude had fled up to their bedroom and locked herself in.

How could I have been so stupid? I'm so cross with myself. I didn't mean to upset her in any way – it just happened. I tried to apologize through her bedroom door but she cried out, 'Oh! Go away, Aunt Biddy!' We haven't spoken since and it is now twenty past ten and I am in bed. I ate some bread and drank some soup, which was delicious although I say it as shouldn't. I left it in clear view in case Maude feels hungry and goes in search of food. I dread tomorrow and the day after that. Will we ever be happy again?

TEN

Two days later Maude plucked up her courage and ventured out of the house, encouraged by Derek Jayson, who had offered his car and himself as chauffeur if she needed it. It went against all her instincts to set foot outside *Fairways* but she did not want to become a prisoner in her own home and the sooner she could resume a place in the outside world the better it would be for her state of mind. Aunt Biddy had protested that it was much too early but Maude, hiding her anxiety, had insisted that she might *be* a victim but she didn't want to behave like one.

As she climbed into the passenger seat she gave Derek Jayson a brief smile. 'I hope you don't object to this outfit,' she said, settling herself and adjusting the veil, which she had arranged from the brim of her neat straw hat to cover the upper half of her face. 'I feel rather foolish but I don't want to . . .' She shrugged self-consciously.

'To be recognized,' he finished. 'I understand perfectly.' He started the engine, stowed away the handle, climbed in and shut the door.

Maude did not add that the veil would also hide her reddened eyes from the curious.

'I expect you thought I'd choose a pleasant run along the beach road, Mr Jayson, but I do feel very concerned about poor DC Fleet. The least I can do is visit him, and Aunt Biddy has made some calves' foot jelly in a jar with a secure lid. At least I hope it's secure. That's why I'm holding it in my lap – to keep it upright. It's most nutritious – if he is out of the coma, that is. If he's unconscious he won't be able to eat it. It doesn't keep well so if he cannot have it I shall ask the nurse to give it to someone else.'

'It's very thoughtful of you, Mrs . . . Miss er . . .'

Maude straightened her back. 'You must call me Mrs Brent

until . . . until I learn otherwise. That is what the solicitor advised when he called in yesterday. If they find my husband's body I shall know I am a widow but will still be Mrs Brent, although . . .' She took a quick breath and plunged on. 'It may be . . . You may have heard the rumours that our marriage may have been illegal. That is going to be investigated when I have recovered some of my energy.'

I shall also have to visit the doctor, she reminded herself, *to discover whether or not I am with child. I think not but would like to be reassured.* It was ironic that she had spent so long hoping for a child and now she was forced to hope it was not so.

He smiled at her. 'At least we have a nice day for the outing. Sunshine and very little breeze. I hope I'm not driving too fast for you, Mrs Brent. You must tell me if I am.'

'No. It's very pleasant. I rarely travel by car. It's usually my bicycle, Shanks' pony or the train!'

'I'm always at your service, Mrs Brent – the hotel business permitting, of course. If you need me at any time . . .'

'That's very generous but you must allow me to reimburse you for the fuel.'

He protested that he wouldn't hear of such a thing.

After a long silence, Maud again turned to him. 'I may take you up on your generous offer,' she said. 'I do rather want to make another call at some time. I want to go and see Alice Crewe.'

'But isn't she in prison?' He was so surprised he narrowly missed colliding with a sheep that had burst through the hedge ahead of them and appeared frozen with fear at the sight of the noisy contraption heading towards it.

As they edged carefully past it, Maude turned to glance back. 'Oh! It has gone back into its field. Thank goodness. It might have caused an accident, wandering about in the road.' She checked that the calves' foot jelly had not leaked and, satisfied, continued. 'Yes, she is in prison, but I want to see her if it's possible. We were very good friends before all this happened and I don't know if she has any friends or family. She might be quite alone in the world.'

He withheld further comment and for a long time they drove along without speaking. Maude, apparently busy with her thoughts, seemed to have lost track of time.

At last he said, 'I'm astonished at how . . . how brave you are being, Mrs Brent. Most women would have crumbled under such a blow. Such a complex set of adverse circumstances. I do congratulate you.'

Maude laughed shakily. 'I have surprised myself, Mr Jayson, if the truth be told. But you see I have my aunt to look after and this upheaval has been very bad for her. She's getting on in years and is easily confused. I realized I have to be strong for both of us or neither of us will recover from it . . .' She glanced round suddenly with recognition. 'Oh! We have made very good time! We are almost on the outskirts of Hastings already. What a marvellous thing, the motor car.'

When she arrived at the hospital and asked to see DC Fleet, she was told that because she was not a family member she would not be permitted to visit him.

'His mother is with him,' the nurse told her. 'He is making progress and has blinked his eyes once or twice but he doesn't respond to speech yet.' She eyed Maude curiously. 'It was a terrible thing that happened.'

'Yes.' Maude found herself feeling guilty simply because she was Lionel's wife – or thought she was. 'How are the other policemen that were injured?'

'PC Adams? Oh he's quite cheerful considering the wound in his neck. We're trying to keep the pain at bay. His wife is with him. A lucky escape if you look at it that way. He might have died from loss of blood and they have a baby daughter . . . The other constable has gone home with his arm in a splint.' She hesitated, glanced cautiously around then lowered her voice to ask if there was any news of Mr Brent. 'I mean, is he dead?'

Inevitably the blunt question shocked her but Maude steeled herself not to overreact. She would have to get used to dealing with such questions. Trying to keep her voice steady she said, 'There is no news. None at all.' Afraid of what might follow she asked quickly, 'Do you think DC Fleet's mother would speak to me? I'll understand if she refuses.'

'I'll ask her. She can only say no.' Pushing open the ward doors, the nurse disappeared briefly behind some curtains then reappeared, followed by a thickset woman. As they drew near, Maude saw from the woman's blotchy face that she had been crying.

'Mrs Fleet, I'm so very sorry,' she cried, stepping forward. 'I wanted to know how your son is and I brought him some calves' foot jelly.'

The nurse, looking nervous, said, 'I must get on with my work,' and hurried away leaving the two women face to face.

'Calves' foot jelly? He can't bear the stuff. Sorry.'

'Oh. Never mind.' Fearing hostility, Maude stumbled on. 'The nurse . . . er . . . She seems very hopeful about your son.'

Mrs Fleet swallowed. 'That blow on the head. They say he'll recover but . . .' Her eyes filled with fresh tears. 'He'll certainly never be a policeman again. It was his life.' Words suddenly tumbled out. 'His father was a police sergeant before he died. He caught pneumonia one winter . . . They were tailing a suspected thief and it was snowing hard. He came home frozen through. Robert adored his father. My son's so like him. Very ambitious.'

She swayed a little and Maude took hold of her arm. 'Come and sit down, Mrs Fleet,' she urged. 'This must have been a terrible shock.'

'Bit of a shock for you as well!'

They found a row of seats and for a few moments sat together wordlessly. Maude didn't know what to say that might be helpful.

Mrs Fleet shook her head wearily. 'I'm not blaming you, Mrs Brent. Please don't think that. That husband of yours has treated you cruelly. He's a monster! I hope he is dead – for everyone's sake! The world will be a better place without him.' She put a hand on Maude's arm. 'Forget him, dear, and start again. We'll have to find a way for my son to make a new life. I shall try to interest him in art. He was good at art when he was in school. I've still got some little pictures he painted years ago.' She smiled faintly. 'Watercolours of flowers mostly. You must do the same. Find a *decent* man, Mrs Brent. Make a new life for yourself. It's all you can do.'

Eagerly Maude told her about the Barlowe Gallery. 'Later on, if your son is interested, write to me and I'll ask Mr Barlowe to look at your son's artwork. I shall still be Mr Barlowe's partner in the gallery and we'll do whatever we can to encourage him and hopefully sell his work.'

They parted company and Maude sought out the nurse and handed over the calves' foot jelly. 'Give it to anyone who needs it,' she told her. 'Anyone who can benefit from it.' She returned to Derek Jayson who was waiting patiently outside in the motor car.

The next day was Tuesday and, true to his promise, Derek Jayson took Maude back to Hastings where she tried to see Alice in her prison cell. The custody sergeant had been adamant that she was not to be permitted to speak with the prisoner.

'Surely five minutes wouldn't matter,' Maude persisted. 'I don't think she has any other friends and her parents are both dead.'

'I'm sorry, Mrs Brent. That's the rules. I'd be in trouble if I allowed anything like that. You see, you're probably going to be a witness for the prosecution and we can't have you—'

'Witness for the prosecution?' Maude tensed. 'I've never agreed to that. I might not be willing. After all, the main person at fault here is my . . . is Lionel Brent.' Her voice rose indignantly. 'He persuaded Miss Crewe to take part in the fraud and if he's not going to be prosecuted, then it's not fair to pin all the blame on Alice.'

'That's for the jury to decide.' Seeing her agitation he added, 'It's a murder, remember.'

'Miss Crewe hasn't murdered anybody.'

'She's party to it.'

'But suppose my . . . Suppose Mr Brent is dead. How can she be charged? He was the . . . the originator of the kidnapping and he killed Jem. Without him—'

He slammed his hand down on the counter. 'Enough! You want answers, you'd better get her a lawyer. I'm just the desk sergeant. It's all beyond me.'

'I might want to give her a character reference.'

'Then you'd be mad!'

They glared at each other.

Sensing Maude's dejection, the policeman suddenly relented. Lowering his voice he said, 'Tell you what, I could tell her you're here. I could give her a message. No-one need know.'

'You'd know.'

'I would only pass on a respectable message. Something personal. Nothing to do with the case.'

Maude hesitated. 'That's kind of you but . . . I've got so much to say. That's the problem.'

He shrugged. Maude stared round at the sombre furniture and fittings which had been considered suitable for the interior of a police station. Nondescript flooring, grey painted walls, small uncurtained windows. A few notices were pinned to a cork wallboard. The place smelled of dust and sweat and something vaguely like disinfectant. She could see a table piled with files and a chair with a dark tunic draped over it.

Maude tried to imagine Alice's cell – small and stifling, no doubt; probably a thick wooden door with a metal grille in it and a slot to push in the food; a narrow bed bolted to the wall and one threadbare blanket. She shuddered.

'How is she?' she asked.

'As you would expect. Quiet. Shocked. Downhearted. Not saying much.'

'If I write her a letter?'

'I'd have to read it first.'

'Is she eating?'

'We sent out for a meat pasty but she brought it up about an hour later and said it must have been rotten. There's gratitude for you.'

'If I bring her some food would you give it to her?' She stared at him across the counter, willing him to agree.

Glancing over his shoulder, he rubbed finger and thumb together. 'A shilling!' he whispered.

Maude regarded him with something akin to disbelief. Her own life, as she knew it, was ending but to him and many others it hardly registered – simply an exciting topic, a few inches of print in the newspapers or, in this case, a way to earn a little extra money.

'A shilling?' she said heavily. 'Done!'

A shilling! The words had an ominous ring to them. This whole tragedy had started with Jem's shilling.

The following morning was cooler and there was a light wind but, ignoring the latter, Maude sat outside at a small table with a notepad, a box of envelopes, a pen and an inkstand. She had forgotten the blotter but decided that the breeze would dry the ink before she could smudge it. Primmy lay beside her, her head on her front paws, giving an occasional wag of her tail. An old tennis ball waited on the grass beside her.

Unable to think how to start the letter to Alice, Maude leaned down to pat Primmy, who immediately jumped to her feet looking hopefully at the ball. When nothing else happened she gave a short bark.

'What's that you say?' Maude teased gently. 'Oh, you want me to throw it for you!' She threw it as far as she could and watched it disappear into the shrubbery with Primmy racing after it.

Thursday 22nd June, 1922
Dear Alice,
What on earth can I say to you? The Alice we knew and loved has gone and we are left with a stranger. I just don't know how or why everything went so dreadfully wrong . . .

That was true, she reflected unhappily. It felt as if malevolent gods had reached down, picked up her life and given it a vicious shaking. Of course Alice had to take her share of the blame but, in her shoes, Maude secretly wondered if she might have been tempted to follow Lionel's lead. Loving someone so desperately tended to minimize the worst of their faults and maximize their good points. Had Alice been led astray against her better instincts?

Primmy rushed back and dropped the ball beside Maude's feet. She threw it again and watched enviously as the dog bounded after it.

'I shall come back as a dog in my next life!' she told herself. It looked so much simpler. Food, fun and sleep. Food made her think of her aunt, busy as usual in the kitchen making goodness knew what. Biddy had always prided herself on her ability to judge people and she had always admired Lionel. She had always considered him the perfect match for Maude and now she had been proved wrong it hurt her pride, and cost her much anguish to remember how she had encouraged Maude to accept Lionel's proposal of marriage.

> *. . . I am presumed a widow and you have been arrested. What a state we are in. I need to talk to you about your marriage to Lionel. Was it legal? I now wonder if he and I were ever truly married. The desk sergeant refused to let me see you but I have found a solicitor to advise me on your behalf as well as mine. He has contacted a private investigator who will try to discover the truth of Lionel's life before he came into ours . . .*

She had also dealt with the ban that had frozen their bank account when Lionel's death was announced, but the solicitor had managed to arrange for a small amount to be released for Maude's use until such times as Lionel's death was confirmed and the estate could be dealt with in the normal way.

Primmy, once more lying beside Maude, sighed noisily and pushed at the ball with her nose by way of a broad hint. Obediently, Maude threw the ball again.

At some stage Maude knew she would have to travel to

London and speak with Frederick Barlowe, but she was waiting for the right amount of energy and so far it had not materialized. She woke each morning exhausted, feeling no relief from her night's sleep. She also preferred to be at home with her aunt whose unhappiness had deepened her confusion. Maude dipped her pen in the ink and continued her letter.

> *. . . Lionel has a lot to answer for and a part of me hopes he really is dead. I never thought I could think that way but even if he lives and is tried in court he will be sentenced to death. Perhaps it would be better for all of us if he did drown.*
>
> *I have been told I can bring you some food and Aunt Biddy is going to make you a rice custard which she thinks will be easily digested and comforting. I shall bring it Friday (tomorrow) with this letter . . .*

On the far side of the lawn a young lad appeared on a bicycle and Maude recognized the butcher's boy. In a flurry of excited yelps, Primmy abandoned her ball and dashed across the grass to greet him. He always brought her a bone and was the dog's favourite visitor.

> *. . . I'm finding it hard to know how to think of you – you deceived me and betrayed my trust and yet you, too, are a victim of Lionel's wickedness, having fallen under his spell as completely as I did. In that respect we are sisters. I shall talk with Aunt Biddy if she seems capable of clear thought on the subject – I do not want to be a witness against you because of my earlier affection for you and because I do not want to feel responsible for the years you may spend in prison. I wonder how I will feel when you are eventually released. If I am not able ever again to consider you a friend I'm sure you will understand my reasons.*
>
> *On Saturday I shall go to the funeral of poor Jem Rider – if his mother is willing to let me join the*

mourners. She may not want me to be there but I feel it is the least I can do. I shall take some flowers and if she refuses I shall quietly withdraw. I don't feel to blame for the young man's death but I do feel tarnished by my relationship with Lionel, who killed him. It is all so difficult. I am having to adjust to seeing the world through different eyes as no doubt you do also. I hope this letter doesn't cause you pain.

Sincerely, Maude.

As Maude folded the letter and placed it in the envelope, the butcher's boy departed with a ring of his bicycle bell and a cheery wave. Primmy returned to her side carrying a large bone and settled to enjoy it.

'Lucky girl, Primmy!' Maude said with a smile.

Yes, she thought wistfully. A dog's life could be rather pleasant.

When the taxi dropped Maude off outside All Saints Church, a crowd of curious onlookers was already assembling in the street in eager anticipation of the event. It was not every day that Hastings could watch the funeral of a murdered man. Maude, her face half hidden by the veil, was wearing a black jacket and skirt and soon realized that this fact was going to make her noticeable, as many of the already assembled mourners at the church door wore a simple black armband and their Sunday best. Shying away from them in the hope of spotting Mrs Rider's arrival, Maude was surprised to see a familiar figure wandering among the gravestones.

'Mr Jayson!' she said in a low voice. 'What brings you here?'

'Ah!' His face brightened. 'I thought you would come. Have you been invited?'

'No – and I may not be allowed to stay. If I'm not welcome . . .' She shrugged.

'Exactly. I thought you might need some moral support and Alison was happy for me to take the afternoon off, so to speak. We sent some flowers. Just a small tribute.'

Maude nodded. 'I did, too, but I don't know how they'll be accepted. Someone may stamp on them! I wouldn't blame them. To them I'm still his wife and he killed their son.'

He squeezed her arm supportively. 'I'll stay with you, if you don't object. We can see it through together.'

From inside the church the organ struck up mournfully and people started to go inside. Almost immediately Emily Rider arrived with what Maude assumed were other family members. Behind them two black horses drew a sombre carriage containing Jem's coffin. A groan of sympathy went up from the watching crowd and Maude hesitated. She didn't want to interfere with the progress of the coffin, which was now raised aloft, but couldn't see any other way to reach Mrs Rider.

Her companion whispered, 'Let's just go in last and sit at the back. No-one will notice us.'

She nodded, wishing that she had decided against attending, but she did feel sad for the young man who had, after all, committed no crime. His only mistake had been to meet up with Lionel Brent.

The service was short but poignant and the vicar spoke of 'the loss of a young life cruelly cut short'.

Maude wondered suddenly how a vicar would speak of Lionel at his funeral. Would there be any kind words for him – and did he deserve any? Tears filled her eyes and she blinked furiously. Lionel must have been born innocent – she believed fervently that this was always the case – so what sort of child had he been? Where along the line had his intentions changed from good to bad? Had his mother noticed the transition and started to worry about her son, fearing that he would come to a bad end? If so, had there been anything Lionel's mother might have done to prevent this outcome?

When the service ended and Jem's body had been laid to rest with due ceremony, Maude and Derek remained undiscovered by the rest of the mourners. Derek told her that Alison had invited her to stay at the hotel for the evening meal if she wished.

'I'd love to,' she told him, 'but my aunt will have prepared a meal – cooking is her only solace at the moment – and I must share it with her. She has taken all this so badly to heart and I worry about her.'

He insisted on driving her home to Folkestone, however, and once there, Biddy insisted that he stay and share the meal that would easily feed three. He accepted with alacrity.

In Hastings, meanwhile, the evening performance at the pier came to an end, the satisfied people who had made up the audience spilled out on to the wooden walkway and, in chattering groups, made their ways home. Twenty minutes later, when the performers finally straggled out of the theatre they found the pier and the beach still washed with the last of the daylight and argued whether it was or was not the longest day of the year. Still undecided, the dancers, giggling and nudging each other, said, 'Goodnight, one and all,' and made their way wearily back along the pier towards their various destinations and bed.

Arturio Loreto walked off without a word and they let him go. Earlier he had confessed that he had had a row with his wife, Jessie, and was probably returning to cold looks and a meagre supper.

'Poor devil!' said Alfie.

Sydney shrugged. He carried his magician's cloak over one arm and his shirt, trousers and waistcoat were rolled up in the carpet bag he carried in the other. His wife would wash and iron them for him ready for the Monday matinee.

Behind them the lights in the theatre were going out one by one and they heard the caretaker locking up.

'All done?' Sydney asked him as he caught up with them.

'Safe as houses!' he replied.

As usual the three of them mooched back along the pier in the direction of the road but on reaching it made their way down on to the beach, crunching along towards what was left of the weekend.

Sydney said, 'Quite a good house, wasn't it, except for the idiot in row two snoring his ruddy head off until the chap behind him shook him awake. I'd have woken him up with something a bit stronger, given the chance!'

'Still, we've had worse evenings.' The comedian smiled into the growing dusk. 'Got a laugh for the Chinamen joke. Sometimes that falls as flat as a pancake.'

'Funny things, audiences. They either make your day or break your heart.'

The caretaker said, 'I've got to have a word with the manager before long. Too much rubbish in the cellar. It's a blooming fire hazard. Go up in a ball of flames, that place would.'

'That would put us on the map!' Sydney swapped his cloak and his bag. 'Not that we need it. We're already in the papers because of the murder.'

'Funny business, that.'

The beach had emptied by this time and the deckchair attendant had collected the deckchairs and stacked them against the wall.

The caretaker said, 'Well, here's where I leave you. Don't do anything I wouldn't do!' and went up the nearest steps.

Three minutes later Sydney also peeled off, leaving Alfie to finish his walk alone along the empty, darkening beach. Ahead he could just make out the shadowy shapes of the town's famous fishing fleet drawn up on the shore below the East Cliff, and he could see the lights on the East Cliff Railway above him to his left. To his right as he walked, the soft waves, breaking with regular monotony, struck him as eerie and he quickened his footsteps.

A couple of hundred yards further on when he turned away from the water towards the town, he spotted a large bundle wedged beneath a derelict fishing boat.

At first sight it looked like old clothes – or maybe a tramp sleeping rough – and he hardly gave it a second glance, but as he passed it something made him peer into the shadow and that's when he saw them – two feet but only one shoe. On closer inspection he saw that the shoe was an expensive-looking brogue. His thoughts moved in slow motion.

'Good God!' he whispered and his stomach churned. 'No! It never is!' Cautiously he leaned closer, breathing rapidly. He saw something else . . . Was it a hand? Almost afraid to look further into the gloom he forced himself to kneel and duck his head. He then realized with a sharp intake of breath that he was looking into a face partly hidden by seaweed.

Almost choking with shock he backed away and, scrambling to his feet, stared round in a growing panic. Seeing no-one who could help him, he tried to run towards the nearest steps, but his weight slowed him and the pebbles hampered his feet. Falling once, he struggled up again, afraid for his thumping heart, and began shouting for help.

Ten minutes later the beach was no longer empty. There was an onlooker in pyjamas and slippers, an ambulance and its driver, a police car and three triumphant policemen – and Ben Hemmings, who was writing in his notebook by the light of a torch held between his teeth.

Alfie, sitting on the ground with his head between his legs, was shattered by what had happened. He wanted to get up and go home but first he had to give a statement to the police. His heart had stopped racing but he felt sick and shivery and was beginning to wonder if he would ever be able again to stand up on a stage and make people laugh. As time passed he became aware of a growing sense of anticlimax among the people around him.

Lionel Brent's body had been recovered. It was all over bar the shouting.

Next morning yet another taxi ride ended. Maude had to identify Lionel's body and with confused emotions she followed the sergeant down to the depths and into the morgue itself. She thought fleetingly that not so long ago Jem's mother had been forced to make the same journey to see her son. As they reached the door the sergeant handed her over to an attendant in a slightly stained overall who said, 'Try not to let it upset you, Mrs Brent. It's not nice but at least your husband is at rest now.'

The sergeant, who had not spoken a word so far, said harshly, 'More than can be said for the policemen he injured!' and gave Maude a resentful look.

In spite of her emotions, anger flickered. 'So you blame me, do you? How on earth did you work that out?'

Taken aback, he said, 'Well, no. I mean not exactly, but he's hardly a hero in our eyes, Mrs Brent – the trouble he's caused us. Not to mention what he did to Jem Rider!'

'None of that is my fault.' Her voice shook. 'I am also a victim, remember.'

The attendant shifted from one foot to the other, obviously trying to think of something suitable to say but, giving up, he led her to the area where the bodies were kept. There were three, each on a separate table and each with an identity tag on one of the toes.

At the last minute Maude's courage failed. Did she really want to remember Lionel as a body on a mortuary slab, she wondered? She said, 'I'm assuming I'm his next-of-kin.'

The sergeant frowned. 'You're his wife.'

'I may not be. I suspect he is – was – married to . . . to the woman we know as Alice Crewe. My solicitor has hired someone to investigate that possibility.'

The sergeant raised his eyebrows. 'A bigamous marriage?' He shrugged. 'Please yourself. I dare say we can get hold of the Crewe woman.'

Maude tried to put herself in Alice's shoes. Would she want to see Lionel like this? It would simply rub salt into the wound, she decided. 'I'll do it,' she said. 'If it's not acceptable Alice can do it later.'

Walking to one of the bodies, the attendant waited for Maude to follow, then pulled back the sheet to reveal Lionel's face.

Maude was relieved to see that he had been washed and his hair combed. She stared at him, unable to speak as she looked for the last time on the man she loved. It was Lionel, and yet it wasn't. His features were the same but the closed eyes suggested sleep. His hair was very dark and he had no moustache. There was not the slightest glimmer of the love, the humour, the passion for life that she remembered. His flesh was pale, his hair a little longer than she remembered. She didn't want to remember him like this, she told herself, but if she remembered only the happy times she would never recover from his betrayal. All that went before, she told herself, was nothing more than a happy dream and it had ended in nightmare. She was wide awake now.

ELEVEN

Five months later, as a dank November mist swirled outside Maidstone Crown Court, Maude and Biddy sat in their seats at the side of the court. The cloudy sky cast a gloomy pall over the room as it filtered through the large windows and the winter heating was not yet in operation. Maude was glad of her warm gloves but her ankles were cold.

Every seat in the room was taken, either with interested parties or members of the press, and the tension in the air was palpable if not oppressive. Grave faces were turned towards the judge's table and only a few whispered comments broke the silence. For a long time Biddy had insisted that she wanted nothing to do with the trial but at the last minute she had capitulated, partly out of curiosity but mainly because Maude had insisted on being a character witness and Biddy felt she needed moral support.

'Conspiracy to commit a fraud by way of a felony, namely kidnapping . . . accessory to murder . . .'

As the words rang out, Maude gasped. Accessory to murder? That was a lie. Alice knew nothing about it . . . Or did she? Maude thought about it and groaned. Of course! Alice had been told in the garden about the murder but had not reported it to the police – which presumably made her an accessory. She closed her eyes but then opened them, determined to watch Alice, who sat next to her brief, white-faced and visibly shaking. If she caught her eye Maude intended to give her a slight nod to reassure her that at least one person in the courtroom did not regard her as a monster. Alice had been booed as she arrived at the court and Maude felt that the jeers should have been for Lionel, not the unfortunate woman he had duped. Because she, Maude, had also been deceived by Lionel's charm, she sympathized with Alice to some extent although Biddy, less charitable, was adamant that Alice deserved all that the court could throw at her.

'Does the plaintiff plead guilty or not guilty?'

'Guilty, my lord.'

Maude was half out of her seat before Biddy forced her down again.

'Will Alice Dora Brent please take the stand.'

Maude sighed, but it was a sigh of relief that it was Alice and not her that was standing in the dock. Maude now had confirmation that her marriage to Lionel was bigamous and thus null and void. In view of what had happened she could only be thankful that she was not, and never had been, the wife of a criminal.

Alice's voice shook as, bible in hand, she took the oath. 'I promise to tell the whole truth and nothing but the truth, so help me God.'

Maude had wondered more than once over the past weeks and months, how she herself would have reacted if she had been in Alice's shoes with the man she loved urging her to help him in what he presented as a daring and exciting plan that would transform their lives financially. If she had been in Alice's position, with possibly very little money and few prospects, she might have been swayed by her feelings for Lionel.

Alice's face was chalk-white as she answered the preliminary questions – name, date of birth, marital status.

Maude glanced across at Emily Rider, who sat grim-faced with her daughter beside her. They had exchanged no words at the funeral of her son and Maude had no idea whether or not Jem's mother had been aware that she and Derek Jayson had been present.

Looking again at Alice, Maude pitied her for the weight of guilt under which she was suffering. Not only had she ruined life for Maude and Biddy, she also had been indirectly responsible for ruining Emily Rider's life. Maude thought back to the first time she and Alice had met – at that fateful interview Lionel had arranged for them. She could think of no way to forgive him his callousness in bringing them together, knowing as he did that, if his scheme worked satisfactorily, it would end in heartache for the woman who thought she was his wife.

Time passed slowly as Alice was questioned and cross-questioned and, as the whole truth emerged, Maude sensed that some of the women in the audience, and possibly a few of the jurors, began to sympathize a little with her position. Emily Rider was called to give her evidence and broke down in tears.

It was half past two before Maude was called to give evidence and the counsel for the defence allowed her to read out a short statement about Alice's behaviour.

'I would like to say,' she began haltingly, but tears blurred the words she had prepared and it took a moment or two before she could continue. With an effort she steadied her voice and read on. 'I would like to say that although Alice's part in this tragedy cannot be excused in any way, I do know that she has a better side to her nature and I truly believe that her love for –' she swallowed hard – 'for Lionel Brent persuaded her to do what she did. The Alice I knew and loved was warm and friendly . . . She was, I am convinced, a sweet person in her own right but was unfortunate to meet a very charming and persuasive rogue who led her astray with disastrous consequences. I hope that in later years she may be given a second chance to make a happier life for herself.'

Emily Rider shouted, 'Sweet words won't bring my son back!'

The judge banged his gavel. 'I will not tolerate interruptions in my courtroom. If you interrupt again, Mrs Rider, you will be led out of the room by court officials.'

Before Maude could return to her seat the lawyer for the prosecution stepped forward. 'If Alice Brent is found guilty of these alleged crimes and is sent to prison, how would you regard her when she finally rejoins society?' Seeing that Maude hesitated, she pressed her further. 'Would you consider re-employing her as your companion, for instance?'

As the court waited for her answer, Maude struggled with her conscience.

The judge said, 'I shall have to hurry you. It's a simple question.'

Not for me, thought Maude, anguished. Finally she said, 'I would not do so. Not because of the alleged crimes but because of the personal issues between us . . . That is the fact that my marriage was bigamous and—' There was a murmur in the court and the judge banged his gavel. Maude caught Alice's gaze and hoped she understood. 'The discovery of Lionel's betrayal caused me such heartbreak that . . .' She took a deep breath. 'The three of us shared a home but I was oblivious to . . . There is just too much between Alice and myself that must forever remain unsaid.'

She was allowed to leave the stand and sank thankfully on to her seat. Biddy patted her hand but she was clutching a damp handkerchief and Maude saw that she had been crying.

Derek Jayson was waiting for them when the session ended and they followed him silently to his motor car. When they were settled on the rear seat he said, 'Alison wondered if you would both have dinner with us at Romilees – in our private quarters, of course. We haven't seen you for a while and it must have been a long day. She thought you wouldn't feel up to preparing a meal after your ordeal. I'll take you home afterwards.'

They accepted the offer willingly. Little did he know, Maude reflected, how desperate they were for some cheerful company. She came to a decision suddenly. She had intended to sit through the entire trial in the hope of giving Alice some support but now she felt unable to do so. Her impromptu answer to the prosecution's unexpected but searching question had cleared her fogged mind. *I've done all I can for Alice*, she told herself. *She must deal with her problems and I must deal with mine. Lionel is dead and we must both face the uncertain future alone*.

Ten days later the jury found Alice guilty on all the charges but the judge, taking all the facts into consideration, handed down a more lenient punishment than was expected. She was going to prison for eighteen months and Maude was grateful that it was all over.

A week later she arranged a meeting with Frederick

Barlowe and on Monday, 13th November, she travelled up to London to discuss the future of the Barlowe Gallery. When she arrived Jane Dyer met her with a tray of tea and some ginger biscuits she had made herself.

'Because I remember that you like them,' she told Maude, helping her off with her coat. 'Mr Barlowe is late back from his bank but I'm sure he won't be long. He asked me to apologize if he was held up.'

She looked anxious, Maude thought. The previous weeks had probably been a strain for her, too, in a lesser way. Outside the sky threatened imminent rain and Maude hoped that she and Jane would have a few moments together before Barlowe joined them.

'I wanted to thank you for coming to Lionel's funeral,' she told her. 'And the beautiful flowers. In the circumstances . . . Well, I was touched. The service was so short and unsympathetic – but then he had killed someone.' She sighed.

Jane regarded her earnestly. 'I expect you guessed.'

'That you were also a little in love with him? Yes, I suspected it but . . . he could be very charming.'

'He was so kind to me. Much nicer than Mr Barlowe. He's a very different sort of man. Not so sensitive. My mother says it was probably the way he was brought up, but she always makes excuses for people.'

Maude finished her biscuit and reached for another one. 'I didn't have any breakfast,' she said by way of explanation. 'My aunt is not at all well at the moment and mornings can be very disorganized.'

'No breakfast!' Jane looked shocked. 'My mother says that a decent breakfast ensures a decent day.' She smiled. 'I sometimes think she's got a saying for everything! I never told her about my feelings for Lio— for Mr Brent. She would never have understood and it would have worried her dreadfully.' She sipped her tea. 'I'm glad I've been given this chance to talk to you. I wanted you to know that even though I was a bit in love with Mr Brent I would never have tried to . . . to take him away from you.' She blushed furiously. 'Not that he would ever have left you . . . Except

. . . Oh dear!' She looked at Maude helplessly. 'What I mean is he never was . . . Oh!' She rolled her eyes.

Maude rescued her. 'If there's a saying for everything, the next one must be, "If you're in a hole, stop digging!"' They both laughed and Maude went on. 'I know what you're saying, Jane, and I understand.' She sighed. 'I wonder how many other hearts he broke. Too many, probably.' She shrugged. 'We have to go on, Jane. I'm sure you'll meet someone much nicer. Someone genuine. You mustn't distrust all men because of what has happened.'

Before Jane could reply, Barlowe rushed in, making his apologies, and within minutes he and Maude were deep in conversation in his office and Jane, with a lighter heart, was talking to the fourth client of the day.

A few weeks later, just as Maude had begun to hope that their life was returning to normal, something happened that shocked her. She woke one morning and glanced at the clock. Ten past six. So what had woken her so early? It was early December and the sun rose much later, which meant that she slept later. This morning, however, she woke with a start and sat up, listening. Maybe the dog had barked at a passing fox . . . No. No barking. So what had woken her? Reluctantly Maude slipped from the warm bed, pulled on a dressing gown and slippers and went quietly down the stairs. At last she pinpointed the sounds. They were coming from the kitchen. She moved cautiously towards the kitchen door and slowly turned the handle.

'Aunt Biddy!'

She could smell cooking.

Biddy, still in her nightdress but with an apron tied around her waist, was busy at the stove. She glanced up at Maude and smiled and Maude's heart skipped a beat. There was something in her aunt's smile – a certain vacancy – that frightened her.

'You're a bit early, Maudie love,' Biddy told her. 'Lunch will be at least another fifteen minutes.'

Maude's startled gaze took in the pan full of sausages, the bubbling saucepan and the pile of shredded cabbage on the board on the table. Was her aunt preparing lunch at this hour of the morning? She said gently, 'What are you doing?'

'Getting lunch, of course. I thought it was about time we had some decent food. A few potatoes and some cabbage – and I'll make some gravy, of course. You need feeding up, Maudie love, after what you've been through, and I said to myself—'

'Aunt Biddy, that was months ago. I've put all that behind me.' She looked around in despair. There was a sheet of rolled pastry on the board. 'Are you making a pie? Something for pudding?'

'A pie? No. I've made a rice pudding the way you like it.' She smiled, turning the sausages as she spoke. Moving nearer, Maude saw that they were burnt. 'Aunt Biddy, it's . . .' She stopped. Her aunt was obviously totally confused. Was it helpful to draw her attention to the fact that she was preparing a meal at least six hours too early?

Aunt Biddy wiped her forehead with a corner of her apron. 'I hate this climate. Summer is so humid!'

With a sinking heart, Maude sat down, her mind working overtime, but it was hard to see a way out of this without upsetting her aunt. For a moment she found herself longing for Alice's comforting presence, but that part of her life was over, she reminded herself. Perhaps they should sit down and eat the meal when it was ready . . . But it might happen again. Biddy needed medical help, she admitted to herself reluctantly. She had suspected this was coming for some weeks but had not wanted to face the truth. The traumatic episode with Lionel and Alice had exacerbated her aunt's earlier vagueness and tipped it over into serious confusion.

She said, 'I was thinking of popping in to the doctor's, Aunt Biddy, just for a check-up. I thought we could both go. We've rather been through the mill, over the last six months.'

Her aunt added the cabbage to the pan of boiling water and put the lid on, half tilted to let the steam escape and stop it boiling over.

Biddy glanced up. 'I'll come with you if it makes you

feel any better.' She smiled. 'Poor Maudie. You always were a worrier.'

The following afternoon Derek Jayson arrived with an invitation. 'We'd love you both to come to the Romilees for Christmas Day and Boxing Day – as our guests. We don't like to think of the two of you rattling around here on your own. You'll be surrounded by unhappy memories and we can't have that.' He looked at her eagerly. 'What do you say Mrs— Oh sorry! You're not Mrs Brent, are you? I never know what to call you these days.'

'You can call me Maude if you wish,' she suggested.

His eyes widened. 'Really? Oh, that's wonderful . . . Maude!' He positively beamed. 'Then please call me Derek.'

Maude smiled but then hesitated. 'Certainly I will, but as to your kind invitation . . .' Briefly she explained the problems that Biddy was experiencing. 'She has become rather unreliable in her behaviour and I certainly wouldn't want to give you or your sister any more problems. The doctor has suggested that I employ a nurse to keep an eye on her and I'm looking for someone. He thinks it might be the beginnings of senile decay made worse by the trouble we have been through, which caused her great anxiety – but, of course, I cannot bear the idea of Aunt Biddy going into a nursing home. Not while I can care for her here, where she feels safe.'

Disappointment was etched in his face and Maude felt for him. She sensed that he was possibly becoming fond of her but could not respond in any way while her feelings were still so raw. She grieved for so many things – the loss of Alice's affection, the shock of losing her way of life as a married woman, the depth of the deception and the sense that she had been diminished by what had happened. The truth was that currently two strategies dominated her life – one was the concern for her aunt, and the other was a fierce desire to forget Lionel and the callous way he had played havoc with her emotions. The latter depended on her own efforts and Maude tried hard to close her mind to anything that threatened to remind her of Lionel Brent, and that included Alice. The former strategy was more complex; Maude had discussed Biddy's prognosis with the doctor and knew that if the disease continued its rapid rate, the vagueness would become a serious problem as Biddy's grasp on reality grew less. Her behaviour was already more erratic and the doctor warned that in the worst scenario, Biddy might even become violent. Maude's heart ached for her but she knew there was little to be done to arrest the progress of the illness. There was no cure for the condition but Maude was determined that her aunt should stay at *Fairways* for as long as possible and while it was still safe for her to do so.

'I have to decline your kind offer,' she told Derek, 'but if you and Alison wish to pop over to Folkestone – maybe for an hour or so on Christmas Eve – we should be delighted to see you and it would give us an excuse to open a bottle of wine. Aunt Biddy will almost certainly bake something for us to nibble. When she is cooking I can still see the real Biddy Cope!' She smiled at him. 'Do come. It would be something to look forward to.'

It was agreed.

Biddy sat up in bed with a pencil and tried to bring her diary up to date. She had said her prayers, kneeling by the bedside, had brushed her greying hair fifty times and had carefully rubbed cold cream into her hands. These lifelong habits gave her bedtime ritual a feeling of order which she increasingly craved. The disastrous events concerning Lionel and Alice had played havoc with her mind and sometimes she realized this with something approaching dread. Now she frowned, trying to concentrate on the task in hand, while her cup of Ovaltine grew cold on the table beside her.

December 15th. I think. Maude will know. So nearly Christmas. We had a shock today and it has upset poor Maude. Alice is having a baby. At least she says she is. I don't trust that girl. It doesn't matter. DC Fleet came in person to tell us the shocking news and we all give thanks to God, amazed at how well he is recovering from his injuries. But his news has upset me. That Alice is having

Lionel's baby even though he is dead and buried! Yes. It is definitely the 15th because it is Friday and we are having fish for lunch. And poor Maude is not at all strong and so she is going to find another companion with nursing experience . . .'

In the next room Maude reread the application letter from a woman called Ivy Benn who had trained as a nurse, worked in the Buchanan Hospital in Hastings for seven years and then given up to care for her mother who had recently died. It was the third application but the previous two were from younger women and Maude felt that as her aunt deteriorated, an older, more experienced woman would be preferable.

She had pretended that her own health was causing her concern. That way she felt sure that her aunt would not protest about the intrusion into their lives.

Maude was trying hard not to think about Alice and the child she might be expecting and outwardly maintained an air of disinterest on the matter, but secretly she wondered how Alice felt about it. Was she delighted to be carrying Lionel's child or sickened by it? The defence lawyer was trying to negotiate an early release on compassionate grounds and Maude hoped that, if granted this release, Alice would have the sense to leave Hastings and take her child away to a part of the country where she was not known. A fresh start. Maude had wondered whether to write a letter to Alice pointing out the advantages of such a move but after some reflection she had changed her mind. A letter might invite a reply and she had no desire to begin a correspondence.

'Leave well alone, Maude!' she had counselled herself and was satisfied she had behaved sensibly.

TWELVE

Thursday, July 3rd, 1930

As the taxi drew to a halt outside the Barlowe Gallery, Derek reached for the door handle and stepped out on to the pavement. As arranged the taxi driver helped him to carry three paintings into the gallery where a smiling Mrs Thomas Marley, once Jane Dyer, held the door open for them.

It was becoming obvious, he thought, that she was expecting a child and no doubt she would soon be giving up her job to become a full-time mother.

'I'm sure you have time for tea and biscuits, Mr Jayson,' she said with a smile as they rested the paintings against the wall. 'Mr Barlowe's on the telephone but I'll make a tray for three.'

She had grown in confidence, he thought with pleasure, and was already wondering what sort of replacement they would find for her.

'How's Mrs Jayson?' Jane asked. 'And your daughter?'

Derek hesitated. 'My wife is well enough but her aunt's death just before Christmas has depressed her. It's depressed all of us, in fact. Our little Amy is still very quiet. Biddy was a very important member of the family.' That was an understatement, he thought ruefully. Their daughter, never very outgoing at the best of times, had retreated further into her shell with the trauma of her great-aunt's death. 'She adored Biddy and sobbed her heart out at the funeral. I wish now that we had refused to let her attend but she wanted to be there and we thought . . .' He shrugged. 'She's nearly five and she understands death and, since it was her wish, my wife felt we should allow her to be there.'

'I think you were right, Mr Jayson. Tears shed are healthier than tears repressed. My mother has always believed that. She says that children worry more about what they *don't* understand and shouldn't be kept in the dark.'

At that moment Frederick Barlowe came out of his office and made his way slowly down the stairs. He now suffered from rheumatism when the weather was damp and 1930 had produced a rather disappointing summer.

The two men shook hands as Jane hurried to put the kettle on. A client came in and chatted to Mr Barlowe for a few minutes then left, promising to bring his wife back after lunch to see the three newly arrived paintings.

Derek wandered round the gallery inspecting the works of art but his mind was elsewhere and his face was set in unhappy lines. Amy had almost died at birth after a difficult delivery but Maude's devoted care had ensured that she survived. She was a fragile child, however, and very shy. Maude had been convinced that she needed a brother or sister but the longed-for second child had never materialized.

'Here we are!' Jane set down the tray, which contained three cups of tea and a plate of biscuits. 'I'm afraid they're not home-made,' she confessed. 'I don't have much spare time these days.'

Barlowe joined them and they chatted until the last biscuit had been eaten. Jane hurried the tray into the kitchen and returned to her own desk to type up the last three letters of the day.

Sitting on the train on his way back to Folkestone, Derek suddenly remembered that tomorrow was Amy's fifth birthday and that Auntie Alison was giving her a birthday party in the hotel. He smiled suddenly, oblivious to the curious looks from the passengers around him. It was a smile that brought a gleam to his eyes. Derek knew he was a lucky man. He had a devoted wife whom he loved to distraction. He had a beautiful daughter who was a constant delight. Thirdly, he had a happy life. No man should ask for more. He knew that Maude didn't like to dwell on the past but he saw things in a more positive way. From all the traumas of eight years ago something good had emerged. He and Maude had met and, eight years later, they were married with a lovely daughter. Without the intervention of Lionel and Alice Brent he and Maude might have remained comparative strangers. Fate works in a mysterious way, he thought, and his smile broadened.

At the moment that he smiled, his wife was answering the door to a complete stranger who stood on the step holding the hand of a young girl.

'Mrs Jayson?' The woman looked about fifty, heavily built and wearing unbecoming clothes that did not flatter her.

'Yes?' Maude glanced at the child, confused.

'I'm Eleanor Surridge. That won't mean anything to you.'

'It doesn't, I'm afraid . . . So what exactly are you doing here?'

The child, a girl, watched her intently. Maude guessed her to be a few years older than Amy. Seven, probably, or eight. She had curly blonde hair and hazel eyes and was neither pretty nor quite plain but had a healthy glow to her complexion and a ready smile.

Maude regarded them curiously but also with some caution. Somehow, for no good reason, the sudden appearance of the woman and child disturbed her and she hesitated. Good manners required her to ask them in but she was reluctant to do so.

Mrs Surridge waited but the child said, 'Please can we come in?'

The woman said, 'Maggie! That's very rude. Say you're sorry to Mrs Jayson.'

'I'm sorry, Mrs Jayson.' She fixed Maude with a pleading look, which the latter found hard to resist.

Maude opened the door wider and said, 'Of course.'

Closing the front door, she led the way into the sitting room and invited her visitor to take a seat. The girl moved to the window and stared out at the front lawn through the net curtains.

Maude said, 'My husband will be home soon. He's been to London for the day.'

'It's you I have to see.' The woman fumbled in her large

handbag and handed Maude a letter. 'We had a housekeeper but she has died.'

'Oh. I'm sorry.'

'She contracted diphtheria – no-one quite knows how – and it closed her throat. The struggle for air weakened her heart and eventually it failed.' She shuddered. 'I did not visit her in the hospital because of the risk. Diphtheria is highly contagious. In ten days she was gone. Poor soul died all alone.' She nodded towards Maggie and mouthed the words 'her daughter'.

The girl must have heard and understood everything Mrs Surridge said but she made no comment. Instead she said, 'There's a big ginger cat running across your grass.'

Nobody answered her.

Mrs Surridge sighed. 'You should read the letter. She wrote it three days before she died and said I should bring it to you. I said I'd send it but she was adamant.'

'Bring it to *me*? But how could she . . .?' Maude stared at the envelope.

Mrs Surridge said, 'Tell her to keep away from the shrubbery.' She smiled. 'That was her message for you. Poor thing. I think she was delirious!'

Already a suspicion had entered Maude's head. 'What was her name, this housekeeper?'

Mrs Surridge lowered her voice slightly. 'She told us she was an unmarried mother but we gave her a chance and she never let us down. Worked hard, bless her, and was very willing. Nothing too much trouble. And she could cook. A dab hand with puddings, especially Bakewell tart, which pleased my husband. No truck with young men, either. Nothing like that, thank goodness. She said she'd learned her lesson. Once bitten, twice shy, as they say. Her name? Oh sorry! It was Alicia Brand.'

Alicia Brand. Alice Brent. Very similar . . . Maude began to pray that Derek would be home on time. Occasionally he caught a later train but today his wife was feeling the need of his support.

Maggie said, 'Mum's name was Alicia Dora Brand and mine is Margaret Ann Brand. I was going to be called

Maude but then she changed her mind. I'm glad she did because I like Margaret better.' She smiled at Maude.

Mrs Surridge rolled her eyes. 'That's enough from you, Maggie. What have I told you?'

'Speak when you're spoken to!'

She had a cheeky grin, thought Maude. So was this Alice's child by Lionel? Was it her imagination or did her own heart now beat erratically?

As Maude began to tear open the envelope there were footsteps in the hallway and Amy came into the room. The contrast between the two children was immediately apparent. Beside sturdy Maggie, Amy was a feather-light girl with long fair hair and blue eyes. Seeing the visitors, Amy at once reached for her mother's hand and, half hidden behind her mother, managed a nervous smile in Maggie's direction.

Maude said, 'Amy, this is Mrs Surridge and Maggie who is . . . a friend of hers. Say hello, darling.'

'Hello.' She eyed them uncertainly.

Primmy trotted in, wagging her tail, and made her way over to Mrs Surridge who obligingly patted her. The dog was ageing and had lost her boisterous ways.

Maggie looked at Amy. 'Is that your cat out there?'

Amy's hand tightened in Maude's but she said nothing.

Undeterred, Maggie persisted. 'The big ginger one. He's sitting in the middle of the grass, washing his paws.' She laughed. 'Come and look.'

To Maude's surprise, Amy slowly released her hand and crossed uncertainly to the window. 'Yes.' She whispered.

'So what's his name?'

'Foxy.' She didn't look directly at Maggie but kept her eyes on the cat.

'That's a good name because foxes are a bit gingery. Did you choose the name?'

'Mummy helped me.' At last she glanced up at the older girl. 'He was my Christmas present. Father Christmas brought him and he had a blue bow round his neck. That's Primmy, our dog, but she's an old lady dog and we have to take care of her.'

It was quite a speech for Amy and, although pleasantly surprised, Maude was still anxious and said desperately, 'You haven't finished your rest, Amy. Perhaps you should—'

'I know but I heard voices, Mummy, and I'm not sleepy.' Amy smiled shyly at the older girl.

Maggie said, 'I can do cartwheels. I might be an acrobat when I grow up and join a circus. I could show you but we have to do them on the grass otherwise we might hurt ourselves.'

Mrs Surridge returned to her earlier explanation. 'We've got a man coming tomorrow from the council about the orphanage. It's sad but these things happen, don't they? It's not ideal but she won't be the first child or the last to find herself in such a place.' She shrugged helplessly.

Amy crossed the room to stand by Maude and tug at her sleeve. 'Can we go out on to the grass, Mummy?'

'But I thought I'd come here first,' Mrs Surridge continued, 'since Alicia was so insistent. She wouldn't tell me what was in the letter but she said you'd understand.'

'Mummy? Please.'

Maude was aware of a moment's irrational panic. First herself and Alice and now Amy and Maggie. Was it history repeating itself? Could it be a recipe for disaster? She had vowed never to think again of Alice or Lionel but it had proved difficult. Seeing this child, who was Alice's daughter, had thrown her off balance – but suppose she was wrong. Suppose she had jumped to the wrong conclusion. She found herself stammering, 'Are you sure you want to do cartwheels, Amy? I don't think you . . . you might hurt yourself.'

Maggie took Amy's hand in hers. 'I'll teach her.'

Mrs Surridge said, 'Maggie'll look after her. She's got a good head on her shoulders.' She sounded impatient and glanced at the mantelpiece clock.

Maude gave in. 'Oh, very well then, but stay where I can see you. Just outside the window.' She was opening the letter with shaking hands.

Was this wavering handwriting Alice's? She took a deep

breath and began to decipher the clumsy, pencilled words which straggled drunkenly across the page.

Dear Maude,
I'm going to die. They say I won't but I feel that I will and I don't want Maggie to go into an orphanage. She doesn't deserve it because she's not to blame for anything that happened. Can you put the past to rest and take pity on my little girl? If not, I will understand but I know you have married and have a daughter so perhaps you will be kind . . .
Alice.

Mrs Surridge watched curiously as Maude wiped away her tears.

Maude handed her the letter and watched as her visitor also struggled with the almost illegible handwriting.

When she handed the letter back she regarded Maude silently. Feeling that the woman deserved an explanation, Maude said, 'We knew each other a long time ago. We were friends but . . . then we parted on bad terms. Something rather dreadful happened . . .'

Playing for time, Maude replaced the letter in the envelope, placed it behind the clock, then sat down heavily. 'I'll show it to my husband when he gets back.' Her heart hammered behind her ribs and she seemed trapped in the chair, unable to get up, undecided what to think and wondering how to deal with an impossible situation.

Mrs Surridge said, 'A bit of a shock for you, I should think. Are you all right?'

'Not really. I don't think we can . . . Really, she shouldn't have asked . . . I mean, it's not something you can do lightly.'

'Not fair of her to ask, Mrs Jayson, if you want my opinion.' She looked round helplessly. 'A bit of a shock – springing it on you like that.'

'But she was dying!' Maude regretted the words immediately. Why on earth had she sprung to Alice's defence? She must not be swayed by sentiment. She would tell Derek that it was out of the question. This was Lionel's child! How could she be expected to love her?

Mrs Surridge crossed to the window and glanced out. A smile played across her face as she watched the children. 'Cartwheels indeed!' she said. 'Maggie is very keen on acrobatics. She's got so much energy. And your little girl is having a go! Oops! She hasn't quite mastered it.'

'Is she all right?' Maude forced herself up from the chair and joined her visitor. Amy's face glowed with excitement as, with her hands held high, she hurled herself across the grass in a vain attempt to produce a cartwheel. To Maude's relief, Amy collapsed laughing and Maggie pulled her to her feet again.

Mrs Surridge said, 'She's nearly there! I didn't think she'd do it.'

Maude saw Derek turning in at the gate and saw the two children rush towards him. Obviously delighted, he allowed himself to witness Amy's attempt at a cartwheel followed by Maggie's more polished version. He glanced up at the house, saw the women at the window and waved cheerfully. Maude wondered just how happy he would be when he learned the identity of the older girl.

So poor Alice was dead, she thought with a lump in her throat. What a terrible way to die. Diphtheria was such a scourge – it was time the scientists found a cure. She could visualize Alice in her hospital bed, near to death, and wondering what would become of her daughter. Alice had been a healthy, cheerful woman with a future ahead of her until she met Lionel Brent – and until he discovered the Barlowe Gallery and the chance of cheating Maude out of a large sum of money! The three of them had been so happy together at the beginning. If only they could have continued . . . If only Lionel had not been a liar and a cheat!

She hurried to meet Derek at the door and thrust the letter into his hands before he could ask about their visitors.

'Read it!' she hissed urgently. 'I don't know what to do.'

He looked at her in surprise. 'You've been crying, Maude!'

'Just read it, *please*, Derek!'

Hovering beside him she watched his expression change – shock and grief followed by the beginnings of understanding.

'Good God!' he muttered. He slipped an arm round her shoulders and drew her close. 'So that child is . . .?'

'Alice's daughter, Maggie. Lionel's child.' Maude clung to him, her thoughts chaotic. If he agreed to keeping Maggie . . . But if he said no . . .

'It's a tough one!' he said, as though reading her thoughts.

'If we keep her, we'll spend the rest of our lives remembering what happened.' She pulled back from him, studying his face.

He nodded slowly. 'But if we turn her away we'll spend the rest of our lives wondering about what has happened to Maggie – so we'll still be remembering!' He shook his head slowly. 'Maude, I've never said this before but, in spite of all that happened, some good came out of it. Alice and Lionel brought us together. You and me. I'll always be grateful for that. Tell me what you want to do, Maude. You've suffered most. I can live with either decision.'

'Can you? With Lionel's child?'

'Yes I could. I would. It's up to you, Maude. I won't try and persuade you either way but I'll support you.' He pulled her close and kissed her. 'Now, put me in the picture, please.'

'The woman's a Mrs Surridge and Alice was her housekeeper – under another name, Alicia Brand.' Quickly she filled him in on the rest of the story and he listened intently.

He said, 'So she was making a new life for herself and Maggie. Well done Alice – Sorry! Alicia.'

There was sudden rush of footsteps and a knock on the door. Derek opened it and the two girls rushed inside.

Amy's pale face was flushed with excitement. 'Please may I show Maggie my room and my teddies and—?'

'And the doll's house!' Maggie prompted eagerly.

Maude was staring at them, her mind churning, and it was left to Derek to say. 'Yes, of course! Off you go.'

As they went upstairs Maggie told Amy, 'We have to be quick because we can't stay long. Mrs Surridge plays cards tonight.'

Maude said, 'We shall have to think this over . . . Take our time . . . Oh! They shouldn't have come!' She stepped back, leaning against the hall stand for support as fresh tears pressed against her eyelids. Her hands balled into fists and she crossed them in front of her chest defensively.

A silence deepened between them. It lasted minutes but to Maude it felt like hours. She said, 'Help me, Derek!'

He took a deep breath. 'I don't believe we have anything to discuss because I think you already know what you are going to do, Maude. We both know it's inevitable.' He reread Alice's last words then gently opened the fingers of Maude's right hand and closed them round the crumpled letter. 'Little Maggie is Alice's child and Lionel's child but they are both gone from us. We have each other and little Amy, but Maggie has no-one. I don't think we can let her go into an orphanage. She can be ours now. An unexpected gift from Alice.'

'A gift!'

'Exactly. She can be Amy's big sister.'

'It may not be as easy as we think.'

'Nothing worthwhile ever is, Maude!'

Maude was smiling through her tears. 'We can love her, can't we?'

Derek held out his arms. 'Love her? Most certainly we can.' Peals of girlish laughter came from Amy's bedroom and they smiled at one another. He wiped her eyes with his handkerchief. 'We'll go and tell Mrs Surridge and then set the wheels in motion.'

Maude nodded, slipping her arm through his. 'Do you think, in a strange way, that it was meant to be?'

'My dearest Maude, I'm sure of it!'